My Life's
A Drag

My Life's
A Drag

Marina's Story

Morven Taylor-Peacock

TO ALL MY LOVELY FAMILY AND FRIENDS

CONTENTS

ACKNOWLEDGMENTS

Thank you to all the lovely, colourful people that I have met throughout my life and career, who were definitely inspiration for some of my characters. Thanks also to all organisations involved in the care of abuse victims. Your work is vital and truly invaluable. Thank you.

INTRODUCTION

It's funny how twists and turns can totally change your whole life, but that's what happened with me and it was all thanks to my love of make-up. In all honesty, I suppose I'm a bit obsessed with it, because I just can't live without it. I know it sounds exceedingly shallow, but I'd rather head outside with no underwear on as opposed to no make-up.

It all started when I was a teenager. Embarrassed of my pale skin and freckles, I started with a little dusting of powder and a slick of lip balm, which quickly progressed to full face, but admittedly, sometimes a bit too heavy, full on make-up. I got a lot of stick and name calling at school, but it didn't bother me in the slightest because I just loved the art of applying it and the transformation it made. Above all else though, it gave me an inner confidence, making me able to face the world.

I suppose that's what lead me to work in the beauty industry. I did a course at night school which taught me the basics and then I managed to get a job in a little salon. The money wasn't great, so I worked in a pub at night which gave me tons extra to spend on my beloved make-up and clothes. Life was good.

I immediately struck up a friendship with Ella, who also worked at the salon and she was an absolute God send when my parents suddenly decided they wanted to up sticks and move to Spain. I had no intentions what-so-ever of going with them. It just didn't appeal to me at all. I mean all that sunshine would only melt my makeup off! Plus, I had developed a really good clientele and I loved hanging out with Ella at the pubs and clubs around town. That's when she had the genius idea that I move in with her.

It was an absolute hoot. The evenings that I wasn't working in the pub, we would get dolled up to the nines and trawl all the good nightspots, having a laugh. It was an absolutely brilliant time in my life and that's how I came to meet Ollie, unfortunately. Ella knew

1

him through an old boyfriend and spotted him across the bar, as we stood one night, sipping at our cocktails.

"Oh, no," she groaned, slurping the dregs of her drink through her straw, "Not him."

"Who?" I asked, following the direction of her eyes.

I physically felt my jaw drop open when I saw the guy she was talking about. He was tall, quite muscular, with floppy blond hair and was very easy on the eye. I could feel butterflies suddenly fluttering wildly about, inside my tummy, making me feel like an awkward little schoolgirl.

"Ollie... he's a friend of Tom... I can't put my finger on it..." Ella said, looking at him very suspiciously, "... but there's something about him I just don't like."

"Oh, I don't know," I said, eyeing him up, as he looked over at us, "He looks a bit of alright to me."

"Oh, yes, he's very good looking and all that, but... oh, hey up. I think he's coming over," said Ella, "Just please promise me you won't be taken in by him."

"I won't," I said, giving him a flirty glance.

But, of course, I was. Hook line and bloody sinker.

"Hello Ella, fancy meeting you here," he said, putting his arms round both our shoulders, "Well... aren't you going to introduce me to your lovely friend then?"

I could see Ella visibly squirm out of his hold, but blindly, I still couldn't see what on earth her problem was.

"This is my friend, Marina... my VERY good friend Marina," she highlighted to him.

"Well, I'm very pleased to meet you, "VERY good friend Marina". I do believe you have the most beautiful eyes I think I have ever seen. So where have you been hiding?" he asked, shaking my hand, while staring intently at my face.

I, of course melted, turning in to an embarrassing, giggling idiot, only managing to say, "Oh... I...well..."

2

Ella on the other hand looked like she was about to spew all over him and I knew she was getting angry, because her Irish accent was starting to get stronger.

"For the love of God, she hasn't been hiding anywhere, you eejit," she said, rather rudely, "We've been painting the town red if you must know."

"Oh, quite right girls. That's what life's for. I must say, I wouldn't mind painting the town red with you," Ollie said, turning around and winking, still looking at me very intently.

"Aye well, it's ladies only tonight," said Ella, pulling me sharply away from him and slamming her glass down on the counter. I naively was still oblivious as to why Ella disliked him so much, but not wanting to cause a scene, I just went along with her anyway. It was already too late though, because I was totally taken in with Ollie's good looks and vomit inducing charm.

"Oh, well, if you change your mind," he said, thrusting a card into my hand and winking again, "then just give me a call pretty lady."

"What a smarmy fecking git," said Ella, dragging me along as we headed to the next bar.

"Oh, isn't he just," I agreed, but of course, in my head I was thinking, "No he's not, he's absolutely, bloody lovely."

The card Ollie had given me turned out to be his business card. He was a building contractor and it had his name and number on it. Due to Ella's reaction, I had absolutely no intentions whatsoever of calling him because I really didn't want to upset her. Of course, a few weeks later though, I was at a loose end and stupidly sent him a text. I was totally bored and lonely because Ella had nipped over to Ireland to visit her family but ended up staying a bit longer than she had intended to. I had nothing better to do and foolishly thought it would be a good idea.

"Hi Ollie," I texted, "It's Ella's friend Marina. It was lovely to meet you the other week…"

Of course, being the true smarmy sleaze-ball that he actually was, he immediately replied back to me.

"Well, hello gorgeous. Great to hear from you. Are you free to go out for dinner or something?"

And that's how it all started. Like a moth to the flame, I agreed to meet him at an exquisite little restaurant and of course, immediately fell for all his slimy bullshit.

"I've only just met you," he said, taking my hand and kissing it, as we stepped out into the street, after our lovely meal, "but I already know I'm in love with you."

Of course, I swooned and swayed, falling for his crummy line, as he swept me into a passionate embrace. No-one had ever said anything like that to me before. He must really love me, I dumbly thought, feeling like a goddess. And that was it. I was head over heels, lock, stock and flaming barrel, totally in love with him.

I floated on a cloud for days and went to mush every time I saw him. We wined and dined and became utterly inseparable, much to Ella's horror when she returned home from Ireland.

"For pity's sakes Marina. Are you absolutely nuts?" she yelled, when I told her the "good" news,

"Did you not listen to a single word I said? He's a bloody creep. He's BAD NEWS."

My mouth dropped open, upset at her response because I was so happy and in love. I wanted to defend him and retaliate, but the words just wouldn't come out. I was totally shocked by her reaction and still couldn't understand her dislike for him.

"Do you not hear me Marina? He's bad news," Ella continued, when I didn't respond, "I can't give you a good reason why, but I just get a bad feeling about him. Pleeeease say you'll not see him again."

"But I'm meeting him tonight," I eventually managed to reply, "He's taking me to a show."

"Well just phone him and say you've got a headache or something," pleaded Ella.

"Oh, but I can't," I said, shrugging my shoulders, "He's spent a small fortune on the tickets."

"Oh, well, carry on then," said Ella, exasperated and started to drag her suitcase through to her room, shouting, "But don't say I didn't warn you."

I felt a bit angry at her outburst because she was kind of spoiling things a bit and I just couldn't see any bad in Ollie at all. Love had made me totally foolish and blind. Obviously, the huge bouquet of red roses that he produced when he picked me up that night totally sealed the deal, as far as I was concerned. Honestly, Ella? What was not to like?

Things were a bit fraught, to say the least, when I started to see him on a very regular basis, but realising that I was a lost cause, Ella was forced to come round thank goodness. I knew that she valued our friendship too much to let Ollie come between us, so she grudgingly accepted that I was evidently going to keep seeing him.

Ollie had managed to charm his way into my life and because I'd never had a serious relationship before, I was totally bowled over by all the attention. The chocolates and flowers scenario continued of course. He made me feel so special when he would just turn up unexpectedly at the pub with a huge bunch of flowers, or out of the blue he'd appear at the salon, then whip me away to some fancy restaurant for a nice, romantic meal.

The great thing was, he had a good income from his job, so money was no object, which made him appear to be even more wonderful. He would never let me put my hand in my pocket for anything, which was so sweet, although I would always offer to pay my way.

He truly made me feel like a princess, so of course when he popped the question for me to move in with him, I absolutely jumped at the chance.

"Oh, Ollie... I can't believe it! Are you sure?" I gushed, squeezing his hands over the table, as we sat in our favourite little restaurant.

"Of course, I'm sure," he said, squeezing my hands in return, "I wouldn't have asked you if I wasn't! I love you Marina for God's sakes."

It was all like a dream come true. I just couldn't believe my luck. Not only was he handsome, with a good job, but he also loved me and now he wanted me to live with him.

WOW!

I came down to earth with a bump though, when I put my key in the lock on my return home to Ella's. I would need to tell her the "good" news and I knew she wouldn't be very pleased. Plus, she had been so kind letting me stay all this time with her. I knew it wasn't going to be easy, but as she was still up watching the telly, I thought I might as well plough in right away and let her know.

"Hello, you," she said, smiling at me as I sat down.

"Hi there," I said, taking a nervous gulp and trying to smile back.

Obviously, seeing the anxious look on my face, her smile turned to a look of horror as she used her usual telepathic powers and somehow knew exactly what I was going to say.

"Oh, no... you're moving in with him... aren't you?" she surmised.

"I'm sorry...," I started.

"Oh, God don't be," she said, jumping out of her seat and hugging me, "You know I don't like him, but if that's what you want then I'm honestly really happy for you."

"Oh, thanks Ella," I said, hugging her back, but knowing full well that she wasn't happy at all about the situation.

"So? When are you moving in then?" she asked, pushing her hair behind her ear and trying to sound enthusiastic.

"Well, I don't actually know. We didn't set an exact date, but soon as, I suppose," I replied and for a split second, I actually wondered if I was doing the right thing because as I looked at her, I realised I would desperately miss our girlie times together.

But, soon as it was. A few days later, I moved in to his posh flat and everything seemed to be rosy. My mum and dad were of course delighted that I had finally found someone and was at last "settling down", especially with them being so far away in Spain.

I played the "good little housewife", making us nice romantic dinners and keeping the flat pristine clean and tidy, while Ollie was very attentive and generous, more or less paying all the bills. I contributed as much as I could towards it all and when I decided that I wanted to do a theatre make-up course at college with Ella, he was fully behind me. He didn't seem to mind the fact that I would need to pack in my job at the salon in order to do it, which meant less money coming in. I kept my job at the pub though, so at least I had some kind of an income.

It had been a lifelong ambition of mine to do theatre make-up, specialising in prosthetics and to be doing it along with Ella was just the absolute icing on the cake. It was interesting as well as fun and we immediately struck up a great friendship with Hannah and William our classmates, who were living the dream along with us.

It was just amazing. I honestly couldn't believe my luck. It was all falling beautifully in to place and living with Ollie couldn't be better. We were joined at the hip as they say, doing everything together. I thought he was the perfect partner.

That is until I started to see a darker side to him…

CHAPTER 1

PSYCHO

We had been really busy at college with assessments to hand in and deadlines to meet so Ella and I decided to chill out and treat ourselves to a nice girlie day in town. That morning though, Ollie announced that he was taking the day off and wanted us to spend the day together. I had already planned my day out with Ella and really didn't want to cancel because I was really looking forward to it. This did not please him at all.

"What? So, I've wasted a day's holiday for nothing?" he moaned, when I was just about ready to leave.

"But you didn't even tell me you were taking the day off," I retaliated.

"Well, obviously I was keeping it as a surprise," he said, looking extremely disgruntled.

"Oh, Ollie I'm really sorry, but I've already arranged to meet Ella today and I don't want to let her down," I said grabbing my bag and heading for the door.

"Oh well, fuck off then," he said sourly.

I was a bit shocked at his language, because he didn't usually swear very often, but thinking he was just joking, I pecked him on the cheek saying, "We can always do something tomorrow."

"Don't think so," he said, slamming the door forcefully shut behind me, as I stepped outside.

What a big baby, I thought to myself but quickly brushed it off because I didn't want anything spoiling my special day and excitedly headed into town, meeting Ella at our favourite bar.

"Oh, my God, you've got no idea how much I've been wanting today to come," squealed Ella, as we ordered some cocktails.

"Oh, me too," I agreed, "We deserve it."

"We surely do," she said, "What a hectic week it's been. I never thought for a minute that doing theatre make-up would be so stressful!"

"Me too, but it's well worth it. I just love it," I said.

"Same. It's absolutely everything I hoped it would be. Right," said Ella, clinking her glass against mine, "Here's to us, bottoms up and all that."

"Cheers," I said, laughing then taking a huge mouthful of delicious cocktail.

"Aaagghh… just what the doctor ordered," sighed Ella.

"Heaven in a glass," I said, totally savouring the taste.

"So… what's Ollie up to these days?" asked Ella, stirring her drink with her straw.

"Oh, you know… just the usual… work and stuff," I said, taking another sip of my drink, "Well… to be honest, he was a bit miffed that I was coming out with you today."

"Miffed?" said Ella, sitting upright in her chair and obviously about to get on the defensive, "How on earth was he miffed?"

"Well, he had taken today off," I explained, "But he didn't let me know until this morning. I told him though, that I had already arranged to meet you and that there was no way I was cancelling."

"Well done you," cheered Ella, holding her glass up in the air, "Here's to girl power. Plus, you'll have a much better time with me!"

"Well, that's what I thought," I giggled, taking another sip.

"Right… drink up. Excuse me bar tender, another two of the same if you please" shouted Ella, then turned to me saying, "I can tell this is going to be a fun day out."

"Me too," I laughed, already feeling a bit tipsy as I guzzled down my drink.

It was so good to be hanging out with Ella and doing what we did best, which was having a great time. I had missed that, which made me want to enjoy it even more, especially after Ollie's reaction this morning. Stuff him!

We finished our cocktails then did a bit of shopping, had lunch, a few more cocktails and generally had a good catch-up. Our day out spilled into the evening when we met up with William and Hannah from college, for dinner.

"Hey guys," yelled Ella, drunkenly when she spotted them coming into the restaurant.

I turned around and waved to them frantically in an equally drunken manner.

"Tut, tut," said William, hugging us both, "Who's had one too many mojitos already?"

"I can see we've got some catching up to do," said Hannah, hugging us too, as they both sat down beside us.

Ella and I giggled like naughty schoolgirls, emphatically and noisily slurping down our cocktails.

"So, what have you two been up to?" asked William, "Apart of course from drinking too much without us!"

"We've just been bloody enjoying ourselves. Haven't we Marina?" said Ella nudging my arm, making me spill a bit of my drink.

"Yip," I agreed, "We've not done it in ages, so we've been shopping, chatting... oh and drinking of course!"

A waiter came over with some menus, while taking William and Hannah's drinks order, then we gossiped and pondered over what to have, eventually settling for a few pizzas to share.

"So, how's your love life William?" asked Ella, inquisitively.

"Oh, well... you know..." he said, sipping his drink, "...could be better. You know that guy I had my eye on in the props department?"

"Yes?" we all said excitedly together.

"Well... turns out he's married," groaned William.

"Oh, William," I sympathised, "That's a shame."

"Oh, never mind," said Hannah, "You'll just need to stay in the singles club with me and Ella."

"...and I think it's about time Marina here was back in the singles club too," commented Ella.

"What?" we all replied.

"Oh, come on Marina, you know you need to ditch that pig of a boyfriend of yours," Ella cried, obviously speaking her mind now, after a bit too much to drink.

I was a bit stunned at her outburst and was just about to defend him.

"What makes you say that Ella?" asked a confused Hannah.

"Well, he only went into a big strop this morning, when she told him she was coming out with me," stated Ella.

"What a big baby," laughed Hannah.

"Sounds like a bit of a control freak if you ask me," added William.

I was just about to give him the benefit of the doubt, but then I felt a bit of a shiver go down my spine when I visualised his angry face from this morning and it made me realise that what they were saying was probably right.

Thankfully the waiter arrived with our food, which diverted everyone's attention and conversation, but it had kind of taken the shine off of my day.

We oohed and aahed as we started to devour the scrumptious pizza, then started discussing the work that we had been doing at college, while at the same time, filling each other in about our classmates.

The evening just flew in and when we realised it was almost eleven o'clock, we all made a mad dash to the station, scared in case we had missed our last trains.

"Oh, I've had such a great time," said Hannah, hugging Ella and I tightly.

"Me too," said William, kissing us both on the cheek, "I just want to know when we're going to be doing it again."

"Bloody soon I hope," said Ella, "You guys take care now."

"See you Monday," I shouted as they boarded their train.

"Oh, Ella, it's been such a brilliant day," I said as we waved them off.

"I know. It's been flaming wonderful and just think… we used to do this all the time. Why did you have to go and fall in love?" she said, looking at me suspiciously, "You are in love, right?"

"Oh, my God Ella, head over heels… honestly," I said, hoping she wouldn't start on about Ollie again, "And it's all thanks to you."

I knew by the look on her face that she was forcing a smile, but I tried to ignore it, saying, "Enjoy your weekend, lovely friend."

"You too," said Ella, "Shit… that's my train. Right got to go. See you Monday."

I laughed, saying, "See you Monday," and waved to her as the train pulled away.

It wasn't long till my train came and as I sat gazing drunkenly out of the window, into the darkness of the night, I had that lovely warm feeling you get, when you're feeling good and you can't wait to get back home to the one you love for a nice cosy cuddle and then maybe more. If I had known though what was going to happen on my return, then I would never have gone home at all.

I got off at my stop and literally floated on up the road, still under the influence of all the alcohol that I had consumed. As I approached the flat, I saw Ollie disappearing through the door in front of me and I felt a wave of excitement and a flutter in my tummy on seeing him. I just couldn't wait to hug and kiss him, so I hurried faster down the street.

"Hi honey, I'm home," I shouted through to him, as I rushed through the door and hung my coat up in the hall.

There was no reply which I thought was a bit odd and when I went into the lounge he was sitting, hunched down in his chair, with his eyes glued to the telly. He was quickly flicking through all the channels, with his face like thunder. I knew right away that he wasn't happy and that something was obviously bothering him. Surely he wasn't still in a mood with me?

"Are you alright?" I asked, as I sat gingerly down.

No reply was the answer. He was still evidently angry with me for going out with Ella and not spending the day with him. How immature and selfish, I thought, but I tried my best to ignore it and continued to be pleasant to him, stupidly thinking that he would brighten up.

"So... did you do anything nice?" I asked cheerfully, but when he didn't answer, I added, "Did you go out with the boys?"

The cold treatment continued though, but I quickly became weary and just couldn't be bothered with his juvenile behaviour anymore. There was no reason for him to be jealous or grumpy. I'd had a great day with Ella and was feeling good and in my opinion, he should be happy for me. It was good to keep in touch with friends and I didn't want his stupid bad mood spoiling my happy one.

I got up off of the couch and started heading for the kitchen to make a much-needed cup of tea. Unfortunately, my huge alcohol consumption had given me false confidence and I made the awful mistake of saying, "Oh, suit yourself, you miserable arse-hole."

He immediately sprung up off the couch, landing right in front of me, like some kind of Ninja warrior, pushing his glowering face straight into mine. It was totally out of character and made me catch my breath with total fright.

"I'M an arse-hole?" he yelled into my face.

13

"What the hell's wrong with you?" I responded, pulling my face away from his, but getting really alarmed by his totally unprovoked bad temper.

"There's NOTHING wrong with ME bitch." he snapped, looking at me with horrible, scary, scowling eyes.

"Well, no need to be so tetchy then." I said, totally shocked by his weird behaviour.

He pushed his face right up against mine saying, "I'm NOT fucking tetchy," and for one blood curdling moment, I actually thought he was going to lift his hand and hit me, but mercifully he backed off.

"Spent all your money on bloody cocktails, have you?" he sneered.

Oh, so that's what it was all about. Not only was he jealous that I had spent time with my mates and not with him, but he was also angry that I had spent a little bit of my money on myself.

"No, of course I didn't spend all my money on cocktails," I retaliated, even though, unfortunately I actually had.

"Yeah well, there's going to be big changes round here. I'm sick of paying for everything while you go swanning about with your stupid friends," he yelled.

Go swanning about? Oh, my God, it was virtually the first time me and Ella had gone out in ages because any spare time I did have was literally all spent with him of late. I now totally regretted it though, the way that he was acting, but still couldn't understand how he could grudge me having a nice time?

I should have known there and then that things had totally changed for good and that there would be no going back. My gut instinct should have made me leave him. Stupidly I didn't though, thinking it was just a one off, but unfortunately things were just about to get worse.

We barely spoke to each other all weekend. Ollie, because he was still in a bad mood and me because I just couldn't forgive him for the way he had been acting. It made things very uncomfortable.

At college on Monday, Ella, William and Hannah were still on a high from Friday whereas I, on the other hand had totally forgotten all about. Ollie had completely wasted it for me.

"Oh, I could just go a slice of that lovely pizza," said Hannah, as we sat in the canteen at morning break.

"Never mind pizza, just bring on the cocktails," said William, holding an imaginary glass in his hand.

"Was Ollie mad at you for being so late?" asked Ella.

I hesitated for a moment, thinking she somehow knew how horrible he had been, but then realised she was just asking a simple question. I desperately wanted to confide in my friends though, but knowing that Ella would say, "I told you so," made me hold back and lie.

"No... course not," I said, avoiding eye contact with Ella, "He was as nice as ninepence."

When I eventually glanced at Ella though, I could tell by her face that she didn't believe me. Thankfully though, it was time for us to go back to class, so no more was said, that is until we were at the station, waiting for our trains.

"You know you can talk to me about anything," Ella said, hugging me when her train came.

"I know," I said, knowing full well that she knew something had happened.

"No secrets," she said, heading towards the train door.

"No secrets," I called and waved her off.

I wanted to run after her and pour my heart out, admitting that she had been right all along, but instead I sat down and waited for my train, not looking forward to going home to Ollie. I couldn't believe it when an announcement said that my train had been cancelled. It meant waiting another half an hour for the next one to come, but at least it delayed having to go back to the flat.

When I eventually got home, I decided just to make something quick because I had been held up and was too tired to make anything fancy, so opted for pasta. I was just bringing it to the boil, when I heard the front door banging shut. Normally my heart would lift at the sound, but tonight it just sank at the prospect of seeing him. It sank even further when he came into the kitchen because his face was like absolute thunder and I knew right away that there was going to be trouble.

No greetings and no hello, he threw his bag down on the floor and came right up to me, glaring into my face. He looked even angrier than he had on Friday, if that was at all possible. I just couldn't understand it. I had never experienced any form of violence in my life before but could feel a sickening fear surging through my whole body, literally from my head, all the way down to my toes, just knowing that something bad was about to happen. He was frightening me like I had never been frightened before.

"Where's my dinner," he roared into my face.

"I'm just making it," I said, hoping that would pacify him.

"You're just making it?" he yelled straight into my face again, actually blowing my hair with the force, "You do fuck all, farting about at your stupid college and you can't even have my dinner ready for me coming home?"

"Wait a minute. It's not my fault it's not ready," I retaliated, "For your information my train got cancelled."

I had barely got the words out of my mouth when he unexpectedly punched me hard in the ribs. I felt the sharp pain of his knuckles hitting my flesh, then the air getting knocked out of my lungs. I immediately dropped to the floor, shocked and unable to breath from the force of the blow, now writhing in pain. I couldn't even speak as he sickeningly proceeded to pour the pot of pasta I had been cooking on the floor, right in front of my face.

"Try getting an earlier one in future," he said, throwing the empty pan noisily into the sink.

I lay on the floor, still shocked and in pain, unable to comprehend what had just happened. My nice, pleasant, loving boyfriend had just turned into a terrifying big ogre, for what I could see, was no apparent reason.

He just left me lying there still unable to speak and still writhing in pain then stormed through to the lounge, slamming the kitchen door behind him. I literally couldn't move and just lay there, watching the steam rise from the scattered pasta. It was a surreal scenario. I felt so hurt, both inside and out. I wanted to shout and scream to our neighbours for help, but I physically wasn't able to.

When I eventually managed to get my breath back, I slowly pushed myself up, holding my painful ribs, still unable to believe my once lovely Ollie could have been so nasty to me.

There was just no logical reason for his violent outburst. It really wasn't my fault that my train had been cancelled. Was he stuck in the Victorian ages or something, expecting me to be the good little woman, at home making his dinner? I was out all day too, after all. I suddenly began to feel really sorry for myself but above all else, I

16

felt absolutely terrified, scared in case he came back through to finish me off.

I anxiously reached for my bag and then began searching manically for my phone. My hands were shaking uncontrollably as I tried to key in my mum's phone number. What help she would have been, I don't know, what with her living in Spain, but then, suddenly out of nowhere, Ollie was there again, whipping my mobile out of my hand.

"What do you think you're doing? Going to tell on me, are you?" he said switching my phone off emphatically, right in front of my face.

"N... n... no, of course not. I... I... just wanted to phone my mum," I said feebly, "You... you're frightening me Ollie."

"Frightening you?" he said, putting the phone down and his face starting to soften into an unnatural, scary looking smile, "Don't be daft."

He then grabbed hold of me, lifting me forcefully up and holding me tightly in an uncomfortable hug, hissing straight into my ear, "I only wanted us to have a nice dinner together. That's all."

I didn't know how to react without aggravating his temper, so I just kept playing along with his madness, while never having felt so afraid in all my life.

"I know... I'm, I'm sorry. But don't worry... I'll make us something nice. It won't take long. Just give me five minutes," I said, slowly pulling myself out of his painfully tight grip.

"That's more like it," he said looking at me suspiciously, but then kissing me roughly on the cheek.

As he went back through to the lounge, I wanted to scrub the wetness of his kiss from my face with a wire brush and bleach, feeling sick at the thought of what he had done to me. Instead, I started to clean up the mess he had made and set about making fresh pot of pasta. Just as I was reaching to get the packet from the cupboard, he was suddenly behind me again. I nearly jumped out of my skin when I turned around and saw him there, fully expecting him to give me another punch in the ribs.

"Don't bother making more pasta," he said, as I turned, warily to face him.

17

"It's no bother," I said, thinking that he was actually trying to be nice.

"I don't want pasta. I fancy pizza, so you can go and get it," he said, folding his arms and looking cocky, "to make up for not having my dinner ready."

I really wanted to say "Oh, for God's sake can you not just drop it?" but instead I protested saying, "But I can't afford it Ollie, I don't get paid till the end of the week."

"Well, you shouldn't have spent so much on cocktails, should you and if you can't afford it, then you better go rob a bank then," he said, threateningly, "Cause that's what I want. O.K.? I'm fed up with you free loading all the time."

"Alright, alright," I said, trying hard to keep the peace.

Glad to be escaping from him, I hobbled through to the hall, grabbing my bag and coat. I wanted to run out into the street as fast as I could, but I was too sore. My ribs ached as I walked along the road and I winced with the pain of every step.

I reached into my bag to get my phone so that I could call someone for help but then I realised it was still in the kitchen after Ollie had whipped it off me. I felt so deflated and vulnerable without it, but continued on my way.

I looked inside my purse as I reached the take-away shop and counted out four pounds and twenty-one pence. That was all the money I had to my name. I knew there was only three pounds left in my bank account so there was no point even trying to use my bank card to pay.

How could Ollie be so mean. He knew it would probably leave me with nothing. Normally if I was skint, he would pay for everything and I would square up with him when I got paid. Why was he being so horrible to me? I just couldn't understand him. Did he really hate me so much that he could do this to me?

Luckily, I managed to get a special deal on a pizza for £3.99, which left me with a grand total of twenty-two pence, then I trudged back to the flat, really not knowing what to expect.

When we sat down to eat however, Ollie chatted away as though nothing had even happened. What a Jekyll and Hyde. I was scared witless but kept playing along with it, while the pain in my ribs made me realise that I would never feel the same way about him ever again. Ella had been right all along. What a creep. He really WAS bad news.

The next morning, I made sure I got my phone back from the kitchen, as I ran about getting ready for college. I couldn't wait to get out of the flat and as I sat on the train, I was desperate to call my mum, to tell her what had happened hopefully, getting some comforting words of advice. I clicked on her name and was about to press call, but then found myself unable to go through with it. I mean, what was the point? She wasn't exactly handy and the last thing I wanted to do was to worry or upset her and dad with them being so far away. They wouldn't have been able to do anything anyway and I knew my mums answer would be to leave him and go to them in Spain. That just wouldn't be an option though, because I just lived for my theatre make-up course and I would miss Ella too much. It was what I had always wanted to do and no arse-hole bully like Ollie was ever going to stop me from completing it.

No, I would just need to knuckle down and accept the situation that I had got myself in to. I had ignored Ella's good advice and had chosen to be with him, so it was all my own fault. Then stupidly, I actually started to doubt myself. Maybe it was me. Maybe I had brought it all upon myself and had encouraged him to hit me. After all I HAD got used to letting him pay for everything and I HAD selfishly spent all my money on cocktails. I managed to convince myself once more that it was a one off and that it probably wouldn't happen again. He loved me… right?

Regrettably, I didn't call my mum and put my phone back in my bag. By the time I got to college my ribs were really aching from Ollie's punch. Every now and again, throughout the day, the pain would make me catch my breath. I just hoped that nobody would notice, but like that was going to happen with Ella about. She had a permanent radar, trying to catch me out and find fault with Ollie.

"Are you o.k.?" she asked, with her usual intuition, as we stood in the lunch queue.

"Yeah, course I am," I lied, but at the same time, wondering why she was asking and scared in case she had seen me wincing with pain.

"Oh, no you're not," she said, grabbing a pack of sandwiches, "I've been watching you. Is there something wrong with your back or something?"

"What? Oh, yeah... yeah, it's my back. I think I've pulled a muscle actually," I lied, putting my hand on my hip and pulling a face.

"Is that moron you're living with got anything to do with it?" asked Ella, looking at me suspiciously.

"No, don't be daft," I said, brushing her off, but totally taken aback by the fact that she actually suspected that Ollie was behind it.

She knew me too well and she obviously knew Ollie too well. Oh, why had I not listened to her warnings? Of course, I could never see anything bad before... but I could see it now. My God could I see it now. It was almost as though Ella could read my thoughts and I was so, so desperate to tell her what he had done to me, but I just couldn't. I was too humiliated, too embarrassed and still too shocked, to be honest. What a bloody mess.

"I tell you, if he ever lays a finger on you... I swear I'll kill him," said Ella, lifting a can of juice.

"Well, actually..." I wanted to say but, instead I just forced a smile, while inside I felt like crying my eyes out and begging for her help, telling her that she had been right all along.

I automatically reached for a bottle of water, but then hastily put it back, as I suddenly remembered that I hardly had a penny to my name thanks to Ollie. Of course, Ella noticed this as well. She just never missed a trick. What a girl!

"Are you not having anything?" she asked, looking at me suspiciously.

"No... I... I'm on yet another diet," I lied.

"Surely you're allowed water, for the love of God," she said, folding her arms and looking at me full on, "Truth please."

"Well to be honest, I've over-spent my budget... again... and I'm absolutely skint," I said.

"Well, could Ollie not lend you some money? Oh, don't. Don't even try to defend him Marina," she said, putting her hand up to silence me before I could even speak a word.

I just stood there with my mouth open about to concoct yet another excuse, but I knew it would be an absolute waste of time as I watched Ella scoop up more sandwiches and a bottle of water for me.

"Well, if that reprobate can't help you out, then I will!" she said, in her thick Irish accent, heading to the checkout, "Come on you."

"Honestly Ella...," I started.

"Sssshhhh," she ordered, "Just you go and get us a seat."

Sheepishly I did as I was told, heading over to an empty table and sat down, waiting anxiously as I watched her pay. I felt like such a sponger. Why did it have to be like this?

"Can't have you going hungry now, can I?" Ella said, dumping the sandwiches and water on the table, as she sat down.

"Oh, Ella thank you. Thank you so much," I said, humbly "You're the best friend ever and I promise I'll pay you back at the end of the week."

"Oh, no you bloody won't. It's my treat," she said, peeling open her sandwich, "But when you can afford it, you can take me out on the raz instead."

"Deal!" I laughed, but then I began to wonder how on earth I'd ever be able to go anywhere again without upsetting the now crazy Ollie.

I was actually scared to go home that night, terrified in case Ollie would hit me again. What an awful situation. Was he really annoyed with me because I didn't put as much money in as he did or was it something deeper? I mean I put in as much as I could afford, but it didn't leave me with that much from my pub wages. At the same time, it never seemed to have bothered him before. I just couldn't understand what his problem really was.

When he got home though, he couldn't have been nicer to me. I was in the kitchen, quickly throwing some dinner together, terrified of a repeat of the night before and froze when I heard the front door banging shut. I had one eye on the cooker and the other looking over my shoulder, ready to defend myself from his blows.

"Darrraghhh..." he said, as he came through the kitchen door, producing a bunch of flowers from behind his back.

"Oh... thanks," I said, trying to look pleasantly surprised and taking the flowers, not really knowing how to react, just in case it triggered his temper again, "They're lovely."

21

"Just like you," he said with his usual vomit inducing charm but even more-so now.

Inside though, I felt like smashing his flowers on the floor and screaming at him, demanding to know why he had flown off the handle last night for no reason. Then the voice in my head held me back, telling me to stay calm and to go along with him, just in case he turned in to a raving monster again.

"Mmmmm ... they smell beautiful," I said, sticking my nose in amongst the visibly cheap, wilting petals, but keeping my eyes firmly on his face, watching his every move, just to be on the safe side.

It was almost as if he actually believed that a poxy bunch of flowers would make everything o.k.

"I know… so what you got cooking?" he asked, sniffing at the air.

"Oh, nothing special… just sausages…," I said still wary of his reaction, "I start at seven so... bit of a rush."

"Great. I'm starving," he said, reaching into the cupboard and getting the plates out.

"Look," I said, warily, "I'm... I'm sorry if you think I don't put enough money in but..."

"Hey, you put in what you can darling," he said with what sounded like a totally fake, sympathetic voice.

"Well, I was thinking that I could maybe get a few more shifts at the pub...," I started.

"Hey, don't even think about it," he said, putting his hand over my mouth.

This action automatically scared the shit out of me. I was expecting him to hurt me in some way and I must have looked like a rabbit caught in the headlights, with my eyes nearly popping out of my head. He didn't hurt me though, thank God and continued the act of Mr. nice guy as we ate our dinner.

Once I had finished, I couldn't wait to go through and get myself ready for work. I had planned to just shout cheerio as I was leaving, but as I headed for the front door, I could hear him in the living room, jumping out of his chair. Before I could do anything, he was there right in front of me. I froze again, not knowing whether to smile or grimace, scared in case he was going to grab me and stop me from leaving. Instead, he bent forward and kissed me gently on the cheek.

"Don't work too hard sweetheart," he said, patting me on the shoulder.

Sweetheart? Really? What a creep.

"Don't worry, I won't," I said, just wanting to get the hell away from him as fast as I could and rushed out through the door.

As I walked quickly up the street, it felt like a massive weight had been lifted from my shoulders and I breathed a huge sigh of relief, so glad to get away from him. I knew though, as I headed frantically for the bus-stop that I was going to live life on a knife edge from now on, never knowing what his mood was going to be like. What on earth was wrong with him? What was with these crazy mood swings?

It was like sanctuary being in the pub that night, even though it seemed to be going in at a snail's pace, with just a few regulars sipping at their pints and the jukebox droning in the background. I didn't mind at all and would have been happy for it to drag in for ever. Seeing as it was so quiet though, I took the opportunity to ask my boss for some more hours.

"Bill?" I said, as he replaced some crisp boxes.

"Yes? What is it love?" he asked, turning to face me.

"Well, I was just wondering if you were needing any more shifts covered. It's just I could be doing with the extra cash."

"Really?" said Bill, looking surprised, "I thought Ollie kept you in the lap of luxury! Well, I dare say we could fit you in for a few. Leave it with me and I'll see what I can do."

"Oh, thanks Bill," I said, gratefully, "I'd really appreciate it."

I tried to busy myself to keep my mind from straying, but it was pretty hard, as the time was going in painfully slow. That is until, out of the blue and extremely unusually, two drag queens made a very grand entrance. They just seemed to burst through the doors then had a good look around but were obviously disappointed at what they saw. Their dresses were colourful, sparkly and figure hugging, while their hair was piled higher than the Empire State building. I noticed right away that their make-up was just absolutely perfect and how they tottered in their stiletto heels defied science!

They were met with ignorant moans and groans from the old men who didn't take kindly to change as they huddled round the bar, nursing their beers. Whereas I, on the other hand was more than delighted to see them. They just lit up the room and I couldn't take my eyes off them as they headed towards the counter.

"What can I get you gent... em ladies," I quickly corrected myself, thrilled that the night had been brightened up at long last.

"Well honey, I don't suppose you do cocktails in here do you? I could murder a tequila sunrise." asked the one with blond hair, looking round at the old men and blowing them a cheeky kiss.

"Though by the looks of it not much could "rise" in here," said the one with the red hair, glancing towards the punters and rearranging his beehive.

The old men just groaned even more, muttering amongst themselves, evidently disgusted by their presence let alone their comments. I, on the other hand, thought they were absolutely hilarious.

"Sorry, no," I said, laughing, "We only do wine, beer and spirits I'm afraid."

"I think there's a bit too much in the way of spirits by the looks of things," the blond one said, glaring comically at the old men, "Looks like they've just been dug up out of the graveyard!"

"Oh, they're just not used to seeing such good looking, glamorous ladies as you," I smiled, encouragingly, hoping they wouldn't be frightened away.

"Oh, bless you honey," the one with red hair said, pushing out her obviously false breasts.

"I love your make-up," I said leaning towards them both to get a better look at their perfectly made-up faces, "It's absolutely flawless."

"Oh, isn't she a treasure Sabrina," said the one with red hair, "We don't usually get compliments... just insults," and she motioned her head towards the old men.

"So, what kind of make-up do you use?" I asked enthusiastically, hoping to get some hints and tips.

"Well, I use only the best products... but Giselle here," Sabrina said, nudging her counterpart, "Uses pure cement with a touch of emulsion!"

24

"Miaow," Giselle said, pulling a funny face and motioning her hands like claws, "She can be such a catty bitch you know."

They were so funny and made me totally forget about all of my recent worries.

"You'll need to share your secrets," I said, gazing at them both, "I don't think I could ever put make-up on anywhere near as professionally as you two."

"Oh honey," said Sabrina, fluttering her eyelashes, "It takes years of practice, practice, practice, I can assure you, but it's so nice to be complimented. You're such a sweetie."

"Anyway," sighed Giselle, looking round the pub again, "There's far too many fossils in here and if I don't get a cocktail soon, I'm going to go into the DT's!"

"Oh, she's such a drama queen," said Sabrina, dramatically holding the back of her hand to her forehead, "Right come on then sugar tits. Think we might have to go to Mexico for that Tequila at this rate."

"Awww," I groaned, disappointed that they were leaving.

"See you round honey," waved Sabrina.

"Toodiloo boys," Giselle shouted to the old men as they started strutting to the door, singing along to the jukebox, strutting even more obviously with their big, long legs.

"Don't you just love Aretha?" Sabrina enthused as they disappeared through the doorway.

And then they were gone. They had made as dramatic an exit as they had made an entrance, leaving me feeling deflated and bored again, as I watched the door bang shut behind them.

"Thank God for that," one of the grumpy old men said, "That sort of thing shouldn't be allowed."

"Their type's got no right coming in here," another one said.

"They should be rounded up and left on a desert island," the really crabby looking one said.

I tried to ignore the old men's nasty, negative comments and I chuckled to myself as I remembered their antics. They were just lovely and had made me feel so much better. It had turned out to be not such a bad night after all. Meeting the queens had really cheered me up and thinking about them helped make the rest of the night fly in.

Bill let me off me sharp and feeling good, thanks to the drag queens, I arrived back home with a massive smile on my face. That was a BIG mistake though. When I walked through the door Ollie was standing in the hall waiting for me, with his arms folded and an angry look on his face, which was now becoming a regular occurrence.

I warily started to take my jacket off, wondering what on earth was going to be the problem tonight, while trying to keep smiling, in the hope that he wasn't actually in a mood and that he might just smile back.

"Are you alright?" I asked, still smiling but feeling like running back out into the street.

"Well, you obviously are," he said, stepping unsettlingly closer to me, "So why are you looking so pleased with yourself?"

"I'm not pleased with myself... I'm just happy," I said, stepping timidly back from him, then trying to change the subject, "Bill's going to try and put me in for some extra shifts."

"Oh yeah?" he said, looking at me suspiciously.

"Yes," I said, trying to stay upbeat, "and you're not going to believe this, but these two drag queens came into the pub and..."

"Drag queens?" he interrupted, screwing his face up and pushing it up against mine, "Do you really expect me to believe that?"

"What?" I said, not understanding why he thought I would be lying.

"So what's his name then?" he continued, "Chatting you up was he… when you were pulling your pints?"

I just couldn't fathom out how he had come to the conclusion, that someone had been chatting me up just because I was simply smiling. For God's sakes I was trying to work extra hours, in an attempt to make him happy by paying my way. What more did he want? Now I wasn't just confused, but I was angry too.

"What the hell is wrong with you?" I started, "It was two..."

"Oh, don't make a fool of me Marina. Drag queens aren't going to come anywhere near your skanky little pub. No… it's all falling into place. Extra shifts so you can see even more of him? Is that it...? Well, I'm watching you," Ollie said, pushing me hard against the door behind me.

Unfortunately, the door handle caught me sharply on my back, making me catch my breath with the pain and stopping me from responding to his stupid assumption. I wanted to run after him as he turned defiantly and walked away. I wanted to push HIM against the door handle and scream madly into his evil face, demanding to know why the hell he was acting so strangely, but my fear of what he might do to me, stopped me from trying to do anything. I felt totally defeated yet again. It was apparent that it really didn't matter what I tried to do or say, because he was only going to twist everything round to suit himself.

I tried my hardest to avoid him for the rest of the night because I just couldn't stand the sight of him and as I got ready for bed, I strained round to look at my back in the bathroom mirror. There staring back at me, was a huge, black bruise which was tender and really sore to the touch. I felt so hurt.

Not only physically, but emotionally too. It made me hate him even more and not able to bear the thought of his body being anywhere near mine, I chose to sleep on the couch that night. Of course, the next morning, Ollie acted as though absolutely nothing out of the ordinary had even happened, playing mister innocent once again.

I just couldn't understand his mentality or let alone his actions. Did he really think he had the upper hand? That he could just hurt me for no reason and then totally brush it under the carpet, hoping that I would forget all about it because I wasn't retaliating?

I was still too scared though to react to him, for the fear of what else he might do to me. I just didn't know him anymore or what he was really capable of. It was just totally bewildering. Although I was desperate to confide in Ella or my mum, I still felt too embarrassed and strangely guilty, almost as though it was actually all my own fault. That I was somehow spurring him on to do these horrible, nasty things. After all, he didn't used to be like this. Did he?

I couldn't wait to get out of the flat that morning and get the hell away from him. It was such a relief when I got to College, to get back to some kind of normality with my lovely friends. We were sketching out different ideas in class when I started to tell Ella how the drag queens had come into the pub the night before.

"Oh, my goodness, that's so random!" she said, laughing, "I wish I had been there to see them.

"Where on earth had they come from?"

"I've no idea, but you should have seen their make-up Ella, it was just fantastic. I've never seen anything so perfect."

"Better than us then?" she joked.

"I'm afraid so," I said, laughing, "We've got a lot to learn."

"Oh my God and here was me thinking we were the best! So... what nasty comment did Ollie make when you told him?" asked Ella.

"I... oh... well... I didn't actually get around to telling him," I stumbled, wondering how on earth she could know that he was nasty to me.

Ella stopped sketching and looked at me in disbelief. I could tell that she knew right away that something definitely wasn't quite right.

"But isn't that the kind of thing you loved up little couples would chat about when you come home of an evening?" she quizzed, obviously trying to get something out of me.

"Well... he was tired... already in bed actually...," I said sketching furiously, so furiously in fact, that my pencil flew right out of my hand.

I quickly bent over to pick it up from the floor actually trying to hide from Ella's scrutinising eyes and hoping that she would change the subject. Ironically, my tee-shirt rode up my back, revealing the big, black bruise that Ollie had inflicted on me the night before. I could hear Ella catch her breath when she obviously had caught site of it.

When I sat back up, I could see the look of horror on her face and I immediately realised why. How on earth was I going to talk my way out of this one?

"Marina how the hell did you get that?" she asked, trying not to speak too loud but obviously angry at what she had seen.

"Get what?" I asked, stupidly pretending not to know what she was talking about.

"Your back... you've got a massive, big bruise," she pointed out.

"Oh, that... I... oh... I... I slipped in the kitchen... caught it on the door," I lied, forcing a smile, "Silly me!"

Ella just shook her head and said no more, but I knew by the way she was looking at me that she was putting two and two together and suspected that something was wrong. I was so, so desperate to tell her what had really happened. Desperate for her pity and desperate for her help but, I just couldn't bring myself to do it. It was too humiliating. After all, I had brought it all upon myself.

Then I felt totally guilty about not opening up and being honest with her. She was my best friend for God's sakes.

What a flaming mess.

The rest of the day went in quite quickly unfortunately and I could feel myself tensing up, worrying as the time got nearer to having to go back home to Ollie. Luckily, we were going to be told where our work placements were that day, so that kind of took my mind off things for a while, as we sat listening with anticipation. We had to get experience working in a make-up department, but it could be anywhere, like a theatre or even a studio. It was really quite exciting.

"I better get somewhere decent," whispered Ella, "Or I'm packing the whole flaming thing in and moving back to Ireland."

"Oh, don't be daft!" I said, "You love it too much and anyway, what else would you do?"

"... Emma White," the lecturer called out, "Independent Performance Studios."

"Bitch!" hissed Ella, "That's where I wanted."

I just smiled at her. I really wasn't all that bothered about where I got, to be honest, so I was only half listening as the rest of the names got called out. Ella grabbed my hand and squeezed it tight as her name came up.

"Ella O'Neil... Minstrels Theatre."

"Yesss!" she squealed, clasping her hands, "Oh my God, I'm so happy."

"Alesha Swinton..." the lecturer continued, "Black and White Studios."

"Bugger," moaned Ella, "That's got to be the best place ever. Now I want that one!"

I giggled at her. She was so funny. We listened as more names were called out. It took a while, but William and Hannah were delighted with their placements too and then last but not least, it was my turn.

"Marina Burton... Tail Feathers Club," announced the lecturer, obviously glad at completing the task.

We just turned and looked at each other blankly.

"Where's that then?" Ella asked with a puzzled look on her face.

"I have got absolutely no idea," I replied, "The back of beyond, knowing my luck. I'll need to look it up."

I felt a tiny bit disappointed because it wasn't actually a theatre or even better, a studio. It was just a club. To be honest I really wanted the Minstrels Theatre because I had been at a show there with Ollie and it looked just amazing. I would never have complained about it though, especially not to Ella because she was so delighted.

"Oh, I'm sure it'll be good," said Ella, reassuringly patting my hand, though I knew she wasn't really caring because she was happy with her lot, (lucky bitch!)

"Now as you all know," continued the lecturer, "Places of entertainment operate mostly at weekends and evenings, so it's up to you to work out your hours. Do NOT let it interfere with your studies please."

Those words suddenly gave me a frightened, sickening feeling in the pit of my stomach, making me feel like I was going to have a panic attack. "Operate in the evenings". After his reaction last night, I just knew it was going to be a nightmare trying to explain to Ollie that I was going to be working more evenings at a club. What on earth was I going to do? I couldn't reduce my hours at the pub because I had just asked Bill for more, plus I desperately needed the money. What a predicament. It was meant to be a happy, exciting time for me, not a stressful one.

The room was noisy with chatter and anticipation for what was left of the day, but I found it really hard to join in with everyone else's enthusiasm. Luckily, Ella was too elated to cotton on to my negative vibes as we said our goodbyes at the station and about to go our separate ways.

"You take care my lovely," said Ella squeezing me tight.

"You too," I said, hugging her back, but not wanting to ever let go.

"And remember," she said, looking seriously into my face, "I'm only a phone call away if you need me."

I wanted to say "But I do need you Ella. I need you to help me get away from Ollie. You were right all along."

But, instead all I said was, "I know. See you tomorrow."

See you tomorrow? Yes, see you tomorrow, that is if Ollie doesn't bloody kill me first.

As I sat on the train, I could feel the tension slowly mounting as I thought about Ollie and wondering what weird mood he was going to be in tonight. With great trepidation, when I arrived home, I put my key in the lock and gently pushed open the door. The flat was empty thank goodness, with no signs of him being in. I couldn't believe my luck. The silence was truly golden.

I flopped down on the couch and let out a sigh of relief, then sat for five minutes, just savouring the tranquillity of being on my own. Before I started getting ready for work, I quickly looked on my phone to see where my placement was going to be. I soon discovered that The Tail Feathers was actually a comedy club, with drag queens mostly at the top of the bill.

I couldn't believe it when I looked at their website, only to discover that Sabrina and Giselle, that had come into the pub the night before, were regular performers there. How funny was that I thought to myself. Now, I felt really excited at the prospect of going to Tail Feathers, just knowing in my heart that I was going to have a ball.

I quickly switched my phone off, shoving it in my pocket, when I heard Ollie's key turn in the door and then pretended to be watching the telly. He looked at me suspiciously as he walked into the lounge, but I just tried my hardest to ignore him and act normally, whatever normal was because I really didn't know any more.

"I'm just going to pop some pizza in the oven," I said, cheerfully, jumping up out of seat and hoping that he wouldn't be angry that it wasn't ready, "It'll just take five minutes."

"Well just bring it through when it's ready then," Ollie said, deliberately standing in my way.

"I'm an early start," I said, trying to squeeze past him, then couldn't stop myself from saying, "I don't really have time for waitress service."

"Well then make time," he said, pushing his face up against mine, glaring at me, "You shouldn't be sitting about watching the telly if you've "not got time" missy."

31

I really wanted to slap his ugly dish, telling him to bugger off and what was with the "missy"?

Terrified though in case he would hit me, I just did as I was told. William had been right. He WAS a control-freak.

"Well let me through then," I said, feebly giving in to his demands.

Thankfully he didn't touch me as he stood aside to let me get past. He then jumped noisily on to the sofa, putting his feet up on the coffee table, still with his mucky big boots on, which he knew would really annoy me. I tried to ignore it though, just so relieved that he hadn't done anything to me and after shoving the dinner in the oven, I quickly ran through to the bedroom to get myself ready for work.

Luckily, the pizza was perfectly cooked just as I was about to leave. I quickly dumped it on to a plate and grudgingly ran through to serve it to him. As I handed it over, I really wanted to smash it on his head, then smear the tomato sauce all over his ugly, big face. I didn't though and he just grabbed it roughly off me, starting to rip into it with not so much as a word of thanks. I didn't care though, as I turned and went to grab my things. I was just so glad to be going to my work and getting away from him. It's strange how quickly your feelings for someone can totally change, turning from absolute adoration to absolute loathing.

Unfortunately, it was deadly quiet in the pub that night, with only a handful of the usual punters, slowly sipping their beer. Not even the old jukebox was playing, which made it unbearably silent.

Every time the door rattled open, I watched in eager anticipation, hoping that it was the two drag queens again, but disappointingly it was always just another regular. I pulled the pints and stood back, absolutely bored out of my mind which wasn't good for me, because I kept finding myself thinking about Ollie. I suppose it was better than sitting at home and actually having to look at him though.

I didn't like using my phone at work because I thought it was a bit rude, but Bill was on his break, so I quickly whipped it out. Ella had sent a text and when I opened it, she had attached a photo of herself, standing outside the Minstrels Theatre. She must have gone for a nosy. Her face was beaming with happiness in the picture and for a split second I felt so envious of her. Not because she had got the Minstrels, but envious of her happiness... her freedom. She wasn't being bullied by a psycho partner. She was free to do as she pleased, when she pleased. I tried to ignore my negative thoughts though and text her back.

"Looking good, gorgeous! See you tomorrow xxx"

As I clicked to send the message, another one was coming through. It was from Ollie. I felt my heart sink at the sight of his name. What the hell did he want? I tentatively opened the message.

"Your pizza was shite by the way," it read.

What an imbecile, I thought. Was that his idea of a joke or was he just intent on totally wearing me down? I wanted to text back, "No YOU'RE shite," but instead I quickly turned off the phone, not giving him the satisfaction of a reply and shoved it in my pocket, just as Bill came walking back through from his break.

I felt utterly sickened as I thought about the text. If he wasn't happy with his pizza, then did that mean that he wasn't happy with me and if he wasn't happy with me then did that mean that he was going to do something nasty again?

I shivered at the thought and really didn't want to go home. I was nearly hysterical when Bill said, "Just you finish up early Marina. There's nothing much doing here tonight so you might as well get home to lover boy."

Lover boy? Oh, my God he was anything but.

I knew he was just being his usual lovely self, but I wanted to scream and shout at him, "No, Bill please let me stay. I'll sleep in the cellar if I have to. Just please don't let me have to go home to that psycho, because I just know he's only going to be horrible to me".

Instead though, I tried hard to force a smile as I said, "Oh, thanks Bill. That's really kind of you."

"No worries pet. You go and have some quality time with that boyfriend of yours," he said.

Quality time? What was that?

I hesitantly gathered my stuff together and said goodnight, then headed for the bus stop. I hoped the buses had all been cancelled as I stood waiting, but of course one eventually came. There was hardly anyone on it which meant it didn't have to stop much, so I seemed to get home in no time at all worst luck.

I looked warily at the door as I approached it and could feel my hands shaking as I put my key in the lock. As I pushed open the door, I noticed the flat was unusually quiet, with no telly blaring in the living room and no radio on in the kitchen.

I cautiously checked each room to see if Ollie was hiding somewhere but thankfully, there were no signs of him. He appeared to be out. I breathed a massive sigh of relief, not even realising that I had actually been holding my breath with fear. I wanted to run and hammer planks across the front door, covering it in barbed wire and electric fencing, barricading myself in so Ollie couldn't get near me when he came home.

Instead, all I could do was soak up the peace and quiet while I could but at the same time, I was anxious about his return, wondering where the hell he was.

As the clock ticked round, I didn't know whether to sit up and wait for him or just go to my bed. I knew in his warped mind that neither scenario would be the right one to choose, so eventually I opted to go to bed, although I knew I probably wouldn't sleep.

I lay awake for a while then must have eventually dozed off, but was rudely awakened by Ollie, clattering noisily into the flat and from the irregular sound of his footsteps I could only surmise that he had been drinking. A lot.

I heard him stumbling into the kitchen and scratching about in the fridge, for something to eat, then he staggered through to the bathroom. He started to do what sounded like an endless, very noisy pee which was obviously the aftereffect of drinking copious amounts of alcohol. When he did eventually finish, he didn't even flush the toilet, then came tottering through to the bedroom. I could smell the stale stench of beer on his breath as he leaned over the bed, peering at me.

"You awake?" he half whispered, wobbling from side to side.
I didn't answer him and kept my eyes tightly shut, pretending to be asleep, hoping that he would just go away and leave me alone. As if that was going to happen.

"Fffff..." he said, swaying backwards a little as he stood back up,
"Wouldn't want to shag you anyway, ugly slag."

I half wanted to laugh out loud. Wouldn't want to shag me? Why on earth would I WANT him to shag me. He was so drunk he probably wouldn't have been able to do anything anyway.

I actually thought that I had got away with it as he started to stagger towards the doorway. I was about to roll over and go back to sleep, when he unexpectedly turned quickly around and came back over to the bed. He lifted one of the pillows and before I had time to do anything, he had put it over my face, weighing it down with all his strength.

"I know you're not sleeping, you stupid cow," he hissed as he continued to push the pillow forcibly down on my face.

I started to panic as I was unable to move or shout, let alone breathe, due to the heavy weight of his body on top of mine. I tried frantically, with all of my might to push him off me, while at the same time trying to kick and punch him, but he wasn't going to budge. I really thought this was it, that he was finally going to kill me this time. I could feel my face burning due to it rubbing against the pillow as I struggled with him some more, but then I began to feel light-headed and faint. I just couldn't fight him anymore.

Everything started spinning and echoing, probably due to the lack of oxygen. When I had finally given up hope of ever breathing again, I felt him bounce firmly on the pillow. The noise of the material scratching at my face rang loud in my ears, then he lifted the pillow roughly away, throwing it on to the floor.

"Not sleeping now. Are you bitch?" he said jumping from the bed and then staggered through to the lounge, laughing triumphantly to himself.

What an evil, sadistic bastard. He just left me lying there, choking and spluttering as I tried hard to breathe oxygen back into my lungs, while struggling to stop myself from passing out. My cheeks were on fire now due to the friction from the pillow rubbing on them. Then I started to shake uncontrollably, as I thought about what he had just done to me, realising that he could have actually killed me. Had that been his intention? Or did he, somehow in his drunken, warped mind, think that it was funny?

I was really shocked at what he had done and felt absolutely terrified, but I somehow managed to pull myself together. I so desperately wanted to phone the police and let them know what a maniac he was and what he had done to me, but I knew that I couldn't. He would hear me talking then probably would take my phone off me, smashing it into pieces, so instead I just lay there, trying to breathe calmly, realising that I just had to accept my lot. He was only showing his true colours and I knew that nothing was going to stop him now. Probably the more I tried to fight back, the more he would hurt me, so I would just have to put up and shut up.

Then my emotions took over and I began to sob, while trying my very hardest not to make too much noise in case he heard me and came back through to finish me off once and for all. The tears were flooding uncontrollably from my eyes though, as I gently dabbed at my face with the bedsheet, still trying my best to keep quiet.

It was a relief to cry and let it all out, but I struggled to stop myself, when I could hear a noise coming from the lounge. I tried not to sniff as I sat up and strained my ears to listen, terrified in case he was coming back through. Fortunately, I realised that the noise I could hear was just him snoring. He must have fallen into a drunken sleep on the couch. Thank God, I thought, feeling relieved as I lay gently back down and pulled the quilt up round myself for comfort.

What I really wanted to do was to grab all my stuff and go running out of the flat, getting as far away as possible so he couldn't hurt me anymore. I knew that in reality though, that I would just have to lie tight and hope that he was in a better mood in the morning. I felt like a prisoner and a slave to his psychotic outbursts.

Luckily for me, he slept the whole night on the sofa, snoring like a distressed pig. I tiptoed around the flat in the morning, trying to be as quiet as possible as I got ready for college, hoping that he wouldn't waken before I left. Unfortunately, he did though. I was in the bathroom, quickly putting on my lipstick when he came rushing through. I still felt traumatised from the night before and cowered back as he stood in front of me.

"Why didn't you waken me?" he asked, putting his hands round my waist, "I think I might have had too much to drink last night."

Was that his means of an apology? I didn't know how to react or what to say for fear of upsetting him. I wanted to ask what the hell was wrong with him. I wanted to demand a real apology. I wanted to punch his horrible face and yell at him, but I didn't. I said nothing and pulled away from him, continuing to apply my lipstick.

"Am I forgiven?" he said, putting on a sheepish look then kissing at my neck as he put his arms back around my waist.

Forgiven? Who was he trying to kid? I really wanted to vomit straight into his face, but just forced a false smile and wriggled back out of his grasp, totally revolted by the touch of his fingers on my body.

"Better run," I said, rushing to the door before he could get his hands on me again.

"Hurry back... and I'll really make it worth your while," he shouted, over exaggerating a wink.

Oh, yuck! Not if I had anything to do with it. What a psycho.

I had to really stop myself from sprinting down the street to get away from him. I was scared to look over my shoulder in case he was there, running after me. I approached the bus stop, but then kept on walking to the next one, still terrified in case he was there, behind me. Still not comfortable, I hurried on to the next one again but didn't start to relax until I got off the bus at the station.

I finally felt safe when I got on the train, but when I got off at my stop, I started to have flash backs of the pillow over my face and feeling Ollie's weight pressing down on me. I felt the tears pricking my eyes as a wave of panic came over me and I nearly jumped out of my skin when I felt a hand on my arm. I spun quickly round defensively, fully expecting it to be him but then started to sob uncontrollably with relief when I saw it was Ella. My friend. My sanctuary.

"Oh my God! What in the name of the wee man's wrong Marina?" she asked, obviously concerned by the state I was in and hugging me tightly, "You look like you've seen a ghost."

I was sobbing so much though, that I couldn't utter a word, my whole body shaking, my face soaking wet with tears and unsightly snot dripping from my nose. Where's a hanky when you need one! I must have looked an absolute mess. Ella comforted me as we sat down on a bench and I forced myself to calm down because I felt so embarrassed, aware that the other passers-by were staring at me.

"It's o.k. ... just let it all out. You don't have to say anything," said Ella calmly, seeing that I actually couldn't speak, "It's him isn't it?" All I could do was nod my head because the words still wouldn't come out, just the tears. I was so overwhelmed with emotions.

"I knew it," Ella said quietly so that no-one could hear her, "has that bastard been hitting you?"

I sheepishly nodded my head, feeling so embarrassed at having to admit it, then just started sobbing uncontrollably again. Ella put her arm round me and held me tight. I felt so safe beside her just knowing that she was there for me, not questioning or probing, just reassuring and once I had finally calmed down, we headed for college.

"Right, I know where we need to go first," said Ella, directing us towards the canteen, "Coffee is definitely the order of the day."

Ella sat me carefully down at a table then went up to get the drinks. This gave me some time to try to compose myself which was pretty difficult because I was feeling a bit hysterical. I managed to give myself a pep talk and had succeeded in calming myself down a bit by the time she returned.

"There you go," she said, handing me a mug and sitting gently down in front of me.

I took a few sips of coffee, the steam swirling soothingly into my face and helping to dry my tears. Thank God for caffeine and thank God for Ella. I was beginning to feel better already.

"You know you don't have to tell me anything if you don't want to," Ella said, squeezing my hand tightly, "But I can assure you one hundred percent, that whatever you tell me will go no further."

"I know," I said, squeezing her hand back, "It's just... well... it's all a bit embarrassing."

"Hey! You have got absolutely nothing to be embarrassed about Marina," said Ella seriously, "Now, please be honest with me. Did he give you that bruise you've got on your back?"

I nodded and sniffed back the tears that were starting to flow again.

"I honestly don't know what I'm doing wrong," I said shrugging my shoulders.

"You're not doing anything wrong Marina. He's a creep," said Ella angrily, "and by the looks of it, a bully too. You know that I've never liked him. I just knew there was something about him, but I never thought for a minute he would hurt you. So, have things been really bad then?"

"Oh, Ella, it's been worse than bad. It's been bloody awful. He's just totally changed," I confided.

38

"That's just it, Marina… he hasn't changed. Unfortunately, the bastard's just showing his true colours. So how did you get the bruise?" asked Ella, anxiously.

"Well… you know how the two drag queens had come into the pub the other night…," I started.

"Yes," said Ella, pulling her chair closer and listening intently.

"Well, I was just trying to tell him what had happened," I continued, wringing my hands and then momentarily brightening up for a minute, as I thought about them, "Oh, and you're not going to believe it, but I looked up the Tail Feathers Club and guess what? Those two drag queens actually do stand-up there!"

"Oh, my God, that's so funny," said Ella, managing a little laugh but then looking seriously at me again, as I carried on with my story.

"But anyway, before I could even start to tell him what had happened," I said, feeling my body tensing up thinking about it, "He started accusing me of seeing someone… just because I looked happy and actually had a smile on my face."

"What an arse," yelled Ella, in disbelief, "That sounds like someone with a guilty conscience to me. He's probably the one that's got a bit on the side."

"I know," I agreed, not really having thought about it before, "but then… then he pushed me… hard against the door… but my back caught on the handle… and that's how I got the bruise."

"Oh Marina, you poor thing. I just wish you had told me," Ella said, squeezing my hand again, "I'm telling you, he's an absolute head case that one. Why would he want to do that to you?"

"I don't know," I said, shrugging my shoulders, "I just can't get my head round it all. It started with him being annoyed at me for not having his dinner ready for him one night. My train had been cancelled making me late getting home… so my punishment was a punch in the ribs… and then he poured the pot of pasta I was making on to the floor."

"Oh, my God, I can't believe you kept that to yourself Marina and what an evil, sexist bastard!
Why should you have to make the dinner," yelled Ella, "He's obviously still living in the dark ages."

39

"I know," I continued, still unable to believe the tale I was telling, "Then he had the audacity to force me to go and get a takeaway, knowing full well I was skint after our big day out."

"For Heaven's sake, so that's how you couldn't afford your bottle of water?" surmised Ella, putting two and two together, "Now it all makes sense. Oh, Marina, why didn't you tell me? You know I'm here for you. Now I just hate him even more."

"Oh God me too," I agreed, "I just can't stand the sight of him. I kept thinking it was just a one off and that it wouldn't happen again. I mean everything was fine up until recently... but now... now I'm absolutely terrified of him Ella."

"Oh, my goodness, you've got every right to be," empathised Ella, "So what happened last night then?"

I took some deep breaths and tried to talk but nothing came out. I was still too traumatised to even think about it, never mind put it in to words. The sheer terror of reliving what he had done to me was putting my whole body in to shock again. As I remembered the terrible ordeal, I still couldn't believe that I had allowed him do it to me or that he could even have done such a thing in the first place. I was suddenly pulled out of my nightmare thoughts by Ella's gentle voice.

"Don't worry, there's no rush Marina," Ella said softly, "Just try taking some deep breaths."

Eventually I managed to hold it together and tried to control my breathing and my shaky voice, because I really wanted to tell her.

"Well, I... I had got off early from the pub and... and when I got home, he wasn't in. I didn't know whether to stay up and wait for him... or just go to my bed. Anyway," I said taking another deep breath, "I decided to go to bed... but when he came in, I could tell by his breath that he had been drinking. I pretended I was asleep, so he wouldn't bother me, but... but he could tell I was faking it and then... then..."

I just couldn't say the words. I still couldn't believe what he had done to me and thinking of what the consequences might have been was absolutely shocking. Ella gently took hold of both my hands and mimicked deep breathing, motioning for me to copy her. I mirrored what she was doing and took some more deep breaths in, with long blows out until I was finally in control again, forcing myself to finish my story.

"... and then... he put... a pillow... over my face," I struggled, unable to believe the words, as they came out of my mouth. It just seemed so hideous and wicked. So unreal.

"Holy mother of God," shrieked Ella, drawing back in horror, but then realising her reaction, she quickly lunged back forward and took hold of both my hands again, listening intently as I continued.

"I thought he was going to kill me Ella. I couldn't breathe... or move. He was on top of me... his body was so heavy. I was petrified," I sobbed.

"Oh, Marina, no wonder, it must have been like your worst nightmare. You do realise this is very serious. You really need to go to the police," pleaded Ella, "The guy's a maniac... you can't let him get away with it."

I totally understood what she was saying, but go to the police? Wasn't that a bit extreme? I just hated any sort of confrontation and would they even believe me? Would they actually be able to do anything? I mean I didn't have any sort of evidence. It was just his word against mine and knowing Ollie, he would just sweet talk his way out of it all. I'd only be wasting their time and what on earth would he do to me if I did go run and tell? It would probably only make things a hundred times worse.

"Marina?" Ella was saying, shaking my hand, "Are you listening to me? You can't live like this. It's far too dangerous."

I couldn't really hear what she was saying. That was, I could hear the words but not interpret them the way that I should have. Oh my God, I didn't know what to think... what to do... I could literally feel the weight of the worry of it all, pushing heavily down on my shoulders.

"Marina? Can you even hear me?" Ella was saying, obviously very concerned, now pulling at my arm to try and jolt me out of my thoughts.

Feeling confused and a bit frightened by her slightly aggressive tone, I wanted to shout at her "Look just leave me alone. I know you're only trying to help but I don't WANT to hear what you're saying. I don't WANT this to be happening to me."

It was obviously just a mixture of emotions flooding my brain, but at the same time I knew she was talking sense and that she was doing what she did best which was being a good friend. God, I needed a friend right now, to help me deal with all of this mess.

"I... I need to leave him... I know," I eventually managed to say, agreeing and nodding my head furiously, "and I will...."

"You're going to be late for class," shouted William popping his head round the canteen door.

"You'll get detention," joked Hannah, standing behind him.

I tried to block them out and kept looking intently at Ella for encouragement, as she shouted, "No worries. Just give us a minute, will you?"

I loved my friend so much, as I looked across the table at her. She was fighting for my side. I desperately needed to listen to her words of advice. I needed her to convince me to do what was best. I smiled at her, knowing she would guide me in the right direction and be there for me – always. I knew she was the one person in the world that I could totally trust.

"First of all, we're going to get to class, because there's no way on this earth he's going to stop you from following your dream. He is NOT going to spoil your chances of a good career," Ella said grasping both my hands, "Then tonight... you're going to pack up your stuff and come back and stay with me. Do you hear?"

I just looked at her wide eyed, wanting to agree but weirdly also wanting to retaliate. I was still scared of Ollie's reaction and what he might do to me for even telling Ella, never mind running away from him.

"Yes... but..." I started.

"Sssssshhh... No buts," said Ella, pressing her forefinger to her lips, "It's sorted, O.K.? It's happening... You're leaving that God-forsaken creep. Now come on, let's get to class before we get into trouble!"

I forced a little laugh, but still wasn't sure that it was good idea and followed like a little lamb as Ella took me by the arm, leading the way. All day I felt totally protected by my friend and I really started to believe that everything would be o.k. now. That everything was going to be good at last.

Luckily, the lecturer was late arriving, so we didn't get into any trouble for not being on time and my thoughts and worries were totally diverted as class started. We were doing scenarios, using each other as models creating strong, theatrical looks. With heavy dustings of powder and exaggerated, lines around our brows and eyes, we all looked a bit comical, but it was good fun. My lips sparkling and red, I felt like a Hollywood film star, even a bit sexy, if that was humanly possible, but definitely a lot more confident and happy as I work and chatted alongside my friends.

"Wo, you look fabulous Marina," said Hannah, standing back for a better look.

"Doesn't she just," agreed William, fluffing my hair up.

"It's actually the perfect combination of my expert technique and Marina's lovely face!" marvelled Ella.

I laughed at them all as they took photos of me on their phones but couldn't help agreeing with them that I looked quite good and as we finished up for the day, Ella kept reminding me of the big plan.

"Now you pack up as much stuff as you possibly can and you tell the bastard what a shit he is as you walk out the door," she said.

"Don't worry! I will," I reassured her but inside I knew I would probably be too scared to say anything at all.

True to her word, she never said anything about it all to Hannah and William, or anyone for that matter and at the end of the day, we rushed excitedly to the station. I felt really positive now about leaving Ollie and was just desperate to get home and gather my things together.

"Now phone me as soon as you're leaving and I'll come and meet you somewhere," Ella said, as we hugged at the station.

"I will," I said, kissing her cheek, "Keep that phone on 'cause I'll definitely be in touch."

"You better be," shouted Ella as we both headed in different directions.

I hurried on to the train, feeling even more positive and excited. As I made my way towards the flat, I turned off the volume on my mobile, just in case Ella might start texting as that would only arouse Ollies suspicions and I definitely didn't want that.

Of course, when I pushed the door open, the aroma of steak and chips immediately teased my nostrils and as I walked into the hall, I noticed a trail of rose petals leading into the lounge.

Unwillingly, I was forced to follow them and once in the lounge I discovered an enormous bouquet of red roses and a huge box of chocolates on the coffee table. My heart just sank. He was spoiling Ella's big plan. I let out a sigh of dismay, but then caught my breath when, like an electric shock, I bounced away as I felt Ollie's hands round my waist.

"OOOhhh!" I yelped, pretending to be HAPPY surprised instead of TERRIFIED surprised.

"Mmmmm. How's my Marina ballerina then?" he cooed, repulsively into my ear, while sniffing annoyingly at my hair.

Ballerina? Fairy elephant more like. As he well knew, I had two left feet and had never danced a step of ballet in my life. Who was he trying to kid? I stayed calm though and just played along with him.

"What's all this then?" I asked, trying hard to look impressed and happy.

"Well, it's just my way of saying sorry," he said, trying to put an apologetic look on his face.

"Oh, lovely," I said, looking at the flowers.

It wasn't what I really wanted to say. I actually wanted to say "Shove your chocolates and flowers where the sun don't shine pal. I've had enough of your psychotic episodes and I'm getting the hell out of here, you absolute nutter."

No, instead I was obliged to sit down at the kitchen table, be forced fed his steak and chips and smile politely saying, "That was utterly delicious."

"Well, if you think that was delicious," he said, taking hold of my hand and looking into my eyes, "Just wait till you see what I've got for afters...."

In the past I would have responded with a girly giggle, knowing exactly what was for "afters", whereas now I tried to force a smile, hoping and praying that he meant he had profiteroles in the fridge. But the kisses he forced upon my neck, as he reached to take my empty plate away, made me realise that profiteroles definitely were not on the menu and I also knew that leaving him tonight wasn't either. It was his perfect, twisted ploy. Be nice to me, then I've got no reason to complain about his strange behaviour let alone be bold enough to even suggest leaving.

I lay like a virgin missionary that night, unable to show emotion or even try to welcome his body into mine. It disgusted me to allow him even to touch me, but at the same time I was overwhelmingly frightened to refuse him. Petting was painful and orgasm was faked, while I felt so guilty for letting Ella down. I hadn't left him and even worse, I had allowed him to have sex with me.

I hardly slept a wink as I lay beside him, scared in case he was going to roll over on top of me again, stopping me from moving, stopping me from breathing, stopping me from living. I felt so frightened and so alone. I was truly like a leaf, floating on the brink of a waterfall.

The next morning, as usual, I couldn't wait to rush out of the flat to get as far away as possible from him and scrambled to get quickly out of the flat.

"Love you," he shouted, as I stumbled out of the front door.

"Well, I certainly don't love you, creep," I wanted to shout, as I pretended not to hear him and hurried on my way.

Due to all of his (unwanted) attention from the night before, I had totally forgotten that I had turned the sound down on my phone and I hadn't even had a chance to look at it. As I sat on the train heading for college, I could see lots of missed calls from Ella and thousands of worried texts.

"What's happening?"

"Where are you?"

"Don't be taken in by him Marina."

"Are you o.k.? Please call me."

Poor Ella, she must have been absolutely out of her mind with worry because I hadn't responded. I quickly text her to put her mind at rest, but I knew it was far too late. I felt so angry with myself for letting him get the better of me, for letting my good friend down.

"Don't worry I'm still in one piece," I text, "On train coming in. I'll tell you all about it xxx"

"Thank God. Speak to you soon xxx" she replied almost instantly.

Ella was waiting for me at the entrance to the college and she ran towards me with her arms open wide when she saw me coming. I couldn't believe she was actually still speaking to me. What a girl.

"Oh Marina, "she said, giving me big hug, "I was so worried about you. I thought he might have done something really awful to you."

"Oh you big dafty," I said, hugging her back.

Ella pulled away, with her hands still on my shoulders, looking intently at my face as if she was reading my thoughts. I honestly didn't know how she did it. It must have been an Irish thing or something, because she definitely had the gift, either that or she'd had one too many bad boyfriends herself and knew all the signs.

"He's been all nice to you. Hasn't he?" she said, frowning. It really was as though she was a mind reader. How could she possibly know this?

"I... emm...," I stuttered, but couldn't speak before Ella did.

"Oh no," she wailed, "Not the chocolates and flowers routine again. You honestly can't be taken in with all that crap Marina."

"Don't worry, I'm not," I said defensively, "But what could I do? He was being all nice to me and I was scared in case he would really go off it."

"But that's why you need to leave him… now Marina... before he DOES really go off it. He's like a fecking ticking time bomb that one and I can't bear to think what he might do to you."

I felt a shiver go through my body as she said those words. It was true. God only knows what he was really capable of. Why did it have to be like this? Everything had been so perfect. Why couldn't he just be normal and nice like the imaginary, fantasy boyfriend in my head? It just wasn't fair.

"Can I come home with you tonight?" I asked timidly.

"Oh my God… of course you can," said Ella, hugging me so tight I thought I was going to burst!

"You'll need to sleep on the couch till we sort something out though... I mean I've got a spare room… but it's full of junk."

"I don't mind. I'll sleep on the floor if I have to… or in the bath!" I said, excitedly, feeling a huge surge of relief,

"But what about all my stuff?"

"Oh, never mind about that," said Ella, taking me by the hand and patting it, "We'll think of something. As long as you're safe... that's the main thing."

Oh, my God. My friend was actually a saint. She always knew how to make me feel better and she had all the answer to all of my problems. She was my absolute saviour.

We hurried into class and all day I continued to feel excited and so relieved that my personal hell was finally going to be over because this time, I was definitely moving back in with Ella. She was on a high too and twittered away, trying to get everything organised. The time flew in and all of a sudden it was time for us to go home. We quickly grabbed our stuff and eagerly headed off down the stairs.

"Oh, I'm so happy. I can't believe you're coming back home with me," chirped Ella, "So, what will we have for dinner tonight? I think we should celebrate and have a takeaway."

"Oh, yes," I said enthusiastically, "... and definitely a glass... no... make that a bottle of bubbly... or two..."

I was depressingly stopped abruptly in my tracks though and Ella along with me. In the distance we could see Ollie, standing at the gate. Why? Why the hell was he there? What was he playing at? He never came to college to meet me. Honestly, one minute he's attacking me then the next he's all over me. What a fucking creep.

"What the hell? I don't believe it. What on earth is he up to?" I said incredulously.

"He's just playing you Marina, that's what he's up to. Now just stay cool and please, please don't be taken in with him," said Ella, pulling me back, "Remember... things are going to get better Marina... you're coming home with me."

"I know I am," I said, positively, but then started to cave, "But what will I say to him though? I don't want to cause a scene. Not here of all places"

"Just say..." started Ella, but before she could finish Ollie was there, right in front of us, taking over the whole situation.

"Hi Marina... Ella," he said in his false pleasant tones.

"Hi," Ella sighed, looking in the totally opposite direction and folding her arms in obvious disgust.

"What are you doing here?" I blurted out.

"I finished early," he said taking my arm and emphatically pulling me away from Ella, "So I thought it would be nice if we could go out for something to eat… just the two of us."

I wanted to be brave and stand up to him… for Ella, but then I honestly didn't know what to say. Why was he doing this to me? It was almost as though he knew that I was plotting to move out. I could see Ella glaring at him then looking at me, obviously willing me to say that I was leaving. I hesitated for a moment, all set to tell him, but then the fear took hold and I just couldn't go through with it. I felt like I was a puppet, with evil Ollie pulling my strings and as usual, the words that I wanted to say just wouldn't come out.

"Marina?" Ella prompted, expecting me to tell him I wasn't going anywhere with him.

"Bye Ella," he said, before I could even answer, looking at her like he had won his prize and waving in a sarcastic fashion, half dragging me away, "Two's company and all that."

"But Marina...," shouted Ella.

I turned and looked at her not knowing what to do, hoping that she would do something to save me. Ollie was looking at her, still with a triumphant look on his face. I couldn't believe it as I realised that he had obviously put the fear in to Ella as well.

"... enjoy yourself...," she eventually said, admitting defeat.

The bastard had beaten us both this time.

Everything had been turned upside down. All our plans had been smashed to pieces. I had gone from feeling totally elated and relieved to feeling confused and threatened yet again but now I just had to go along with his warped master plan as he went in to his "nice" act.

He took me, or should I say half dragged me to a beautiful little restaurant, which any other time would have been so romantic and sweet, but tonight it just turned my stomach. I forced myself to eat my meal, but ended up chasing it round the plate, as I listened to him drone on about nothing in particular and trying to act like the perfect boyfriend. He dragged it out as much as he could and then I was forced to walk, arm in arm with him all the way back to the flat.

I hurried into the bathroom as soon as we got home. I really wanted to be sick to empty my stomach of its contents, put there by his horrible scheming and then scrub my whole body after having his dirty hands touching me. Instead, though, I got ready for bed, then walked through to the kitchen. He was there, getting a mug of water at the sink.

"So... did you enjoy your surprise dinner then?" he asked, looking round at me.

I should have said, "Yes... it was lovely thanks," to suffice his twisted, warped mind, but for some reason, my mouth actually said what my brain was thinking for once.

"No... I didn't to be honest," I said, shocked at myself for saying the truth, but immediately regretting every word and wanting to take it all back.

"Oh?" he said, turning right round and looking at me full on, with his scary eyes.

I couldn't back down now. I had to continue, no matter what.

"It's just... It's just I don't understand you any more Ollie. One minute your... Mr. Nice Guy then the next minute your..."

"Sshh, sshh," he said, taking me in his arms, "I know I've been difficult lately... but it's work Marina... I've been stressed out... too many deadlines and stuff."

"That's fair enough Ollie, but you're frightening me," I said, pulling away from him, "I never know what you're going to be like. You're constantly like a ticking bomb, just ready to explode."

"I'm truly sorry Marina... you've got to believe me... I'll make changes... I promise," he said, pulling me to him again.

"But the thing is... I don't think I want to be with you anymore," I said defiantly, but then instantly regretting my bravery and truthfulness, when his face looked like thunder.

He immediately pushed me forcibly away and picked up the mug he'd been drinking from.

"Aaaarrhhh," he roared, smashing it on the floor, "You NEED to stay with me... I said I'll make changes. You know I love you Marina."

"O.k., o.k.," I said, backing down, scared in case he would strike out with his bad temper.

"I know I've been all over the place lately, but it won't happen again. I promise," he said, obviously trying to force some crocodile tears.

I didn't believe a single word he said but just pretended to be taken in by his lies. I reluctantly put my arms round him and hugged him, while resenting every single minute of it. He sniffled back his false tears, nuzzling his face into my neck. I felt totally repulsed by him, but I knew I just had to fake it till I could work out another plan. I was really pleased with myself though for saying the truth. For finally standing up to him.

CHAPTER 2

TAIL FEATHERS

It was the weekend and everything felt so strange and wrong. Ollie was continuing the being "nice" act, which was really beginning to irritate me, while Ella was totally ignoring all my texts. This was making me feel really isolated and vulnerable because right now, I needed her friendship and support more than ever.

I still hadn't managed to go to the Tail Feathers Club to get my induction and work out my hours. To be honest, I had actually totally forgotten about it with all the things that had been happening. When I eventually did muster up the courage to tell Ollie where I was going that afternoon, he was still putting on the "nice" act and seemed to be alright about it.

"No bother. That'll work in well because I'm going for a game of pool with the boys," he said, pecking me on the cheek, "Just try not to be working too many weekends though so I can have some time with you too."

"No worries," I said, walking out the door, while in my mind I was thinking "As if! Time with you? I don't think so."

I would be making sure I was definitely working EVERY weekend so that I DIDN'T have to spend some time with the complete weirdo. As soon as I was out in the street, I got out my phone and called Ella's number. It rang out though, going straight to her voice mail. I tried again and again without any joy. I was just about to give up when I tried one last time and was so relieved when she actually answered.

"Hello," she said drily.

"Hi Ella, how's things?" I asked.

"O.k. I suppose," she said, "How's things with you? Alive, thank God!"

"Yes," I laughed nervously, "Listen, I'm going to the Tail Feathers Club to sort out my placement. I don't suppose you want to come with me?"

"Oh, I don't know. I mean am I allowed to? You're not going to come chained to that moron boyfriend of yours, are you?" she joked.

"No, of course not," I laughed, nervously again, "I'm just on my way to the bus stop, so I could get you at the station if you like?"

"Really? O.k. Possibly see you soon then?" she said, sounding a bit doubtful as to whether Ollie would allow me the freedom to get there.

I didn't have too long to wait for my bus to come and managed to get a train as soon as I arrived at the station. When it reached the centre of town, I sat down on a bench, knowing Ella would take a little longer because she stayed a bit further away than I did. I was surprised at just how quickly she appeared though. Surely that must bode well, I thought, that she had come so fast.

I felt a bit awkward when I saw her. I knew she wasn't pleased with me because I hadn't left Ollie and quite rightly so, but I just wanted everything to be normal between us. I needn't have worried though. As soon as she saw me, her eyes lit up and she came running over with her arms open wide. It was so good to get a genuine hug from someone that really cared about me. I could feel the tears suddenly pricking my eyes with happiness and relief.

"Oh Ella," I said, trying hard to fight back my emotions, "I love you so, so much."

"Oh, me too," she said squeezing me so tight, I thought I was going to pop, "So is he still trying to butter you up then?"

"Oh my God, it's stifling Ella. I don't know which is worse. Him being nice or him hitting me!" I said as we walked on to the platform, waiting for our train.

"Well, Marina, I can't make any decisions for you, but I think you know as well as I do, that you need to leave him," she said, "He's not going to be nice for ever and you know what they say... a tiger never changes its spots."

"Leopard!" I laughed, correcting her.

"What?" she asked, not realising her mistake.

"A leopard never changes its spots, not a tiger!" I giggled, "You're so Irish!"

"Oh, shit, spots or stripes, you know what I mean," she laughed, "But seriously though, you really need to leave him. I worry about you, constantly… thinking about what he might be doing to you."

"Oh, Ella, please don't worry. I promise I will leave him, but I just need to wait for the right moment," I said reassuringly, "I just can't risk having him going off on one."

"I can understand that and you know that I'll always be here for you," she said, reassuringly, "but please don't wait too long. Anyway, we're not going to let him waste our precious time together. So where is this Feathers Club?"

"Tail Feathers," I laughed, "I'm not 100% sure but I've got a rough idea."

Our train eventually came and between us we worked out where to go with a little bit of help from our phones. We got off at our stop and after a few wrong turns we eventually managed to find it. Up a little back street, there it was, The Tail Feathers Club with its name flashing in bright lights just welcoming us in.

"Oh no, it looks a little bit seedy," I said as we approached the entrance.

"I think it looks flaming amazing," enthused Ella, "It's so bloody exciting. Come on, I can't wait to see what it's like inside."

Her excitement was infectious as we headed through the door. It was just so full of atmosphere with chandeliers hanging from the ceiling and plush carpets under foot. It was like a rogue's gallery on the wall, with pictures of all the acts that obviously played there and most of them drag queens.

"Wow," said Ella, pointing at one of the pictures, "Look at her. She looks absolutely stunning. Her make-up is just breath taking."

I looked a bit closer at the photo and then recognised the familiar beautiful faces.

"Oh my God, that's Sabrina … and that's Giselle," I said pointing to the picture next to it.

"Can I help you ladies?" a voice shouted to us from the box office.

We both looked over and at first, I wasn't sure if it was a man in drag or if it was a woman heavily made up. I'm embarrassed to say it turned out to be the latter. Her abundant cleavage was the give-away. Ella pushed me forward, so I had to do all the talking.

"Hello there," I said, feeling a bit self-conscious, "I'm Marina Burton. Emmm… I've got a work placement here... in the make-up department?"

"Make-up department?" echoed the woman, then laughed, "Oh, I think that'll be with the queens. If you just hold on a minute and I'll give someone a shout."

"Oh thanks," I said timidly, now feeling really nervous and awkward. I glanced at Ella and she gave me a reassuring smile as the woman lifted the phone, pressed a couple of numbers, then waited for an answer.

"Mark?... Hi, it's Molly," she said, "Listen I've got a Marina Burton here... Says she's been given a work placement or something?... Oh... o.k.... see you in a minute."

We waited eagerly as she put the phone down and then rearranged her bottom on her chair, sticking out her enormous breasts.

"If you just have a seat," she smiled warmly, "and Mark will be with you in a couple of minutes."

"Oh, that's great thanks," I said, then we headed over to some fancy, plush couches.

"I think I'm going to wet myself with excitement," squealed Ella, "I wish I had got this place now. It's just got such a great atmosphere and Molly seems lovely."

I still wasn't convinced that I was going to benefit from working here, but when the door in front of us opened and a tall man with striking blue eyes and black hair came walking towards us, I suddenly totally changed my mind. He was stunningly handsome and I just couldn't take my eyes off of him. Neither could Ella. Her chin had literally hit the floor and I could see that she was absolutely mesmerised by his good looks.

"Hi," he said, reaching his hand out to me.
He firmly shook my hand and I didn't want to let it go, hypnotised by his beautiful eyes but then he turned to shake Ella's hand. When I came out of my trance, I could see Ella melting in front of him.

"I'm Mark. Actually...," he said, looking intently at me, "Don't I know you from somewhere?"

"I don't think so," I said, looking back at him shyly.

"Oh, I know what it is. Don't you work at the Anchor?" he asked.

"Yes," I said, but it still wasn't ringing any bells.

"I was in the other night... with Sabrina...," he smiled, pointing at her photo.

"Oh right," I said, then it suddenly clicked, "Oh my God... are you Giselle?"

"Yes," he said, "My alias!"

"Wow, that's so funny," I laughed.

Suddenly realising that we had been so taken by his good looks, that we hadn't even introduced ourselves I said, "Oh, I'm Marina by the way and this is my class-mate Ella."

"Hi there," beamed Ella enthusiastically, raising her hand up in a wave.

"It's so great to meet you both," said Mark, clapping his hands together, "So you're here for work experience?"

"Yes," I nodded, enthusiastically.

"That's great. I'm pretty sure you'll enjoy it here. We run a pretty good ship and everyone's lovely. Well, come this way and I'll give you a guided tour," he said, waving us to follow him.

We scurried behind him like a couple of little lambs as he took us down the long corridor and through the huge, gilded doors that opened into the main area. Tables and chairs filled the floor with the stage at the far end and the bar at the other. It just looked so brilliant.

"Wow, it's absolutely fabulous," gasped Ella, "You're so lucky Marina."

I was speechless. I couldn't believe I had actually landed so lucky and Mark seemed so nice.

"So, this is it," he said, folding his arms, "This is where it all happens. The punters get their drinks at the bar over there, sit at these tables and hopefully we make them laugh."

"It looks fantastic. So, is it all drag acts?" I asked, not really knowing what else to say.

"Well mostly," Mark said looking at me, with his lovely twinkling eyes, "But we get a few stand-ups and dancers. It's great. The best job in the world to be honest!"

"So how long have you worked here Mark?" asked Ella, evidently not wanting to be left out.

"Oh, let me think... God it must be a couple of years now. The time just flies in! Right," he said, turning and heading for the huge doors again, "Follow me and I'll show you the dressing rooms."

Now he was talking, after all that was why I was here. He took us back out into the main hall, to the door that he had previously come through, then got out his swipe card and unlocked it, waving us both to go through. We followed him up a set of stairs which led to a landing with lots of doors going off. It was so exciting.

"And this is where everyone gets transformed," he said, opening one of the doors, "This is usually my room when I'm performing."

We peeked in and could see wigs hanging on dummy heads, a rail holding lots of colourful costumes and of course a mirror with a dressing table weighed down with tons of make-up. It was absolute eutopia. Mark grabbed the red wig and flung it on. He turned around with his hands on his hips and wearing a big pout.

"Does this ring any bells now Marina?" he said in his best drag voice.

"Oh my God yes," I laughed, "Now I recognise you!"

"Thought you might," he said winking at me, then pointing to the make-up "and these are all my lovely magic potions."

"Goodness there's loads" I said, "I'm well jealous."

"I've never seen so much make-up," added Ella, with her eyes nearly popping out of her head.

"Well, Giselle doesn't get to look like a super model without a little bit of help and if you play your cards right, she might just share some of her secrets!" Mark said, winking at me again.

"That would be great," I said, still unable to believe that I had been lucky enough to get such a good place.

"So, have you both seen a drag act before?" asked Mark, hanging his wig back on the dummy head.

"No," we both said at the same time, looking at each other.

"Well, I think it would probably be a good idea for you to come and watch us tonight then you'll be able to get an idea of what we're all about."

I felt so excited and grateful to be given the chance to actually watch the queens perform, but then my excitement was quickly quashed when I began to think about Ollie. I knew he wouldn't be at all happy about me socialising on a Saturday night.

"Oh my God, that would be so amazing," Ella said to Mark, then I could feel her looking suspiciously at me when I didn't immediately respond, probably knowing what I was thinking,

"Wouldn't it, Marina?"

I hesitated for another moment then stuttered, "Yes… yes that would be great Mark."

"Brilliant," he said rubbing his hands together, "Well, the show kicks off about nine and I should be on about 10. It'll be really great to see you both."

"Oh, thank you so much," I said, trying to sound delighted but inside my stomach was churning, thinking about how on earth I was going to explain it to Ollie, without him going off on one.

I tried to avoid looking directly at Ella but could tell she was a bit angry with me as we followed Mark back down to the main entrance and back over to the box office.

"Molly," he said, leaning on the counter, "Marina and Ella are coming to the show tonight for some work experience, so would it be o.k. to just let them go straight through?"

"Of course it's o.k. Mark. Anything for you my love," she said winking at him and shouted to us,

"I'll see you later girls."

"Thanks Molly," we both shouted.

Mark politely saw us to the door then waved us off and once down the street we started giggling hysterically like naughty little schoolgirls.

"Oh my God he's absolutely gorgeous," said Ella, taking my arm.

"Isn't he just," I agreed, "Those blue eyes..."

"…and his beautiful dark hair. Awww, why do all the best-looking guys always have to be gay?" moaned Ella.

"Who's to say he's gay?" I pointed out.

"Oh, come on! You don't dress up like they do and fancy women. It just doesn't seem right," said Ella.

"Don't be so narrow minded. I'd be willing to let him dress up in my clothes!" I said, "And anyway, anything goes these days."

"Oh, I know, but you know what I mean… I mean... oh shit, I don't know what I mean. What am I like? Anyway, what are you going to wear tonight?"

Then unfortunately I remembered that I would have to tell Ollie and gain his approval. How on earth was I going to tell him?

"Oh, to be honest, I really don't know if I...," I started.

"Don't even go there," said Ella, holding her hand up at me, "You're coming tonight and he can't do anything to stop you. It's your work placement for God's sakes. It's not like you're just gallivanting about."

"I know... but what will I tell him?" I asked, feeling weak and helpless at the prospect of facing him.

"What will you tell him? You'll tell him the fecking truth, that's what," Ella said, with her hands on hips and her Irish accent intensifying with anger, "Oh, it makes me so annoyed that he's doing this to you Marina. He's got you right where he wants you. He's nothing but a control freak. Remember… if you don't stand up to him then he's going to win. Do you want ME to phone the bastard?"

"Oh, God please no," I said, stopping suddenly in my tracks, "I don't want him to know that I've even told you anything... just in case he holds it against you... or me for that matter. No Ella... you're right... I need to man up… I'll tell him the bloody truth."

Ella backed down, pleased that I was finally seeing sense and took my arm again.

"That's my girl," she said, contentedly as we continued down the street.

We headed back to the station and worked out a time to meet up later, then went our own separate ways, although I would have much rather been going home with Ella. When I got off the bus I walked warily towards the flat, trying to compose in my head what I was going to say to Ollie.

"By the way, I'm going to a drag club tonight... for my work experience..."

"I've got my work experience tonight... it's at a drag club..."

"You know my work experience? It's tonight... at a drag club..."

I climbed hesitantly up the steps to the door and unlocked it. Nervously I pushed open the door, stepping into the flat but there didn't seem to be any signs of him. I looked at my watch. It was twenty past four. Reluctantly I text him to see when he would be home. He replied immediately, saying that he was having a great time with the boys, playing pool and that he wouldn't be back till late. Great! I couldn't believe my luck. It was my get out clause not to have to tell him face to face that I was going out tonight. I could just text him. So much less of a challenge and after all, what was the problem? If he was out, then surely it was o.k. for me to go out too?

"No bother," I texted him, "I've got my theatre placement tonight, so I'll not be home till later too xx"

"Great," he replied, "Have a good time."

Phew! What a relief and not only that, I had the whole flat to myself to get ready, with no weirdo lurking in the background to unnerve me. Yahoo! I turned the music up full blast, singing along to my favourite tunes.

Then I got into my comfortable pyjamas and set about totally pampering myself. I perked up my hair, painted my nails and applied the all-important make-up. I felt so excited and just couldn't wait to get to the Tail Feathers Club. I couldn't believe I had managed to get completely ready without Ollie suddenly coming home to annoy me. I put on a nice little dress that I had never had the chance to wear before and of course the all essential heels. I hadn't got this dressed up in ages and actually felt quite good about myself. Confident even.

When I was all set to go, I rushed out of the flat as fast as I could, just in case the psycho unexpectedly appeared and tried to put me down or stop me. I walked as quickly as my high heels would allow, till I got to the bus-stop. Luckily, I didn't have to wait too long for the bus to come and when I got to the station, Ella was standing waiting for me. We hugged each other enthusiastically.

"You look fantastic," squealed Ella.

"So, do you," I said, looking her up and down.

"What in these old rags?" she joked, "Anyway let's get a shifty on. I just can't wait to get there."

"Oh, me too," I agreed, "It's so exciting."

"Well… what did that moron say when you told him you were going out tonight?" asked Ella, taking my arm as we got on our train.

"Well, thankfully he wasn't home," I started, "He was still out playing pool with the boys, so I didn't actually have to talk to him. I just text him saying that I had my work experience tonight."

"Did he not even ask you where it was?" asked Ella.

"No, he just text back, "Have a good time!" thank goodness."

"Oh, that was nice of him," Ella said sarcastically, "And a good time we shall definitely have my dear. Come on you."

When we got to our stop, we hurriedly made our way to The Tail Feathers Club and joined the big queue that was already forming outside the main door.

"I never thought it would be as busy as this," I said, as we shuffled slowly forward with the crowd.

"Me neither, but I suppose that's a good sign," pointed out Ella, "They must be really good."

As we moved steadily towards the door, Molly at the box office spotted us and motioned for us to come in, shouting, "Just go on through girls."

We looked at each other then, hesitantly stepped forward, scared in case it wasn't actually us she was calling to. We felt a bit guilty not having to pay AND skipping the queue but as we squeezed past everyone, we felt like VIP's! We were met with some tuts and sighs from the other customers who were waiting in front of us, but what the hell, I was a member of staff after all!

"Thanks Molly," I shouted, giving her a thumbs up as we hurried past her.

We went through the big, gilded doors and could see that the club was pretty full already. It was obviously a very popular place. Scanning the room for a seat, Ella spotted a table in a nice little corner. We literally ran over just in case someone would beat us to it and parked our bottoms firmly on the seats. There was a band already playing on stage, who sounded absolutely brilliant. It was just so exciting and such a great atmosphere. Quite surreal to be honest.

"Right, I'll go and get the drinks in," said Ella, standing up, "Don't let ANYBODY steal my seat or I swear… I WILL kill them."

"Don't you worry! Your seat is safe! Wait," I said, reaching for my bag, "I'll get these ones."

"Oh no, you won't," she said, firmly, "It's my treat because after all, I wouldn't be here if it wasn't for you. Just the usual?"

"Oh, thanks Ella. Yes, just the usual," I said, gratefully.

Although I had just got my wages, I knew that Ollie would be looking for the money that I "owed" him and was scared to spend anything at all, so I secretly felt relieved that Ella had offered to get the drinks in, but a bit guilty at the same time. I watched her as she went up to the bar which had a queue a mile long and I felt so blessed to have such a good friend. Gazing round the room, I totally soaked up the wonderful atmosphere, feeling like a prisoner released. It felt absolutely amazing. Everyone looked happy and excited to be here. I was just so lucky to get such a good placement.

After a while though, I realised that Ella seemed to have been away for ages and I started to feel a bit conspicuous, sitting on my own. A wave of panic came over me as I unfortunately started thinking about Ollie, terrified in case he came barging into the club and spoiling it all. I visualised him crashing, drunkenly through the doors then stomping towards me and dragging me by the hair out of the club, into the street. Luckily, I was jolted out of my thoughts by Ella's sweet voice.

"God, I thought I was never going to get served," she moaned, laying down the tray which was loaded with glasses, "What a queue. I just got us a few rounds to save us having to go back up again."

"Excellent idea Ella!" I said lifting the glasses off the tray still feeling guilty but relieved to be back in reality, "This should keep us going for at least ten minutes! Cheers!"

"Cheers!" said Ella clinking her glass against mine, "Here's to us and a great night out."

And a great night it was indeed. When the band had finished their set, they left the stage to a huge applause, then the compere, who was called Big Ron, strolled on and began to introduce the next act. He was honestly as broad as he was tall but looked very vibrant in a colourful stripy suit.

"Weren't they amazing ladies and gentle-bottoms," he said, clapping his hands, "It's so lovely to see you all tonight... though I have to say... you're a bloody ugly bunch!... Only kidding! Now you're going to love this next act. He's thinner than a sheet of paper. Seriously... I found him outside the club, hiding behind a lamp post! But all kidding aside, I actually met this guy at weight watchers. As you can see it didn't work that well for me... I think I should get a refund! So, ladies and jelly bottoms, please put your hands together for Skinny Jim."

The audience laughed and clapped as Skinny Jim came on and boy, was he skinny. He shook hands with Big Ron who turned his back to the audience as he started to walk back behind the stage, only to reveal, pretty disgustingly, that his suit only covered the front of his body, while his back was naked apart from a tiny thong and visible bra-straps, showing off his vulgar bulges. This of course was met with hysterical laughter from the crowd and from us!

Skinny Jim was hilarious too, poking fun at himself the whole time. At one point we couldn't move for laughing which was great. There was no better therapy than having a laugh. Just what the doctor ordered and when Skinny Jim finished his act, Big Ron came back on, clapping his hands.

"Think I'll need to go back to weight watchers!" laughed Big Ron, "Either that or get a gastric band! To be honest… I'll eat anything! Now, next up we have two very beautiful, young ladies. They've spent all day in make-up and look absolutely out of this world. First up is the lovely Sabrina."

She came floating on, in a lovely billowing pink dress to absolutely rapturous applause. The crowd obviously knew her well. She looked utterly beautiful and had obviously spent hours doing her flawless makeup. Boy, was I going to learn a lot here.

"Well, hello there boys," she said fluttering her eyelashes at the audience as she glided about the stage, "Girls... you can just all go home now..."

Hey, we weren't going anywhere!

"My God... Skinny Jim... I could just about hide him in my cleavage," she said, pushing her fake breasts together, "Big Ron on the other hand..."

Sabrina turned her back to the audience and stuck out her bottom, giving it an enticing shake. Her act was absolutely hilarious and had us in stitches. When she left the stage, Big Ron came back on, clapping enthusiastically, then took Sabrina's hand giving it a noisy, slobbery kiss.

"Wasn't she brilliant everyone," he said, "Give it up ladies and gents for the very gorgeous Sabrina."

The audience cheered then Big Ron turned back to them saying, "Next up is an equally stunning young lady, who goes by the name of Giselle… though she's so slim and elegant, I think she should change her name to Gazelle!"

Everyone yelled with delight as Big Ron departed the stage and Giselle strutted on in absolutely death-defying heels, wearing the tightest, shiniest silver hot-pants I think I had ever seen. With raunchy music blasting out in the background, she turned her back to the audience and stuck her bottom out as far as it possibly could go.

"Does my bum look big in this?" she said, gyrating her hips sexily as the audience laughed and cheered, with wolf whistles galore.

"People often ask me what my sexual preference is...," she continued as she stood back up and faced the audience, fluttering her huge eyelashes,

"I just tell them... four times a day, twenty-four seven. What's yours honey?"

The audience absolutely loved her. She was obviously well known and adored by everyone as they roared with laughter at all her naughty jokes and hilarious wise cracks.

"They are such a tonic," laughed Ella as Giselle left the stage at the end of her act.

And so they were. I had never experienced anything like it in my life before and it helped me to totally forget about all my worries and stresses. I felt so much better than I had done in ages. Their good humour had put me on a high, along with a little help from the alcohol. Laughter really was the best medicine.

The acts that followed were just as funny and I was having such a good time, I just didn't want it to end. I wanted tonight to last for ever, but then regrettably I started thinking about Ollie again and it began to fill me with absolute dread.

"Suppose we better start thinking about heading," I said, starting to panic a bit, "Don't want to push my luck."

"Awwww, but the show's not finished yet..." moaned Ella, but then realising that I was getting a bit anxious, she said, "but I guess you're right. Will we see if we can say goodbye to Mark before we go?"

"I suppose we could... if we're allowed that is," I said, but starting to feel really worried about the prospect of having to face Ollie on my return.

We quickly finished our drinks and squeezed past all the tables making our way towards the big doors. Molly was still sitting at the box office and smiled as we headed towards her.

"Well... did you enjoy the show girls?" she asked.

"It was just hilarious," Ella replied, enthusiastically.

"We had a great time," I beamed, "I haven't laughed so much in years!"

"Oh, I know. They're a comical lot," said Molly, "and I just never tire of Sabrina and Giselle. They're just lovely."

"We were wondering," I started gingerly, "If there's any chance that we could pop up and see Mark before we go?"

"Why, of course you can girls," she said, "Just wait a minute and I'll get the door for you."

She jumped off her stool and came out from behind her desk then headed to the door, swiping her card to let us in.

"They're you go girls?" she smiled.

"Thanks Molly," we both said at the same time.

Excitedly we headed up the stairs towards the changing rooms and could hear a lot of talking and laughing. The door to Mark's room was open, but I timidly knocked first, looking apprehensively at Ella, who was just about wetting herself with anticipation. The talking suddenly stopped and Mark or should I say Giselle, pulled the door open.

"Ladies," he said with his arms open wide then kissing us both noisily on the cheek, "Come in, come in. So... what did you think? Were we any good… or do we need a bit more practice?"

He ushered us in as Sabrina came floating over to greet us, saying, "Don't hold back now. Remember … honesty's always the best policy… but we don't mind a few little white lies!"

"Oh, my goodness you were awesome," I gushed.

"Totally hilarious!" enthused Ella, "You had us in stitches."

"Well, as long as we didn't have you in plaster," joked Sabrina.

"You girls are so kind! We always aim to please," said Giselle, turning slightly and sticking her back end out, "...and DID my bum look big in this?"

"Definitely not," I laughed, "It looked fantastic… and so did your make-up."

"Oh, you're so sweet," said Giselle, kissing me again on the cheek, "I just love you darling!"

"But your bum's not quite as small as Skinny Jim's," piped up Ella.

"Oh, oh. I think we've got a bit of competition here," said Sabrina, raising her eyebrows, "But then again, no-one's ass is as skinny as Jim's!"

We all laughed and suddenly I was aware of the creaminess of Mark's thick lipstick on my cheek and it felt strangely good. I knew I would have a lipstick pout stuck on my face, but I didn't even attempt to wipe it off. I wanted to keep it, almost like a tattoo.

"So, when are coming for some... experience?" Sabrina asked with a cheeky wink.

"Well, probably next Saturday if that's o.k.?" I said, giggling.

"Well, of course it's o.k. Are you coming too honey?" Sabrina asked Ella.

"Oh, God I wish I was," she said, "No, unfortunately I've got a placement somewhere else."

"Your loss sweetheart," said Sabrina with a down turned mouth and cupping her hand under Ella's chin, "Tail Feathers is soooo the place to be."

"I can see that," laughed Ella, "I'm so jealous."

"Anyway, we better let you get on," I said, suddenly starting to worry about the time, "Thanks again. We've had a really brilliant time and I can't wait to work with you both."

"No bother at all," said Giselle, "Look forward to seeing you gorgeous."

Gorgeous? Me? No one had EVER called me gorgeous. Not even when Ollie and I were in the first throes of romance. Mark was just so lovely.

Ella and I both left on an absolute high, laughing all the way down the street. Giselle and Sabrina had been so funny AND so nice. It was such a great combination. We chattered away non-stop on the train and when we got off, we went our separate ways.

"You take care now honey and any problems at all just give me shout," said Ella hugging me tight,

"O.K.?"

"But I've got a huge problem," I wanted to shout, "I've to go home to Ollie."

Instead though, I just said, "Don't worry, I will. See you Monday."

"See you Monday," she said, hugging me again.

As she started walking away, I just wanted to run after her and beg her to take me to the safety of her home, as I began to think more about Ollie, but I just turned and headed towards my train which was sitting waiting. It seemed to get to my stop in no time and when I got off, I reluctantly walked towards the bus-stop.

I looked at my watch. It was quarter past eleven. The bus wasn't due for another twenty minutes so I decided to just start walking because it would probably be just as quick. The more I thought about Ollie though, the quicker I began to walk. Would he be in one of his moods? Would he be "nice" or would he want to hurt me? Thinking about him totally spoiled the warm, happy way I had felt back at the club.

When I eventually got to the flat, I could see there were no lights on. I felt an enormous wave of relief because after all he had said he was going to be late. I turned the key in the lock and slowly opened the door, listening intently for any sounds, but couldn't hear anything. The flat was silent thank goodness. I let out a grateful sigh and walked through to the kitchen, turning on the light.

"Boo!"

I almost jumped out of my skin when the light revealed Ollie, sitting at the kitchen table. What a screwball, sitting in the dark, just waiting to catch me out and frighten me.

"What the hell are you doing?" I shouted angrily with the shock.

"Saving electricity," he said, standing up and coming over to me then shoving a letter into my face,

"Cause you've been using too much."

"What?" I said, not having a clue what he was talking about.

I strained my eyes to see what the letter was. It was the electricity bill. As I looked at the words and the figures, I was even shocked at the amount. We'd never had a bill quite as high, but it wasn't my bloody fault.

"It's a lot of money... isn't it… and guess what? You can pay it," he said, snatching the bill away from my gaze.

"What do you mean I can pay it?" I demanded, shocked at his statement, "We'll split it... just like we usually do."

"Oh no we won't," he said, with the mad look coming over his face, "You've never got that flaming hair-drier off or your straighteners and as for that annoying music... well! So, it's your call."

I was too scared to retaliate any more, but how on earth was I supposed to cover the cost? What I got paid from the pub would hardly cover it, let alone pay for everything else and fine he knew it.

I felt totally deflated, but his eyes looked really scary, so I didn't dare argue any more with him.

"Anyway... where the hell have you been?" he yelled, "Spending more money were you?"

"I was at my work placement... remember?" I said, squeezing carefully past him and reaching for the kettle.

I turned the tap on, but he came up behind me and roughly turned it off, saying, "Bit late, aren't you? Surely you didn't have to be there this long?"

"I told you I would probably be late in my text," I said, turning and looking at him.

I wondered why he was scrutinising my face so much but then remembered I still had Giselle's lipstick on my cheek, as I could suddenly feel its creaminess on my skin. Oh my God. What was he going to think but more's to the point, what was he going to do?

"What the hell's that on your face," he said, grabbing hold of my chin and pulling me up close, so that he could get a better look, "Been kissing your girlfriend, have you?"

Oh shit, how was I going to reply to that? I knew what I wanted to say, but it didn't really matter though what I said, because he would just end up twisting it around to suit himself.

Mustering up some courage, I finally managed to say, "Oh, for goodness sake, it was the drag act we were watching..."

"Drag act? Oh, come on, what kind of an excuse is that? So, is it you and Ella then?" he sneered, holding my chin painfully tight, "Couple of lesbians now, are you?"

"Oh, don't be so flaming ignorant," I said, trying hard to pull my face out of his tight grasp, "It was..."

"Always thought she was a bit of a dyke that one," he said pushing me away then leaning back against the worktop and putting his hands in his pockets.

"Oh, there's no point in even talking to you," I said, angry at his stupid juvenile comments about me and my best friend.

I turned my back to him and started filling the kettle. He had come right up behind me though and started rubbing roughly at my breasts.

"Prefer the feminine touch do you," he said, nuzzling his face in my neck, "Come to think about it, that's quite a turn on... you and Ella... girl on girl..."

"Oh, get off me, you disgusting scumbag," I said putting the kettle down and pushing him away, feeling totally repulsed by him.

"Emm, no I think you're the scumbag, bitch," he said, grabbing me round the waist so that I couldn't move, "Kissing girls, now that's REALLY scummy."

"I wasn't kissing flaming girls." I screamed.

I tried in vain to struggle out of his hold, but he was too strong and the next minute his hand was down the front of my pants. I felt agonising pain as he started to yank roughly at my pubic hair. I still tried to push him off, but it was no good. I just couldn't move out of his now really painful grip.

"Stop it, you freak. You're hurting me," I yelled at him, "Why are you being such a moron?"

"Because you're making a fool of me you stupid, useless piece of shit," he hissed into my ear, giving another sharp, painful tug.

"I'm not making a fool of you," I cried, tears starting to roll down my cheeks with the pain.

"Lesbian," he roared.

"I'm NOT a flaming lesbian," I shouted, "If you would just let me explain... It was one of the drag queens that kissed me on the cheek."

He gave one last rough tug and then forcefully pushed me away, like a useless piece of dirty rubbish.

"Jesus Christ... that's even worse," he yelled, "Hanging out with a bunch of trannies AND kissing them. What a little weirdo."

"No... I think you're the weirdo Ollie," I yelled angrily, straightening up and facing him.

Oh no. The words were out of my mouth before I could stop them and unfortunately there was no reversing the process. I tried to cower away from him as he stood menacingly over me. He just stared at me for a while and thinking he was going to punch me in the face, I lifted my hands ready to defend myself. Instead, he called my bluff and kicked me hard on the shin. I buckled over with the pain, then he came up behind me, grabbing my arms from behind and pulling them painfully up my back.

"You're a useless piece of shit... What are you?" he yelled in my ear.

I said nothing in reply but then he yanked my arms painfully up my back again and hissed in my ear again, "What are you?"

I was forced to reply, before he actually broke my arm.

"A useless... piece... of... shit...," I managed to say, as he twisted my arm even tighter.

"That's my girl," he said, as soon as the words were out of my mouth and then threw me, roughly to the floor.

Hesitantly, I looked up, scared in case he was going to do something else to me, but then watched him as he disappeared out of the kitchen. I listened intently as he went through to the bedroom and then, thankfully heard him jumping noisily into bed.

I sank slowly down on to the floor, my arms aching from the strain and then sat nursing my leg, which was now bleeding. I started sobbing, unable to control my emotions and tried hard not to make a noise. I really wanted to wail and moan because I felt so violated and abused. How could he be so crude and so cruel? I just wanted it all to stop. All this strange, awful behaviour. All this unnecessary and unprovoked violence. Surely the neighbours could hear us shouting? Why did no-one try to intervene or at least call the police? I felt so scared and so alone.

CHAPTER 3

BREAKING POINT

We didn't really talk to each other over the next few days. I couldn't stand looking at Ollie never mind speaking to him, after what he had done and luckily for me, he didn't have any more vicious outbursts.

Of course, I was far too embarrassed to tell Ella what he had done to me this time. I mean how could I even bring it up in conversation? It was just too personal and too horrible. How could he have done such a vile thing? I couldn't tell her why he had done it either. She would totally explode if I told her that he had called her a dyke or a lesbian.

Then my emotions and thoughts all got a bit confused as usual. Did it make me a lesbian because I loved my friend so dearly and felt a bit attracted to a drag queen? No, of course it didn't I reasoned with myself, because it was Mark I was attracted to, not Giselle and I pined to be with Ella because she was my best friend in the whole wide world, who gave me comfort and security when I most needed it and on whom I could depend upon. Absolutely nothing else.

Ollie had succeeded in turning me in to a bundle of nerves, with no confidence or self-esteem left in my system, terrified of the next assault and yet again with absolutely no money. Ella, as usual sensed something was afoot because she kept probing and urging me to move in with her.

"Has he been nasty to you again?" Ella quizzed, obviously sensing something was wrong.

How could she possibly know? It never failed to amaze me how she could tell. She must be able to see a change in my body language or something. God only knows. I was still convinced she had the gift.

"Oh… we've just not been talking… that's all," I lied, sipping from my bottle of water as we sat in the canteen.

"I'm telling you Marina, you need to leave that creep... NOW," she warned, "Look at you, you're an absolute wreck."

"I know Ella and I will leave him. I honestly don't think I can take it anymore," I said, wearily putting my bottle down, "But I need to work it all out. I mean I know it's his flat, but I've bought tons of stuff, like cushions and curtains..."

"That's a fair point. I hadn't really thought about that," said Ella, nibbling on an apple, "But you know, happiness and peace of mind is a hundred times better than a pair of old curtains."

"Oh, I know," I agreed, "But I'm just so scared Ella... cause I've no idea what he's going to do next."

"Oh my God! What an awful situation," empathised Ella, "You know what you need... some retail therapy. How about we go shopping later. That'll cheer you up."

"Oh, well... I...," I stuttered.

"What?" cried Ella, "He can't stop you from spending your own money you know."

"Well... that's just it... I haven't actually got any," I said, feeling ashamed and embarrassed.

"But I thought you just got paid?" Ella pointed out.

"I did but... but...," I stuttered again.

"But... but what Marina?" she mimicked, "And I want the truth now."

"Well, we got the electricity bill in yesterday... and it was a little bit higher than usual...," I started.

"It can't have been that extortionate surely?" questioned Ella.

"Well, no, not really... but Ollie blamed me, for using my hair dryer... and listening to my music too much," I explained.

"Holy mother of God," said Ella, pretending to pull her hair out, "please don't tell me he's making you pay it?"

"Well...," I started.

"Oh, for heavens sakes, Marina... he is, isn't he?" she wailed, "Marina, you really need to get a grip and stand up to him. You need to leave this arsehole. He knows he's got control and he's just going to keep playing you."

"I know," I agreed, pathetically.

Of course she was absolutely right, but truthfully, I was terrified of leaving him, because I knew he would probably never give me any peace. It was a terrible situation, but thankfully we didn't need to talk any more about Ollie because it was time to head back to class. It really helped us both to stop thinking about things and turned out to be a great afternoon.

We had been learning how to do prosthetics and were practising on each other. I had previously moulded an enormous, knobbly nose which Ella was now comically modelling and she was now applying the nose that she had moulded for me. We couldn't stop laughing at each other and at William's enormous ears and Hannah's massive chin that they had made for each other. We kept taking photos of each other because we all looked so bizarre and funny! The time just absolutely flew in and it was honestly just the best therapy ever.

"So? Are you coming home with me?" asked Ella, as we left college.

"Oh, Ella, I promise, as soon as I get things sorted out, then I'm definitely moving back in with you," I reassured her.

"Oh, Marina, I'm worried sick about you now. You need to do it sooner, rather than later" she warned, hugging me, tightly, "You're in too deep now."

"Oh, don't worry... it'll be fine," I tried to reassure her but knowing full well that it probably wouldn't be.

As usual when I went home to Ollie, any happiness I had was totally flattened, but I tried my best to ignore him and to just get on with things. As Saturday grew closer though, I could feel myself getting more and more anxious, scared of how he was going to react to me working at the Tail Feathers again, but then I decided I had to try and get tough. I had to get stronger to fight against him and his demons. I was going to my work placement and he would just need to deal with it. So, on the Friday night I made him a nice dinner and when we were nearly finished, I tactfully tried to remind him.

"So... is you're dinner o.k.?" I asked him, gingerly.

"It's not too bad," he said, not looking up as he took another mouthful.

"That's good. Don't forget I'm on my work experience again tomorrow night," I said, boldly but not really knowing what to expect in reply.

"Oh, yeah... I forgot," he said, chasing the last bits of potato round his plate, "With the laaadeeez..."

I tried to ignore his shallow remark but really wanted to plant one on him as I lifted my plate into the sink. Ollie took the last mouthful of his dinner and then jumped up out of his seat, dumping his plate on the work top. I honestly thought he was going to turn around and hit me, because I hadn't reacted to his comment, but instead he asked, "So where is it you're working again?"

I hesitated, not actually wanting him to know exactly where I was going, but then I forced myself to say, "It's a club… called The Tail Feathers?"

"What kind of a stupid name's that?" he said, ignorantly, "I suppose I'll need to sort my own dinner then?"

"Well…," I started, stupidly about to offer to make him something, before I went.

"Don't worry, I'm playing pool with the boys, so I'll just get a takeaway or something," he interrupted, "At least it'll taste better than your disgusting offerings."

"No worries," I said, totally ignoring his insulting comment, just relieved that I didn't have to do anything nice for him and turned back to the sink, still half expecting him to thump me.

Thankfully he didn't though. He played the "nice" Ollie for the rest of the evening and the next morning, I tried to stay out of his way, by going to the supermarket and getting the shopping. I took longer than I normally would have, just to prolong my time out of the flat away from him but was mortified when my card was rejected as I tried to pay. I had totally forgotten the electricity bill had completely drained my bank-balance.

My heart sank but then, luckily, I remembered I had a secret little savings account that my mum had set up for me for absolute emergencies only. I knew that there was more than enough in it to cover the shopping but because I didn't use the card much, I was mortified when I couldn't remember the pin-number. It was so embarrassing, holding up all the other customers behind me. I just wanted the ground to open and swallow me up. Then, thankfully the number suddenly came to me and I quickly tapped it in. Phew!

I felt really stressed and stupid now and couldn't wait to get out of the shop. As I struggled home, my arms were aching with the weight of the groceries. When I got back to the flat, it was relief to put the bags down on the step, as I wrestled with my handbag, desperately trying to find my key.

As I battled my way through to the kitchen, I could see Ollie lounging back in the living-room. The lazy bastard didn't even budge off his chair to come and give me a hand. In the past I would have been really annoyed by his idleness, shouting for assistance, whereas now I was more than happy that he wasn't coming anywhere near me. I really wanted to point out to him that I HAD actually paid for all the shopping and that I WASN'T free loading off him. Of course, I didn't though, just desperate to keep the peace.

When I had finished the mammoth task of putting it all away, I tried to busy myself doing some cleaning. Not that I really wanted to, but just so I didn't have to go through and look at Ollie's big, ugly face. I could hear him rustling about in the bedroom. He was obviously getting himself ready to go out, with the overpowering wreak of after-shave that was wafting through.

"That's me away," I heard him shout a few minutes later, as he walked noisily down the hall.

"O.k. See you later," I called, then heard the front door banging loudly shut behind him.

"Fucking dickhead," I added, under my breath.

I hated swearing but he just forced it out of me with his strange behaviour. Why could he not just go away and never ever come back? That would be so good. I suppose I had to be thankful for small mercies though. At least I had the flat all to myself for a little while. I relished the freedom, but mostly the silence. It was such a relief not to feel fear or anxiety and never knowing what on earth Ollie's mood was going to be like.

I put my feet up for a little while, exhausted from the stress of shopping and housework then a bit later on I started to get myself ready to go to The Tail Feathers. I knew that I didn't need to get too tarted up because after all it was work, so I put on some practical clothes and shoes, trying to look professional. I desperately hoped that I was going to get a chance to do the queens make-up and stuff and not just to be observing.

After a quick bite to eat, I grabbed my phone and my bag but as I was about to leave the flat, I hesitated for a brief moment. I had a sudden strong urge to fling all my earthly belongings into a suitcase with a vision of going straight to Ella's from The Tail Feathers and never ever coming back.

Foolishly though, I dismissed the idea from my thoughts and headed out into the street, but as I sat on the bus, I felt really annoyed with myself for not following my heart. Why on earth did I have to be so weak?

When I got to the Tail Feathers Club though all of my worries and troubles just melted away and all I could think about was seeing lovely Mark again, which made me feel so much better. Molly was at the desk and she greeted me with a huge, warm smile which was very welcoming and encouraging.

"Hello Marina, my love!" she said, coming out from behind the counter and swiping the door open for me to get up the stairs, "On you go up pet. Mark's not in yet, but he shouldn't be too long."

"Oh, thanks a lot Molly, that's great," I said, heading through the door.

I ran quickly up the stairs but felt like an intruder though as I pushed open the dressing room door. No one was in, so I gingerly sat down, not really knowing what to do with myself while I waited for the queens to arrive. I looked around the room at all the costumes and wigs and it immediately brought a smile to my face, thinking of Giselle and Sabrina. They were both so nice and so funny.

I looked at all the make-up sitting on the dressing tables. There was absolutely gallons of the stuff. It was my own personal heaven! I leaned forward and was about to pick up a bottle of foundation when I could suddenly hear their voices coming towards the door. I quickly jumped up out of the chair as they came in, standing to attention to welcome them.

"Oh, look Ricky... it's Cinderella," joked Mark.

"Alright Cinders?" Ricky said, walking over to me and winking as he shook my hand.

So, Sabrina was actually called Ricky. I hadn't even thought about what his real name was! They both looked uber cool and handsome, dressed casually in tee-shirts and jeans. Ricky had naturally dirty blond, floppy hair and had almost as twinkly blue eyes as Mark, if that was at all possible! Their beguiling looks were quite over-whelming and I suddenly felt strangely self-conscious being in their presence. I don't think I had ever been in the company of such handsome looking men before.

"So how are you darling?" asked Mark, coming over and hugging me.

"Oh… I'm fine thanks," I said, hesitantly, trying hard to sound confident and nonchalant, "How are you guys?"

"Raring to go," said Mark sitting down and motioning for me to sit down next to him, "Raring to go. I just hope it's a good crowd tonight."

"Oh, I'm sure it will be… They'll just love you," I gushed as I sat down, "If last week's anything to go by."

"Oh, aren't you a sweetie!" said Ricky, standing over me and ruffling my hair.

"Isn't she just," said Mark winking at me, "So are you ready to watch us transform ourselves into gorgeous, beautiful ladies then?"

"Oh, God, I can't wait," I said, smiling broadly and brimming with excitement.

"So, what do they teach you at that college then?" asked Ricky.

"Oh… well… lots of things really. We learn about anatomy… good maintenance of the skin...," I started.

"Oh yes, skin maintenance is VERY important," said Ricky gently stroking his cheek.

"... how to apply a good base," I continued, "colouring, contouring, shading, all that kind of stuff. Oh, and we've been learning how to do prosthetics."

"Prosthetics?" said Mark, "You could be doing with some prosthetics Rick!"

"Cheeky!" said Ricky, cupping his chest and sticking it out to make it look like he had breasts while pouting his lips big time.

"But honestly, that sounds like fun. So, have you got any pictures of your work then?" asked Mark.

"Oh, it's brilliant fun," I said, lifting my bag and searching for my phone, "We took loads of funny photos the other day."

I quickly found them, then proudly held my phone up so Mark and Ricky could get a good view.

"Wow! It's amazing what you can do with a bit of play dough," joked Ricky.

"Oh, miaow!" said Mark, "Just ignore his bitchy remarks darling. No honestly... that nose makes you look ten times better!"

"Oh, miaow!" I said in response, "Who's the bitch now?"

"Only joking!" laughed Mark, nudging me, "It really does look amazing."

"Think we might have a bit of competition here Marky," said Ricky.

"You might have a point there," said Mark, "Right let's get started then and we'll let you see what WE can do."

"Great!" I said, "After all, that's what I'm here for."

I watched as Mark and Ricky piled on their make-up. It was very thick, but very effective and it was nothing short of magical to see the transformation. How lucky was I to be getting such great experience.

"Hey Marina! Are you any good at doing eyebrows?" shouted Ricky, "I'm afraid that's the one thing I'm really not good at."

"Yes," I said eagerly and searched amongst the piles of make-up for eyebrow pencils, "How do you want them? Thick, thin, arched...?"

"Oh, decisions, decisions," said Ricky, twiddling his fingers, "I think I'll go for a thick, arched look please darling."

"No bother at all," I said, starting to shade them in.

"So, what make-up would you recommend for us?" asked Ricky.

"Oh, I don't know. What you're using looks fantastic. I know that water based is good for quick changes because it's easy to remove," I said, trying to sound like I knew what I was talking about.

"Well, we like thick and unbudgeable, so it stays firmly in place!" joked Mark, leaning into the mirror as he applied his eyeliner, "Once it's on, we just don't want it to come off."

"To be absolutely honest, I wouldn't change a thing. What you're doing looks utterly perfect to me," I said, complimenting their good work.

"Correct!" yelled Ricky, throwing his hands up in the air, "This girl's a quick learner Marky!"

"She is indeed," agreed Mark.

I finished Ricky's eyebrows and stood back to get a better view.

"How's that?" I asked, pleased with the result but at the same time scared in case he didn't like it.

"My God Marina, what have you done?" said Ricky, taking a closer look in the mirror.

Thinking he wasn't pleased and that I had made a mess, I blurted, "Oh no… I'm so sorry…"

"Sorry? What for? They are positively fantastic. My eyebrows have never looked so good! What do you think Marky?" Ricky said, swivelling round on his chair.

"Wow! I think they look absolutely fabulous darling," said Mark, scrutinising them, "Right come and see what you can do with my lashes Marina."

"No bother," I said and quickly grabbed the false lashes that Mark was waving in his hand.

I dusted them with a bit of glittery eyeshadow and with an extra slick of mascara, once applied, they made Mark's sparkling blue eyes look even more stunning, as if that was humanly possible.

"What do you think Ricky?" asked Mark, fluttering his eyelashes, emphatically.

"Well… Daisy the cow does come to mind," he joked, "No but honestly though, they look absolutely stunning. Well done Marina."

It was so satisfying and such a pleasure to be working with Mark and Ricky because they were so comical and lovely, appreciating everything that I did. Once their faces were completed, I helped them on with their wigs, then they changed into their costumes which totally transformed them into Sabrina and Giselle. I really felt like I had achieved something tonight and was proud that I had, in my own small way helped them.

"Wooo," said Sabrina, doing a little twirl, "How do we look Marina?"

"Oh, my goodness you both look gorgeous!" I said, clasping my hands and gazing at them in awe,

"Is it o.k. if I take a picture?"

"Why of course it is," said Giselle, grabbing hold of Sabrina and pouting her mouth towards hers.

"Make love to the camera Gizzy," pouted Sabrina, sexily.

I took a few shots of them in different poses. My God they certainly knew how to work the camera!

"Oh, darling, be a gem and send them to my phone, will you please?" begged Mark.

"Of course I will. What's your number?" I asked.

He rhymed it off, then I sent the photos as they went to do a rehearsal before the show began. I looked around, wondering what to do next then started to busy myself clearing up the dressing tables and folding their clothes. I felt really happy and content to be here, especially when later on I could hear Giselle and Sabrina once they were out on stage, doing their act.

This was everything I had ever dreamed of doing. Experiencing the thrill and excitement of being back-stage, knowing that I was a part of the bigger picture. It was a great feeling. I was so very blessed and so lucky. As I sat in the big swivel chair, marvelling at my good fortune to be working with two lovely drag queens, I started singing happily along to the radio.

I smiled broadly when I heard the door opening, fully expecting to see Giselle and Sabrina returning from their performance, but my smile very quickly turned to a horrified gawp when I saw Ollie come strolling in. What in the blazes was he doing here? And more's to the point how on earth had he got passed Molly and through the security door?

"What the hell are you doing here?" I yelled at him as I jumped up out of my seat, utterly appalled at the sight of him.

"Wo, that's no way to welcome the man that you love," he said sitting on one of the chairs and then roughly spinning on it.

The man that I love? Who was he trying to kid?

"How did you even get in here?" I asked, annoyed that he had dared to invade my territory.

"Easily," he said, stopping spinning and looking directly at me, "That fat bitch at the desk let me come up no bother... she was really friendly and helpful... a real push over. I just said that I was your boyfriend and that I was desperate to see you, then hey presto!"

"You've got no right doing that Ollie. Well, you better go and wait outside. I AM working you know," I reminded him, "and for your information Molly's NOT fat by the way and she's NOT a bitch either."

"Well, for YOUR information, I'm not waiting outside. Embarrassed to show me off are you," he said standing up, right in front of me, pushing his face towards mine, allowing me to smell the alcohol on his breath and see his ugly face just a bit too close up for comfort.

The very sight of him totally repulsed me and yes, I WAS embarrassed to be associated with him in any way or form, but especially so at my place of work.

"Look, I'm really busy Ollie and anyway, what is the point of you even being here?" I asked, "You know that you'll see me when I get home, plus you really shouldn't be in here. It's a changing room you know."

"Didn't look like you very busy to me and anyway, it's not like I'm going to see anything I haven't seen before.... but then again...," he said, looking in disgust at the wigs and the dresses.

I was sickened by his narrow-minded comment, but just then I could hear Sabrina and Giselle talking and laughing out in the corridor thank goodness. The next minute the door flew open and they both came strutting in, but stopped suddenly in their tracks, staring in surprise at Ollie.

"Why, who have we here then?" asked Sabrina, eyeing him up and down, "One of our many admirers are you darling."

"I don't think so mate," scowled Ollie and put his arms round my waist, pulling me roughly towards him, making me yelp with shock, "I'm Marina's boyfriend."

"Oh, that's a pity," said Giselle, obviously sensing his negativity, "Thought we were going to have a bit of fun for a minute there. Maybe a little threesome... with you in the middle."

Ollie had definitely met his match with these two and didn't have a clue what to say as a come-back, but I could see by his face that he was totally humiliated and repulsed by them. I felt so embarrassed and pulled myself away from him. How could he do this to me. What on earth was he getting from it?

"Are you finished then?" Ollie asked, turning and looking at me.

"Well, not really. I need to help the guys...," I started.

"The guys?" he mocked, looking sneeringly at Sabrina and Giselle.

Oh my God. How could he be so blatantly obnoxious? I could see Mark's expression immediately turn to absolute disgust and for a split second I really thought he was going to plant one on Ollie. If only he had. That would have made me so, so happy.

"If you've got a problem pal then maybe you shouldn't even be here," Mark said in his own voice and stepping forward, "You can get off now Marina. Don't worry, we'll tidy up here."

"Are you sure?" I asked, but really hoped that he would say, "No Marina, just you stay here, safe with us."

"You heard what he... SHE said," Ollie mocked, putting his arm round me again and pulling me roughly towards him again, "It's time to go home darling."

He kissed me on the cheek, but it just made me want to pull away from him and wipe off his slobbers. What I really wanted to do was rip my nails down his face and yell at him to "Fuck off and stop spoiling everything for me" but of course I didn't. Instead, I just stood there taking it like a stupid dummy, but I could tell by the looks on their faces that Giselle and Sabrina were definitely not one bit impressed by him.

"Thanks again for all your help honey," said Sabrina, as we walked towards the door, "You play your cards right and we might just have to give you a permanent job!"

"Not on my watch," Ollie muttered under his breath, pulling the door open.

I just drew him a dirty look as he pushed me forward, obviously in a hurry now to get out of the dressing room.

"Same time next week?" asked Giselle questioningly, obviously realising that it might be a problem with Ollie now.

"Same time next week," I bravely said, forcing a smile but really feeling like sinking to the floor and sobbing my heart out with anger and embarrassment, not actually knowing if I would be there next week, if Ollie had anything to do with it.

He kept a tight hold round my waist until we got downstairs and into the foyer. I could definitely now smell from his breath that he had been drinking and obviously a lot by the way he was behaving. As we passed the box office, Molly shouted, "Goodnight you love birds!" with a beaming big smile on her face as she watched us shuffle past.

"Stupid old cow," Ollie muttered rudely to himself.

I loved Molly but I was so angry with her for letting Ollie in and just wanted to scream back at her, "Why the hell did you let this maniac come anywhere near me and spoil my night?"

Instead, I just tried to smile back and said nothing, giving her a little wave as Ollie virtually dragged me out of the club. Once out in the street Ollie practically pushed me away, no longer having to put on the "lovely boyfriend" act. I hated him so much at that moment and wanted to run far, far away. He just didn't want me to be happy. I knew he had only done all this to make a total fool of me. He seemed to get some sort of pleasure out of making me miserable. He couldn't just be happy for me and let me enjoy the job that he knew I so wanted to do, without interfering and spoiling it all for me. I was absolutely raging with him.

"Why did you have to do that?" I asked bitterly.

"Do what? So, am I not allowed to come and see you when I want to?" he said, grabbing my arm and digging his nails in to my skin. I winced with the pain but firmly shook off his grip.

"You've no reason to come and see me at work," I said, trying not to shout, in case people could hear us.

"Oh, is that what you call it?" he ridiculed, "Hanging out with a bunch of queers..."

"Yes, it is work," I said defiantly, "It's MY work and they're NOT a bunch of queers... they're drag queens for your information."

"Same thing isn't it?" he said, insultingly with a sneer on his ugly, horrible face.

"Oh, what's the point? You're just a total bigot," I said despairingly, starting to walk away from him.

"Hoy," he said, coming after me and grabbing my hand, obviously just to annoy me, "Don't you dare speak to me like that. I went to the bother of coming to see you bitch, so the least you can do is walk nicely with me."

He grabbed hold of my hand squeezing it so tight that it made me squirm with pain, then he more or less dragged me along the street. Not knowing which way his mood was going to go, I was forced to go along with him praying that he wouldn't touch me when we got home. Luckily by the time we got back to the flat he appeared to be tired. The alcohol had thankfully taken its toll on him.

"I'm bushed," he said, as we walked in through the door.

He disappeared through to the bedroom then I heard him audibly crashing out on the bed. Relieved, I just let him go and went wearily through to the lounge. I put on the telly but turned the sound down low, so as not to disturb him too much. God knows, that was the last thing I wanted to do.

Staring at the screen, I could feel the hot tears slowly trickle down my face. I just couldn't understand the whole point of Ollie's performance tonight. All I had wanted to do was make a good impression but instead, he had totally humiliated me in front of Sabrina and Giselle, but then I guess that was his cold and calculated plan. In the process though, he had made me realise that I couldn't take much more of him and his strange behaviour. I'd honestly had enough now. It was just one step too far.

He was slowly crushing me, turning me into a total wreck and making an absolute fool of me to boot. The tears kept on coming and I tried hard not to snort and sniff in case he heard me and came through to gloat. When my phone beeped with a message, I almost jumped out of my skin with shock. I quickly turned the sound down just in case it beeped again and disturbed an obviously, but now thankfully, snoring Ollie. I expected it to be Ella or my mum, but when I looked at the screen, I didn't recognise the number, so I warily read the text.

"Great photos Marina. Are you o.k.? Me and Ricky are a bit worried about you?"

Then I suddenly realised that the text was from Mark. I quickly brushed away my tears so I could read it more clearly and looked at the text again. My heart was truly lifted, knowing that they both genuinely cared about me and I could feel the warmth of their concern.

"Glad you like the photos. I'm fine thanks," I text, "Ollie sleeping thank goodness!"

"That's good. Hate to say it but we really don't like him," Mark text back.

"Funny, I don't like him that much either!" I replied.

"Well, if you ever need a shoulder..."

Just then I could hear movement coming from the bedroom and quickly shoved my mobile into my pocket. I listened intently, half expecting Ollie to come barging through in a mad rage and smash my phone to smithereens, but thankfully he didn't. He must have been rolling over in bed. I waited for a few minutes though, just to make sure and then when I knew the coast was clear I whipped my phone back out.

"Thanks Mark. That's good to know. Better go now," I text, "See you next week."

Once the message was sent, I immediately switched my mobile off and put it away just to be on the safe side. I climbed up on to the couch and felt happier, safer even, knowing people out there genuinely cared. I knew I wasn't alone, thank God. I didn't even contemplate going through beside Ollie. The very thought of it filled me with repulsion. I just hated him so much. Instead, I curled up on the sofa (again) and fell fast asleep.

Sunday was awkward and uncomfortable. Of course, the next day Ella was horrified when I told her that Ollie had appeared uninvited at The Tail Feathers, totally embarrassing me.

"He what?" she yelled, "That eejit is seriously as mad as a bag of spanners."

"Tell me about it," I agreed.

"You are leaving him now… Right?" begged Ella.

When I didn't answer and looked sheepishly down at the ground, I seriously thought she was going to have a meltdown.

"For heavens sakes Marina," she barked, "You can't go on like this. It's just not healthy."

"I know, I know…" I started, but luckily William bounced over to us, cutting into our conversation.

"What's not healthy?" he asked.

"Chips," Ella said, glaring at me, heading to class.

I knew that she was only looking out for me and that she was now genuinely worried, but I was so scared of upsetting Ollie and of making things even worse. Ella understandably, was getting extremely annoyed with me now and I desperately didn't want to lose her support because I really needed her now, more than ever. It was just such an awful situation to be in.

She wouldn't let it go though and nagged me at every given opportunity. Luckily her thoughts were diverted when we were given details about the end of term competition. Our class had to showcase what we had learned by producing a catwalk type of show and we were divided into groups of four.

Our job was to decide what we were going to use as a theme, prosthetics, make-up, models and all that kind of stuff. It was all very exciting but best of all, it was a distraction.

Luckily, Ella and I had been paired up with William and Hannah. We were going to be the dream team and immediately started discussing options, jotting down some ideas. However, we just couldn't totally agree on a final theme. It was good though, because it really gave me and Ella something to concentrate on other than Ollie.

"What about zombies?" suggested William, "I think that would be good. Scary faces and blood oozing everywhere. The prosthetics would be amazing to make."

"Nah. It's a bit too obvious," sighed Hannah, looking up at the ceiling for inspiration.

"Too frightening more like," said Ella, "Don't forget there might be kids in the audience. No, I think something more glamorous would be good... like...like... Oh God, I just can't think... Wait a minute... like Mardi Gras or something. Now that would be fun."

"Well at least we've got plenty of time to choose," I said reassuringly, "I think what we need to do is to go away and just have a good old think about it before we decide on anything."

"I think you're right Marina," agreed William, "I mean, we don't want to rush into it and make a mess of things. We want to win!"

"Aliens!" shouted Hannah, triumphantly, not really listening to what we were saying, "We could make really grotesque prosthetic faces to show off our wonderful talent."

"Grotesque prosthetics? God that's not easy to say!" joked Ella, "Hey wait a minute that's a great title... Grotesque prosthetics... or wait a minute...what about a Grotesque Mardi Gras? That would be a good mix of scary but glamourous!"

"Brilliant idea Ella," yelled William, "I'm up for that."

"Me too," squealed Hannah, "Oh God, I can't wait to get started. It's so exciting."

They were all enthralled with the idea, but I had to admit I still wasn't really getting it. Perhaps it was all the stress with Ollie, finally taking its toll. I went along with the idea none the less and scribbled down some sketches. They loved them and before we finished up we had more or less agreed on everything. The hard part would be trying to get clothes which would obviously have to be bright and colourful and of course getting people to model for us, but we would just have to cross that bridge when we came to it. The main priority at the moment was working out the make-up and prosthetics.

It made for a quick week thank goodness, with the focus now being on the end of term show. Ollie's mood had thankfully been pretty even, but when I was getting ready to go to the Tail Feathers that Saturday, he unfortunately didn't seem to be "going out with the boys" as he had been the last couple of weeks.

He was in the living-room watching T.V., while I was getting ready in the bedroom, putting my make-up on. I felt a bit uneasy as I applied my lipstick, just somehow sensing that he was going to do something horrible. My premonition was right, as it turned out, when in he came and stood behind me with his arms folded, looking at my reflection in the mirror.

"You're needing to stop putting so much of that muck on your face," he said nastily, "You're beginning to look like those bloody queers you're working with."

What an arsehole. Why did he have to say such a stupid, senseless thing just to irritate me? I loved my make-up and he knew that. It was my life, my job and I was furious that he had referred to it as "muck" but I tried to push away the negative feelings and calmly turned a deaf ear to him because I knew that was the desired effect, just to make me angry. I carefully put the lid back on my lipstick then stood up and headed towards the door.

"Hoy! Are you ignoring me?" he said, standing in my way, "I said you don't need all that shit on your face. Do you hear me? It doesn't make you look any better you know. You're still fuck ugly."

Oh, my God. Just how far was he going to push me? Part of me wanted to laugh at his stupid comment, but mostly I really, really wanted to punch him in the face and say, "Just bugger off you big waste of space. You're not so pretty yourself".

I didn't want to jeopardise getting to the club though, so instead I tried to stay calm and still said nothing as I attempted to get past him. Obviously, he was annoyed by my lack of response to his horrible, unnecessary nastiness. He suddenly grabbed me roughly by the shoulders and then before I could retaliate, he had firmly wiped his hand all over my face and eyes. I could feel the make-up all being dislodged from my skin in the process, then he dragged his thumb across my mouth, removing all my lipstick. For me, it was the ultimate violation, removing my confidence mask. It was actually worse than getting a slap.

"There," he said, standing back, admiring the mess he had made, "That's much better. Now you don't look like a flaming drag queen."

Instead of feeling angry, I just felt so sad and so defeated. It was almost as though I had come to expect and accept him doing something like this. He knew he could do what he wanted to me now and get away with it because I was too scared to fight him. He also knew that I was desperate to get to work, because I actually happened to like it and that was probably why he felt compelled to hurt me.

What the hell was wrong with me? Why was I letting him do this to me? What I really wanted to do was to yell in his face. Punch his chest. Scratch his face so hard it stripped his skin off, but then, that would be lowering myself to his depraved, violent level, so instead I still said nothing and squeezed gently past him. I quickly grabbed my bag and phone from the kitchen and lifted my jacket as I headed to the front door. Suddenly he was standing there in the doorway, blocking my way again and I started to panic, scared in case he wouldn't let me get out.

"Say hello to the poofs for me," he said sarcastically, again knowing that it would annoy me, then he stepped aside to let me past.

I just ignored him and wrestled with the door, now desperate to get outside. He banged the door noisily shut behind me and as I virtually sprinted up the street towards the bus stop, the tears started pouring from my eyes yet again.

It was bad enough when he was threatening towards me, but somehow this was much worse. I just couldn't understand how he could be so evil and horrible for absolutely no reason. He was so clever and knew exactly how to get to me. Even though I was determined he wasn't going to totally destroy me, I felt so emotional, so upset and at my wit's end. I shouldn't be feeling like this. It should be an exciting, happy time for me, going to The Tail Feathers and hanging out with the queens but yet again he had succeeded in making me feel stupid and worthless, while making me look an absolute sight.

Sitting on the bus, I took my little mirror out of my bag and looked at my face. It was a total mess. My lipstick was all over my chin and my mascara was smudged to kingdom come not just from Ollie wiping it off, but also from my tears. I tried to do a quick fix before I got to my stop, but I didn't really have enough time. I just felt so fed up and heavy hearted.

I was tempted to just stay on the bus and not ever get off, too embarrassed to show my face to anyone let alone the queens, but then I started to get angry. Why should I let the monster win? I continued on my travels but by the time I got to the club, I was feeling even angrier and not just with Ollie. How could Molly have let him in last week? Just what on earth was she thinking of? When I went into the foyer, I marched up to the box office where she was sitting, fiddling with her phone. When she looked up, she welcomed me with her usual big, beaming smile, which made it pretty difficult for me to maintain my irate demeanour.

"Hello Marina, my love," she said, but immediately saw that my face wasn't too happy (and a sight into the bargain), "Is everything all right pet?"

I really wanted to shout and swear at her, demanding to know why the hell she had so stupidly allowed Ollie up to the dressing rooms last week, but when I looked at her lovely, friendly face, I suddenly realised that all this mess wasn't her fault. She had only done what she thought was best, because she had been totally taken in with him. It wasn't her fault that Ollie was a psycho, that he had wiped my precious make-up off my face or that he was doing his best at totally ruining my life.

"Oh, Molly...," I started, but then I couldn't even speak, just couldn't get the words out as my emotions took over as usual.

"Oh Marina, what on earth's the matter?" she said, reaching her hand across the counter and comfortingly touching mine.

She was looking intently at my face, knowing that something was wrong as yet again the tears flooded down my face, though I tried my hardest to sniff them all back.

"Just... please don't ever let Ollie... my... "boyfriend" ever get in here again," I finally managed to say.

"Oh Marina," she said, still holding my hand tightly and looking searchingly at my face, "I totally understand and I'm so, so sorry I ever let him through. It's just... he said he was desperate to see you and I believed him."

"That's the trouble... he's so convincing. I'm sorry Molly, you weren't to know," I said, backing down, "It's not your fault..."

"Oh, but I feel terrible pet," she said, "I must admit, I didn't really like the look of him. My first husband was a monster too. Don't you worry Marina. If he comes hanging around here again then I'll get security to chuck him out... or the police even!"

"Oh, thank you Molly. I just hate being a pest," I said apologetically.

"Being a pest?" a voice said out of nowhere, "You could never be a pest!"

I quickly turned around and discovered Mark standing behind me. I didn't expect him to be here already and felt mortified that he was seeing me in such a state. I had hoped to nip up to the dressing room before he arrived, so that I could touch up my make-up. I felt so weak and helpless, with tears welling up in my eyes yet again.

"Oh my God Marina, are you o.k.?" he asked earnestly, reaching his arms out, then immersing me, in a lovely warm hug.

Of course, that just made me snivel even more and before I could get my words out, Molly had whispered to him, "It's her boyfriend."

"Say no more, I knew he was worth the watching," said Mark squeezing me tight and soothingly rubbing my back, "Come on, let's get you upstairs and you can tell me all about it."

I didn't want him to ever stop hugging me because it felt so good, so comforting but I reluctantly pulled myself away from him and followed him up to the dressing rooms. Surprisingly, Ricky was already in there, applying his make-up, but immediately stood up with shock, when he saw the state I was in.

"Oh my," he said scrutinising my face, "What do we have here?" Obviously, knowing it might upset me to speak, Mark put his finger to his mouth saying, "Ssshh Ricky, darling. I think Marina just needs a few minutes. Come on sweetheart... sit yourself down."

I plonked my bum on the big swivel chair, but instead of feeling all emotional and like crying again, I suddenly felt loved and cared for because I knew that they were both genuinely concerned about me.

"It's that awful boyfriend of yours, isn't it?" surmised Ricky, "I didn't like him one single bit."

"I... oh my God," I laughed, ironically, "How is it that everyone can see he's horrible, but I never could?"

"Ah well," said Mark, leaning on the dressing table, "Love is always blind."

"Love!" I laughed, ironically again, "Love doesn't come into it. I flaming hate him!"

"Honey, we don't even know him and we hate him. He looks absolutely Knutsford to me," said Ricky, "Anyway, stupid question... but why DO you hate the arse-hole?"

"I wouldn't even know where to I start?" I said, holding my head in my hands, "Well... he's moody, unpredictable and..."

I hesitated, not knowing if I could actually share with them all the gory details but I needn't have worried.

"Let me say it for you darling," said Ricky, "... and violent? I can tell his type a mile away. I had a boyfriend like that once... just loved to use me as a punch bag."

"And look what he did to my face," I wailed, pointing to my messy make-up and then found myself helplessly crying again.

I immediately felt really stupid and must have been an awful sight to behold, but again I needn't have worried because Mark and Ricky threw their arms round me in a great big group hug.

"Don't you worry for a minute about that," said Mark, "You've got us... the make-up queens. We'll soon have you looking a million dollars. Just you wait and see."

"But I'm supposed to be helping YOU guys," I said, laughing and crying at the same time.

"Well, there's plenty of time for that once we've got you sorted," said Mark, getting the baby lotion out, "Now let's start by wiping away those tears."

"I don't know what to say," I said, sniffing and trying hard to smile at the same time.

"You don't have to say anything," said Ricky, massaging my head, "Just sit back and relax."

Mark twirled my chair round so I wasn't facing the mirror and then Ricky placed a towel round my neck. I just felt so special and pampered as they busied away making me feel totally human again.

"You have beautiful skin," said Ricky, dusting my cheeks with powder.

"...and beautiful eyes," said Mark, brushing on my eye shadow.

"Oh, thanks guys," I said, feeling a bit embarrassed and not really believing them, "You're far too kind."

"Oh shit, don't you just love make-up," said Ricky slicking my lips with the shiniest gloss I had ever seen, then shrieked, "Oh my God, I've just had a horrible thought. Imagine if there was an apocalypse and all the make-up in the world was just totally wiped out!"

"Lord, I wouldn't want to survive it," squealed Mark, "Life just wouldn't be worth living if I didn't have my war-paint."

"Tell me about it," agreed Ricky, "Oh, my God and all that mess would simply wreak havoc with my O.C.D.!"

I laughed at their craziness, a bit hysterically, I have to admit, feeling so fortunate to have them both in my life. They really knew how to make me feel better and when they had finished doing my face, Mark twirled my chair back around so that I was facing the mirror, allowing me to see the fantastic results.

"Wow!" I gasped, looking closer at my reflection, "I look absolutely fabulous."

"Why of course you do," mocked Ricky, "You've only been done by the best."

I couldn't stop looking at my reflection. I honestly had never looked quite so amazing! It was just utterly breath taking.

"Right you stop admiring yourself and get out of that chair," said Mark, "It's our turn now!"

"Oh, no bother," I said jumping up, "Thank you both so much."

"Now, I definitely want my lashes the way you did them last week" said Mark, opening his big eyes as wide as they would go.

"... and I definitely want the same gorgeous eyebrows!" said Ricky, raising his brows unnaturally high.

"It'll be my absolute pleasure," I said, quickly grabbing all of the essentials.

91

I happily did their lashes and brows while at the same time, trying to catch sneaky glimpses of myself in the mirror to check out their fantastic handy work. I dabbled with some shading and contouring on Mark and glittered over Ricky's vibrant blue eye shadow. I actually felt a pang of jealousy as I looked at them, all done up and ready to go, in their colourful, sparkly dresses. I could never look as perfect as they both did and actually wished I was going out on stage with them.

"You both look stunning," I said, feeling so happy for them both.

"O.M.G., you've worked your magic on us yet again Marina," said Sabrina, doing a little pirouette.

"You are nothing short of an angel," said Giselle, planting a big kiss on my cheek, "Wish us luck sweetie."

"Break a leg," I laughed in return.

"But for Gods sakes not a nail!" said Sabrina, heading to the door and waving his hands madly up in the air.

"And remember," said Giselle, "If that creep dares to show up just scream as loud as you can and we'll come running."

"Don't you worry, I will," I said, following them to the door, "Enjoy yourselves."

I watched them disappear through to the stage and then went back into the dressing room, closing the door behind me. I noticed that it actually had a bolt. I hesitated for a moment. Would I lock it or wouldn't I? I knew in my heart that Molly would never let Ollie through again, but there was no question about it. I quickly bolted it shut and felt so relieved for doing so.

Sitting back down, I looked at myself in the mirror, admiring my make-up again. I noticed there was a lipstick stain on my cheek where Mark had kissed me. I gently rubbed it and could feel the rich, creaminess. It gave me a strange pleasure as I touched it and though I really didn't want to, eventually I slowly blended it into my skin, realising that in some odd way that I was beginning to feel a strange attraction towards Mark.

There was just something special about him. He was so good looking and kind. For a moment, I wished that I was a man, so that he would fancy me. I tried really hard though, to divert my thoughts and feelings by busying myself with some tidying up. I had a look at all their colourful dresses and costumes. They were stunning and there seemed to be piles of them, each one even more vibrant and beautiful than the next.

As I gazed at them, I suddenly had a light bulb moment. The queens would be absolutely perfect models for our entry in the college show and they would be able to use their own clothes which would save us a fortune. I couldn't understand why I hadn't thought of it before.

Just as I was about to sit down my mobile beeped with a message. It made me freeze, scared in case it was from Ollie, with one of his weird and nasty texts, intent on bullying me. Warily I read it but breathed a sigh of relief when I realised that thankfully it was from Ella.

"Is everything ok?" it read.

"Yes," I replied, "The queens have done my make-up and I look gr8!"

I attached a selfie and she quickly replied, "Oh my God! You look absolutely gorgeous! When can they do me!"

I text back, "I've just had the most amazing idea! Why don't I ask Mark and Ricky to be our models for the show?"

"That's just a fantastic idea! Why didn't I think of that?" Ella text, "Let me know what they say"

"Don't worry I will do," I text her.

It helped me to pass the time and before long I could hear Sabrina and Giselle chattering noisily as they came back off stage. I looked towards the door expecting them to come floating in, but instead heard them wrestling anxiously with the door handle, because I had stupidly forgotten to unlock it.

"Marina?" shouted Giselle obviously distressed.

"Marina? Are you o.k. honey?" Sabrina yelled, hammering on the door, with all of his might.

"Oh no... I mean YES," I shouted, running over and unlatching it, feeling really foolish.

Sabrina and Giselle virtually fell into the dressing room as I pulled open the door. They were both looking me up and down, making sure that I was alright, then their eyes were darting nervously all over the place.

"I'm so sorry," I said, clasping my hands, "I just locked it to be on the safe side."

"Oh, quite right darling," said Giselle, still looking round the room to make sure Ollie wasn't there.

Realising that he wasn't she said, "For one awful minute I thought that creep was holding you hostage or something."

Just then an older looking drag queen came running in to the changing room behind them, puffing on an e-cigarette, with a worried look on her face.

"What's all the commotion?" she asked, surveying the situation.

"Oh, Matron, don't worry. Everything's fine," Giselle assured her, "We thought we were going to have to knock the door down to get in, but Marina here had just locked it!"

"Marina?" Matron queried, checking me out.

"Oh, sorry we haven't introduced you," said Sabrina apologetically, "Matron, this is Marina. Marina, this is The Matron."

"Marina's our work experience girl," added Giselle.

"Oh right... very pleased to meet you," she said, firmly shaking my hand, "They call me Matron because I'm... er... older... and wiser. Well, not exactly older, but definitely wiser."

"Oh, come on Matron! Everyone knows you were around long before the dinosaurs," joked Sabrina.

"Oh, it's lovely to meet you too," I said, noticing that her make-up wasn't quite as perfect as Sabrina and Giselle's and that there was a tiny bit of stubble popping out of her chin, making her foundation look a bit caked and rough, but lovely non the less.

"Work experience eh? Well now, if there's anything you need to know just come and ask me," she said winking her wrinkly looking eye, "I've been around the block once or twice, so I definitely know a thing or two!"

"Oh, that's very kind," I said, gratefully, really appreciating the kind gesture.

"Anyway ladies, I'll see you later at the club," she said, making her way to the door.

"Look forward to it Matron," said Giselle, blowing her a kiss.

"Matron!" echoed Sabrina and saluting.

As she disappeared out through the door, Sabrina and Giselle turned quickly back around and looked at me again.

"So, you're sure you're definitely o.k.?" Giselle asked anxiously.

"Yes, yes, I'm fine," I assured them, "So how was the show?"

"Oh, it was simply brilliant," said Sabrina, gliding about with pride, "The audience just loved us! Didn't they Gizzy?"

"Indeed, they did!" Giselle said, fluttering her eyelashes, that I felt so proud to have done, "indeed they did."

"Oh, that's great!" I said, feeling really pleased for them both.

"Now listen," said Sabrina seriously, stopping in front of me, "We're going out clubbing now, but we're walking you to the station first, to make sure you're safe."

"Oh, honestly, there's no need," I said.

"No... we insist," said Giselle, holding up her hand, "We can't risk anything happening to our precious little princess Marina!"

"Oh, thanks so much. I really appreciate it and I was also wondering....," I said hesitantly, scared in case it wasn't the right moment, "emmm... well... that is, the guys at college were wondering... if there was any possibility that you could be models for our end of term show?"

"Well, I don't know about you Gizzy... but I think that sounds fabsolutely marvellous darling," said Sabrina, enthusiastically.

"We would be truly honoured," said Giselle, bowing gracefully.

"Oh, that's brilliant," I said, hugging and kissing them both, "Thank you so much. I'll just text Ella, if that's o.k. to tell her the good news."

I could just imagine her dancing about the place with delight, as she immediately replied, "Wooooo. I can't wait xxxxx"

The queens and I gathered our stuff together and headed for the stairs, waving to Molly on our way out. As we walked down the street arm in arm, I felt so proud and lucky to be accompanied by Sabrina and Giselle who were still in full drag. I could just imagine the horrible, snide remarks Ollie would have made if he had seen us, but in a way, this made me feel even more defiant and happy to be with them. I really felt like I had finally found my niche.

It was actually just as well that I wasn't on my own because it was very quiet and I would have felt really vulnerable walking all by myself. When we reached the station the queens both stopped to embrace me.

"Now remember," said Sabrina, holding my chin gently, "Do NOT take any shit from that horrible boyfriend of yours."

"I won't," I promised.

"And do NOT be frightened by him," said Giselle, elbowing Sabrina out of the way, so she could get in for a cuddle, squeezing me tight.

"I won't," I said, hugging tightly back.

They were like my own, protective fairy godmothers and stood waving me off as the train pulled away. I laughed to myself thinking how ironic it was that I had a couple of drag queens for body guards, but also how lucky I was that they cared so much. I was just so grateful to have them in my life.

As the train trundled down the track my thoughts quickly turned to Ollie though and how he had nastily wiped my make-up off before I left. For a split second I began to panic and was about to start taking off the make-up that Sabrina and Giselle had so perfectly applied but then I suddenly felt rebellious again. He was a horrible pig and everyone knew it. Why should I remove it?

I bravely kept it on and when I got home, I marched confidently in to the flat. He was in the lounge watching the telly as usual, so I walked quietly in and sat down on the couch waiting to see if he would even speak to me. He ignored me at first. Not a "Hello", not even lifting his eyes from the screen, so I said nothing but when the adverts came on, he turned the sound down then looked straight at me, sneering in his usual vulgar way.

"I didn't know the circus was in town," he mocked, "You look just like those stupid clowns you're working with."

I had fully expected an ignorant comment like that. I was angry that he was determined to knock my confidence and happiness but still felt strangely defiant. My brain told me to ignore him and say nothing, but unfortunately of course, my mouth had other ideas.

"Do you know Ollie… actually I think it's you that's the clown," I said, unable to stop myself, but then, as usual, totally regretting it.

"Oh, do you now?" he said jumping up out of his chair.

I froze with fear as he sprung right in front of me and unable to move, I watched in slow motion, as he lifted his arm up in the air.

"Maybe this'll make you think differently, bitch," he said, punching me hard in the mouth.

I didn't have any time to duck out of the way and then felt the searing pain of his knuckles whamming my bottom lip into my teeth. As he pulled his hand triumphantly away, he looked down at me in disgust, then just left me to mop up the blood that was now dripping down my chin. I looked at my bloodied hand in utter disbelief and then I could feel my body starting to shake with the shock. Why on earth had I even bothered to come back home? How did I think I could ever win with him and why the hell was I so stupid?

"I'm going out clown," he shouted from the hall then slammed the front door noisily behind him.

I sat frozen to the spot, still traumatized. As I sat there in the silence though, I began to feel so relieved, that he had actually gone out. I tried to ignore my pain, hoping and praying that he would never ever come back.

"There is a God," I said to myself.

I was weary and so tired of his crazy outbursts. Normally, I would feel all emotional and start to cry, but oddly, once the initial shock of the punch had worn off, I just picked myself up and trotted through to the bathroom. I suppose it was now just all getting a bit predictable.

I peered into the mirror to see what state my lip was in. It was now big, fat and purple with a bit of blood still oozing from the corner. It was weird, but I felt no emotion at all as I saw my reflection. I suppose it was acceptance with a hint of misery, but then as I looked over the rest of my face and saw that the queens hard work was actually still intact, I began to feel strangely strong and content.

My make-up really was my strength and I felt happy knowing that I had lovely people in my life. who had tried to make me look beautiful and wanted to help me instead of continuously hurting me.

I dabbed my lip again then went through to the bedroom. I quickly looked out one of my big bags and calmly started packing all my most important things into it. That was it. I was definitely going this time. The punch in the mouth was the final trigger. I just couldn't take it anymore.

I stood looking desperately round the room to see what else to take but was stopped in my tracks when a thought came into my head. What if he was pretending that he was going out just to test me and then suddenly came back just as I was leaving? He was so warped and would probably do something nasty like that. I had visions of him chasing me down the street, then punching and kicking me before throwing me in the gutter. The more I thought about it, the more scared I felt and stupidly decided that I just couldn't risk it.

Despairingly, I started unpacking all of my things, deciding that it would probably be a better idea to wait until tomorrow to leave him. To run off tonight would be a little too obvious, making him think he had won and that I was the weak and defenceless little person that he wanted me to be.

Whereas if I waited until tomorrow, I could tell Ella and give her some warning that I was moving back in, instead of just landing on her doorstep tonight. I could then come back to the flat one day when he was at work to get my stuff, without fear of him catching me in the act or trying to stop me.

To phone Ella tonight would be too risky too, because I knew she would be round here in a flash to help me but, again I was scared in case Ollie appeared and caused a big scene. No, waiting until tomorrow was definitely the best option, I tried to convince myself.

Reluctantly, I put away the unpacked bag and was just about to wash off my lovely make-up but then defiantly decided that I was keeping it on. It was like my very special comfort blanket from the queens. I got my pyjamas on and guessed that Ollie would probably assume that I wouldn't want to sleep beside him and that I would sleep on the couch. In another act of defiance though, I climbed into bed, hiding under the covers and unexpectedly went straight to sleep, probably exhausted from all the emotional and physical trauma.

I woke up the next morning, a bit earlier than usual and tiptoed through to the bathroom, hoping not to make a noise, just in case he was in. I glanced hesitantly through to the lounge as I passed the door and there he was, sprawled over the couch, out for the count. He must have crept in last night, but thankfully didn't come near the bedroom, then flaked out on the sofa.

I quietly proceeded to brush my teeth, looking at my lip in the mirror. It was even bigger and fatter this morning than it was last night. I felt so angry, but was excited at the same time, knowing that today was definitely going to be the day for me to break free.

I tiptoed back to the bedroom and touched up my make-up, which was still fairly intact, trying hard to disguise my lip with tons of concealer and powder. I couldn't make my mind up if it made it look better or worse but anyway, it would just have to do for now. As I started to get dressed, I could hear movement coming from the lounge, then the bathroom door getting slammed shut. I struggled quickly into my jeans and grabbed my bag as I ran through to the hall. I had managed to get my boots on and was just reaching for my jacket when Ollie came back out of the bathroom, pulling up the zip of his trousers.

"You're up early," he said, coming menacingly towards me.

"Yes," I said, trying to get my arm into the sleeve of my jacket while wracking my brains to find an excuse for being up early on a Sunday morning, "Me and Ella are going to do some extra work for our assessments and stuff."

"Oh, no you're not," he said, infuriatingly blocking my exit.

The wind was taken from my sails yet again and feeling exasperated, I sighed as I said, "What?"

"You're not going anywhere today... because I've planned a surprise treat for you," he said, almost gently taking hold of my chin and looking at my fat lip, "To say sorry for doing that."

No! That's not supposed to be what happens. He was spoiling my big plan yet again. My great escape. I couldn't let him ruin it all.

"Don't be silly," I said, pulling my chin out of his tight grip, which was now starting to hurt, "I don't need any treats. Honestly... you're forgiven."

"No, no. I insist," he said, turning and heading for the bedroom, "Just give me a minute to get freshened up."

In my mind I was quietly opening the front door then running down the street at top speed to get as far away from him as possible. In reality though, I just stood there like a stupid dummy, not able to believe that in his own twisted way, he was stopping me from going through with my plans to leave him. He was the victor yet again. I began to feel really angry as I waited for him. I hated him so much and didn't want to go anywhere with him. He only seemed to have been in the bedroom for a minute when he came running back through.

"Oh... and go and wash your face... you know you don't need all that slap on," he said.

"But I don't want to take my make-up off," I responded, shocked at his request but determined to keep Giselle and Sabrina's handy

99

work intact, especially as my big, fat, ugly lip needed to be camouflaged.

"Now, now, don't annoy me," he said menacingly, "It really doesn't do you any favours and you know I prefer you with your natural looks."

"I'd rather keep it on if you don't mind," I insisted, feeling really exasperated with him.

"Wash it off," he said firmly, half glaring, but half smiling in his usual threatening way.

Terrified of what he might to do to me if I didn't, I reluctantly went through to the bathroom and washed my face. There was no way I could go out looking like that, I thought to myself as I looked in the mirror, not only with a big fat lip but also because I never ever did no make-up. I cheated by dabbing bits of concealer here and there, then lightly coated my lips with lipstick and put on a light brush of eye shadow. It wasn't brilliant, but it was better than none at all and hopefully he wouldn't really notice it.

"Now that looks much better," he said, as I walked back out into the hall, then he took my arm as we walked outside, "You're going to absolutely love this."

Oh no I bloody wasn't. Why on earth would I want to have any interaction with him after what he had done to me last night? I knew it was not going to be good but unwillingly I was forced to go along with his madness yet again, for fear of what he might do to me if I didn't. I felt naked though, having to go out into the street with hardly any make-up on and felt really angry with him for making me do it. He knew fine well that I never ever went out without my make-up on, but then that was his plan. He was just wanted to make a complete fool out of me.

"Now, before we do anything… first we get our phones," he said, raising his in the air and motioning to me to get mine out.

I did as I was told, reluctantly reaching into my bag and slowly lifting it out, dreading that he was going to smash it to smithereens on the ground. I just wanted to use it to phone my mum, Ella, Mark, anyone to come and rescue me, but instead I just meekly followed his instructions.

"Then… on the count of three," he said, "we switch them off… because we don't want any annoying interruptions, do we?"

I shook my head slowly in agreement but felt panic and fear, not wanting to turn it off just in case I needed to use it in an absolute emergency. It was my only means of contact to the real, sane world. What on earth was he up to? I played along with him though and hovered my finger over the off button.

"One... two... three...," he said, emphatically switching his off and watching me to make sure that I was doing the same.

I showed him the blank screen to prove it was off, but I desperately wanted to turn it back on. I felt so vulnerable now, even more than usual.

"That's my girl" he said, taking my arm tightly again, "We don't want any distractions. Do we now?"

I knew he was referring to Ella, but just ignored his remark and said nothing, as we continued down the street. Things were a bit strained to say the least, because I didn't want to even try to make any conversation with him, let alone be with him.

We eventually came to the station and when we got on the train I literally cringed as he sat with his arm round me the whole journey. What the hell was he playing at? There was no love involved with his attentions, because again I knew that he was just doing it to irritate and get to me. Not only that, I felt so ugly without my full make-up on and thought that everyone was staring at me in disgust.

We ended up at the coast and he took me, or should I say, dragged me to a beach where we had once had a "romantic" picnic, before things had become so fraught between us. He had picked up some food on the way and even though it was blowing a gale and absolutely freezing, he insisted that we sit on a bench looking out to sea to eat it.

"Do you remember this place?" he asked, as I sat next to him, shivering and totally uninterested.

"Yes," I said, purposely not expanding my answer because it wasn't a very happy memory for me now.

He unwrapped the sandwiches then held one up to my mouth saying, "Open wide."

"What the hell are you doing?" I said, pulling my face away from him and saying, "I can feed myself, thanks very much."

I put my hand out to take the sandwich off him, but he held it out of my reach.

"A-ah," he said, holding it higher above his head, "I just want to look after you Marina. I want to prove that I'm truly sorry for what I've done to you and I want to make up for the awful way I've been acting. I know I've been hard to live with lately."

I wanted to say, "You sure have, you cretin," but instead I just said, "I told you... it's fine," not really knowing what to say in case I tipped him the wrong way.

He was still holding the sandwich annoyingly up in the air, but I just couldn't be bothered with his silly little games. I was too cold and now far too hungry.

"Just give me the bloody sandwich," I said, feeling totally exasperated with him.

"Kiss me first," he said, leaning towards me, "and then I'll let you have it."

Yuk! The very thought of his lips being anywhere near mine, totally turned my stomach, putting me right off wanting to eat anything. I knew it would probably hurt because my lip felt really tender, but knowing that I had to keep him level, I reluctantly pushed my face towards his. He kissed me gently at first but then his kisses turned heavier, pressing unnaturally hard on my mouth. I allowed him to do it for another second but then pulled away when it became unbearably painful.

"Right, that's enough," I tried to joke, as my mouth throbbed, "Just give me my sandwich now."

"There you go," he said, handing it to me, but then raising it back up in the air, "What's the magic word?"

I really wanted to say, "Fuck off, per chance?" but instead I forced a smile, saying, "Please?"

"There you go," he said, finally giving me the now very floppy, unappetising looking morsel,

"You've earned it gorgeous."

Gorgeous? Who was he trying to kid? Could he actually see the state my face was in? I didn't even want the bloody sandwich now, feeling totally and utterly repulsed by him. I just wanted to vomit all over his stupid picnic, but instead I was obliged to politely nibble at his food, trying to keep my mouth busy, so that he didn't dare attempt to kiss me again.

He continued the "romantic" act, making me walk arm in arm with him on the beach, while he showed off skimming stones. It was agonising and felt like we had walked for miles. Then he took me for lunch in a lovely little restaurant. If it had been with anyone other than Ollie, then it would have been quite nice, but because it was with him the whole experience made my flesh creep. I felt frightened and threatened the whole time, wondering what on earth he was going to do next. I just didn't know what was going on in that mad, scheming mind of his anymore.

I felt really self-conscious and ugly again, seeing all the other women in the restaurant, looking pretty, with their nice clothes on and perfectly applied make-up, while I was virtually bare faced and with an ugly fat lip to boot. He certainly knew how to torture me, did Ollie.

As I looked at him across the table, I could actually now see the evil eyes that Ella had always commented on, the evil eyes that I had never actually noticed before. Until now that is and as I watched his mouth as he spoke, I could totally see why Mark, Ricky and Molly didn't like the look of him either. Why had I been so blind and naïve?

I found myself totally zoning out, totally bored as I listened to him droning on and on about nothing in particular and then I found my thoughts wandering to my lovely friends. As I did so, I suddenly felt a surge of panic again, wanting to run as far away as possible from him and get to the safety of Ella's flat. However, I realised that I couldn't. I had to sit it out, held captive in a restaurant by my psychotic boyfriend. The only thing that helped me deal with it all, was sinking countless glasses of red wine which I knew was probably the wrong thing to do, but it was the only way that I could cope with the situation.

When we eventually finished our lunch, he continued the whole awful experience, by insisting that we go for another walk back on the beach. I knew it was just to annoy me even more. As if we hadn't walked enough. I grudgingly agreed and I don't know if it was the effect of all the alcohol that I had consumed, but I actually allowed him to maul me, his hands all over my body, soaking my face with his unwanted, horrible, slobbery kisses.

"Oh my God, I can't wait to get you alone," he whispered in my ear, as we sat on the train going home.

Get me alone? I wanted to scream, "You've got to be joking right? I never, ever want to be alone with you, ever, ever again. O.K.?"

Instead, I just smiled sweetly, hoping that he would be too tired by the time we got home and just fall asleep before he was capable of doing anything.

Unfortunately, though that wasn't to be. As soon as we got into the flat, he was tearing my clothes off, dragging his mouth over my neck and his hands were all over me like an octopus. I was too scared to fight him off, as he pulled me through to the bedroom and then revoltingly, I allowed him to aggressively make love to me, looking triumphant as he came. It was painful. Not just physically but mentally too. As usual, I faked an orgasm just to speed up the gruesome process, but then he held me uncomfortably tightly in one of his bear hugs as we lay on the bed. It was truly awful.

"Just like old times, eh?" he said, pulling his face back to look at me, "I love you Marina. You do know that don't you?"

"Of course I do," I said, through gritted teeth, closing my eyes and hoping he would just go to sleep and shut up.

Thankfully he did. I didn't sleep much however, feeling appalled with myself for everything that we had done together, because I hated him so, so much. I pretended I was still sleeping when he rolled out of bed in the morning and before he left for work, he crept back into the bedroom.

"Love you," he said, as he kissed me on the forehead.

I kept my eyes tightly shut though, pretending to still be asleep until I heard the front door closing firmly behind him. I waited for a minute just to make sure he was definitely away, then very warily got out of bed. I went straight to the front door, to check that it was securely locked, then quickly started getting ready for college.

When I looked at myself in the bathroom mirror, visions of Ollie gruesomely having sex with me came to mind. It made me feel totally disgusted with myself and I immediately jumped into the shower, scrubbing my whole body, in a frantic attempt to wash all traces of him well away. I quickly got dressed and put some make-up on, caking my lip with lots of foundation, and concealer, trying my hardest to hide the mess it was now in, after enduring Ollie's unwanted, frantic kisses.

Suddenly, I remembered my phone was still switched off. Panic-stricken, I ran through to the kitchen and whipped it out of my bag, quickly turning it back on. I had that horrible sinking feeling when I realised it had been off since yesterday and of course, there were loads of anxious texts from both Ella and my mum, obviously worried because I hadn't replied to them. I sent them both a text to say that everything was o.k., hoping that would pacify them, then hurried back through to the bedroom to get dressed.

I knew that I could tell Ella in more detail exactly what had happened yesterday when I saw her at college and when I thought about it, I began to feel really excited about telling her I was finally leaving Ollie. That I was definitely moving back in with her this time.

When I left the flat, I kept checking nervously all around me as I walked down the street, half expecting Ollie to suddenly jump out in front of me, in his usual warped fashion. Luckily, he didn't though. Feeling so thankful, I climbed aboard my bus and headed for the station. I couldn't believe that I was now actually able to look forward to the future.

I was desperate to see Ella, because I knew she would be as excited as I was. I cheerfully got my little mirror out and started to apply my lipstick. I was absolutely horrified though, to see the state my lip was now in. I had hurriedly put my make-up on earlier and hadn't really looked closely at it, but now, seeing it in broad daylight, it was visibly all crusted over and looked really awful with the foundation and powder now caked solid. Ollie's rough, horrible kisses with his jaggy, stubbly face had made it a hundred times worse.

By the time my bus got to the station, unfortunately I had totally lost my nerve. There was just no way on this earth that I could go into the college looking like this. What on earth would everyone think and poor Ella would probably get right on her high horse, making me go to the police or something.

What a bloody mess.

CHAPTER 4

TURNING POINT

I was so disappointed and angry with myself for not having the confidence to prove to the world just how violent and awful Ollie really was. As proof I should have gone to college and put my battered face on display to everyone, showing them the mess that he had made. I was so annoyed that I felt too embarrassed even to show my best friend what the evil monster had done to me, let alone the whole college. Now I just didn't know what to do or who to turn to. Then stupidly, yet again, I began to think that maybe I deserved to be punched, that I WAS to blame.

Instead of running into the station to get my train, downheartedly I turned and walked in the totally opposite direction, heading instead towards the shopping mall. It wasn't too busy because it was still quite early. As I gazed in shop windows, I kept catching sight of my reflection, with my deformed mouth standing out like a sore thumb. I looked absolutely awful and felt like everyone was staring at my ugly face.

I definitely didn't want to go to back to the flat, but I had no idea what on earth I was going to do now. I just continued to trudge aimlessly around the shops for a while, hoping for a miracle, but then of course I started getting lots of texts from an obviously now very anxious Ella, because I hadn't turned up for class.

"Where are you? Is everything o.k.?"

"Why are you not replying?"

"I'm getting worried Marina. Please answer xxx"

I immediately text her back saying, "Yes, everything's fine. Don't worry. Just not feeling too good. Think it's something I've eaten."

"I hope you're not hiding anything from me...," she texted back suspiciously.

"Of course not!" I lied, "Hopefully I'll be back tomorrow."

That seemed to pacify her, but then I realised that I would need to face her at some point today. It was all just so overwhelming and depressing. I continued walking round the shops, but I felt so guilty and angry for not being honest with Ella, or myself for that matter.

Smelling the sweet aroma of coffee coming from a coffee shop, I suddenly felt my tummy growl with hunger, realising that I hadn't even had any breakfast. I automatically headed towards the door to go in, but then remembered that I was absolutely skint, thanks to Ollie. I pulled out my purse and counted out a couple of pounds which I hoped would be just about enough for a small coffee but it definitely wouldn't be enough for any food. My hunger would just have to take a back seat.

It felt so cosy and warm as I stepped in through the door. It was a relief to see that it was fairly empty because I really didn't want to give anyone the opportunity to stare at my ugly, battered face.

I went up to the counter and ordered my coffee but could feel the assistant's eyes gawping at my lip, making me feel very uncomfortable and self-conscious.

"Would you like any cakes, pastries or toasties?" he asked, cheerfully.

I really wanted to say, "Oh, yes please. I'll have the lot," as I was now absolutely ravenous, but obviously because I had no money for such luxuries, I was forced to say, "No, I'll just have the coffee thanks."

The smell of all the lovely food teased at my nostrils and I couldn't wait to grab my drink and get as far away from it all as possible, so that I wasn't tempted. I found a table over in a nice, little corner and felt strangely relieved as I sat there anonymously, out of anyone's view, while getting a much needed shot of caffeine.

It gave me some time to think too. Time to reflect on the enormity of all the misery that Ollie had brought upon me and how he had ruined everything that we had. Why could he not just be normal and nice to me? Why did he have to be such a vicious creep?

A shiver went through me as I remembered the awful experience with him from the day before, culminating in a revolting sex session. I felt so ashamed of myself and actually felt physically sick as I remembered the awful, graphic details. It turned out to be good in a strange way, because it helped me to forget about my now aching hunger pangs.

I sat sipping very slowly at my coffee in an attempt to make it last longer. It was really hard though, because it tasted so good and I had to keep stopping myself from drinking it too fast. My attention was diverted thankfully, as I watched a delightful looking elderly couple come walking into the shop, demonstrably still very much in love with each other. The man held the door politely open for his wife, then put his arm lovingly round her shoulder as they went up to the serving area to order.

It was so lovely to watch, but then I felt deeply saddened and a little envious to see them so evidently still in love with each other, probably after decades of marriage together. Then I felt ashamed of myself, realising how stupid and irrational I was being. Just because I wasn't in a loving relationship didn't mean that everyone else had to be unhappy too. As I kept watching them, their obvious contentment and adoration for each other started to make me feel really happy for them. How lucky they were to have each other, without loathing or fear.

It was actually quite nice to people watch, just passing the time, not thinking about my worries and problems or Ollie for that matter. I kept looking towards the door as people came in, wondering what kind of lives they were leading. Were they married, divorced? Working or between jobs? Happy or sad? It was quite fun actually and totally absorbing.

I sipped at my now almost finished coffee, trying to eke it out as long as possible and looked over to the door as the next person came in. I was utterly shocked and caught my breath when I realised it was Mark that was walking into the shop. What were the odds? I quickly looked away hoping he hadn't seen me and tried to hide behind the menu. No way did I want him to see me in this horrifically ugly state.

I soon realised that it was too late though. He had spotted me right away and came rushing over. I leaned my elbow on the table with my cheek resting on my hand, half covering my mouth,
desperately hoping that he would just say hello then get on his way. Like that was going to happen! He was too nice and friendly to just say hello.

"Fancy meeting you here," he said pulling a chair out and sitting down, "Shouldn't you be in college... or are you having a sneaky day off?"

"Emmm...," I started, not really knowing what to say, still trying to hide my deformed mouth. I could tell by the way he was looking at me that he knew something wasn't quite right and he continued to probe, not taking his eyes off of me for a second.

"Is everything o.k. Marina?" he quizzed, when I didn't freely enter into any conversation, while at the same time totally scrutinising my face.

Before I had time to answer though, he had leaned over and gently lifted my hand away from my mouth. I felt vulnerable and totally helpless, because I knew I couldn't stop him. There was just no way I could hide the mess I was in. My heart sank and I wanted to cry when I saw the horrified look on his face as my fat lip was revealed. Why did he of all people have to come in? He was the last person I wanted seeing me looking like this.

"Now don't tell me you walked into a cupboard door," he said in a quiet, gentle voice, "Cause I just wouldn't believe you... Ollie did this to you, didn't he?"

That was all he had to say for the floodgates to fly open and then there was just no stopping the deluge of tears. I must have looked a really pathetic site as I sniffled and snorted back my tears. I felt so embarrassed and stupid. So exposed. Thank goodness the tables next to us were still empty. It would have been even worse with an audience listening in.

"That's good Marina. Just let it all out," he said holding my hand with both of his, "It's nothing to be ashamed of you know. You've done absolutely nothing to deserve this."

"I know," I sniffled, "But he just makes me feel so useless."

"Stop right there" said Mark putting his hand up, "You are anything but useless Marina. You're a beautiful, talented young woman with a fantastic future ahead of you and don't you ever forget that."

"Oh Mark," I laughed and cried at the same time, "You're so kind."

"It's not kindness," he said, shaking my hand, "It's the bloody truth. You're a wonderful person Marina and I think it sounds like he's probably actually jealous of you or something. Now listen to me... you need to leave this monster... before he grinds you down any

109

further... and before he really hurts you. God knows, he's done enough damage already by the looks of it."

"But that's just it," I said, trying to compose myself, "I WAS leaving him. I had it all planned out... I was going to ask Ella today if I could move back in with her... just till I get myself sorted. Only... only... I just couldn't face everyone seeing me looking like this."

"But that's where you're going wrong Marina... You SHOULD be letting everyone see you looking like this and let them know just exactly what he's doing to you," Mark said, looking at me earnestly, "You shouldn't be hiding it. In fact, I think you should seriously consider going to the police. It's GBH Marina. That nutter's dangerous and shouldn't be allowed out on the streets."

The word "police" just filled me with horror and dread but at the same time I knew that what he was saying was absolutely true but I just wanted it all to go away. I didn't want to have to face up to the truth. I just wanted to be normal, whatever normal was because I really didn't think I knew any more.

"Right, don't you go anywhere," Mark said, standing up, "I'm just going to go and grab us some coffees, then we can talk some more. O.K.?"

"O.K.," I said, forcing a smile and rubbing my now cherry nose with a napkin.

I suddenly felt totally safe and protected as I watched him head over to the counter. He was like my very own knight in shining armour, appearing out of nowhere, just to rescue me. He was so lovely, kind and caring. He was also so good looking, which at the same time was a bit depressing. It just made me wonder why on earth all the really nice guys are always unavailable?

Before long Mark was back at the table, weighed down with coffees and yummy looking cakes. It was just what the doctor ordered because I was now feeling absolutely famished.

"There you go," he said, pushing a coffee and one of the cakes towards me, "It might not take away all your troubles... but it's guaranteed to make you feel a lot better!"

"Oh, thank you so much Mark," I said, taking a sip of the lovely hot coffee and eyeing up my cake.

"Oh... and it's completely calorie free!" he joked.

"I wish," I laughed, "You're an absolute tonic. Do you know that?"

"Well, I've been called a lot of things in my life! Nothing quite as polite as that though!" Mark laughed, as he bit into his cake, "So you're going to stay with Ella then? That's brilliant. I don't want to put a damper on things though, but don't you think Ollie might put two and two together and guess that's where you are? It's just, you don't want him hanging about, hassling you or anything."

"Oh, God, I never really thought about that. It's just I've no-where else to go," I explained, "My mum and dad are in Spain, so it would be a bit too big a commute to college every day… on the other hand I suppose if I'm staying with Ella then at least I'll have her for back up if he comes anywhere near me."

"That's a good point," he agreed, "You can never have too many witnesses that's for sure. Unfortunately, I never had that luxury."

"What do you mean?" I asked, not really understanding what he was getting at.

"Well, I was in the same situation as a kid," he said, taking a sip of his coffee, "Just to put you in the picture, I was an only child. No brothers, no sisters... Just me. My poor mum ended up being the main bread winner when my dad suddenly left his job, which meant she was out working all hours, leaving me alone... with him. He had been very high up in the army but then out of the blue, for some unknown reason, he took early retirement. Now this was the man that was absolutely married to his work. A real man's man, so it was all a bit strange. I was never told why he had suddenly quit his job and nothing was ever said about it but I'm pretty sure it was due to some sort of mental instability, because I saw a side of him that no one else ever saw. Oh, he was always polite and lovely to everybody... everybody but me that is... he was a monster Marina... just like Ollie."

Mark took another sip of his coffee as I listened to him intently, now fully captivated by his story.

"Anyway, he was always wanting me to do the obvious macho things that he loved like rugby and football, but I had no interest in them whatsoever and to be honest I was never any good at them. I loved all the gentler things in life like art and music and all things creative, which totally annoyed the shit out of him. He forced me to play rugby though," Mark continued, sipping at his coffee again, "and of course whenever I played badly, which was like all the time, or if I didn't man up enough for him any other time then he would just knock seven bells out of me. Obviously, no one ever suspected anything... not even my mother. She was totally oblivious to what was going on. He would just blame my black eyes and bruises on rugby injuries or pretend that I had been fighting with other boys to make me look like the tough little boy he wanted me to be. I was desperate to tell my mum what he was doing to me, because I hated him so much, but I knew he would just threaten me with more of the same if I dared to open my mouth and I knew my mum would be broken hearted if she found out. I just couldn't do that to her."

"Oh, that's terrible Mark. I just can't believe he could do that to you. I mean... your own dad? What a bastard," I said, absolutely stunned by his words.

"Tell me about it. You see, what I'm trying to say is, I fully understand what you're going through... I honestly feel your pain Marina. I know exactly what it's like to be abused, to constantly be living in fear of someone. To be trapped. Never knowing how or when they're going to hurt you... and not just physically either," he said, his voice breaking, taking another sip of coffee and his eyes visibly glistening with tears, "That's why you've just got to do something... and fast. If Ollie can punch your face in then there's just no way of knowing what he's really capable of doing to you."

"Oh, Mark, I know," I said, feeling all emotional for him but just so grateful that he had opened up, sharing his own very personal experience with me and that he fully understood the misery of what I was going through.

"Anyway," he said, obviously trying to sniff back his tears, "My dad was desperate for me to follow in his footsteps and go into the army... the same as him. I think he thought if he bullied me enough, then I would just give in... but there was just no way on this earth I was ever going to be doing that. I mean a platoon of "my dad's"... all out to get me? It was just never going to happen. Not ever. So as soon as I left school, I went straight to drama college. Of course, he would never come with my mum to see me in any of my performances, but still at every given opportunity he thought he had the right to batter the living daylights out of me. Saying that I had "let the side down" or that I wasn't a "real" man. What an arsehole."

112

"Mark, I'm so, so sorry. That really is awful for you," I sympathised, still trying hard not to cry for him.

"Well, it's not really all bad," he said, leaning towards me over the table, "You see, I get the last laugh. I knew that nothing would fill him with more hate and loathing than the thought of me being gay or even worse... dressing up in women's clothes. So that's half the reason I decided to go into drag. I knew that it would totally disgust him knowing that his one and only son was a drag queen!"

I laughed with him at the irony of it all.

"The truth is though," he continued, "I absolutely love my job. Not only that I make a fantastic living out of it AND the audience totally adores me... which is more than my father ever did. So he actually did me a big favour. Of course, I always make sure my mum's around when I visit now, so he's forced to be pleasant to me and I ALWAYS go in drag. It's great watching him writhe and squirm and even better than that, my mum is so proud of me and what I've achieved. She's behind me all the way and she's got my photos all over the house which totally rubs his nose right in it, but there's not a single thing he can do about it or he knows that the truth will finally come out and bite him in the bum!"

"I only wish it would, the horrible pig," I laughed, "and I hope you always take your boyfriends home with you just to irritate him even more. That would be really funny!"

"Well... you see that just wouldn't happen," Mark said looking at me intently, "I don't have a boyfriend... because I'm not actually gay! Although God knows I've questioned it many times and yes... I admit, I've dipped my toe in the water so as to speak but no, I think I am honestly totally heterosexual... but just love women's clothes... oh and make-up! I adore make-up. That's why I love drag so much. Although I must say it is very tempting to bring a random home... just to get to annoy him and keep him wondering!"

I honestly didn't know what to say at that point. It was all a bit too much to take in, my beautiful Mark wasn't gay? It had been really narrow-minded of me to assume that he even was in the first place, but at the same time, I couldn't believe it! What a turn-up for the books. This day was turning out to be even more bizarre than ever!

The only thing I could think to say was, "Cool," which was really naff, but then I suddenly felt really self-conscious and embarrassed, as if he could now tell that I had feelings for him. I honestly couldn't believe that my kind, beautiful friend was suddenly a love possibility.

Wait a minute... my face has just been bashed in by my violent boyfriend and I looked an absolute mess so why on earth would he fancy ME? Better calm down and take one step at a time. Try and get my life together, THEN think about hooking up with Mark. Hold on, hooking up with Mark? Oh my God, what the hell was wrong with me? I really had lost the plot. Why on earth would he be interested in me?

"Are you O.K. Marina?" Mark asked, obviously noticing my silence as he ploughed through my crazy, unrealistic thoughts.

I had been so busy planning out my love life in my head, that I had completely forgotten that he was even there, right in front of me. My beautiful, lovely Mark. My breathtakingly, beautiful, lovely Mark.

"Marina?" he asked anxiously.

"What? Oh... yes... yes, I'm fine thanks," I said rubbing my head, realising how absurd I was being, "Just a bit tired... actually... exhausted to be totally honest with you."

"No wonder, you poor lamb," he said, looking deeply into my eyes and stroking my hand.

Oh my God, please don't do that I was thinking... I like it too much. It was very comforting but sexual at the same time. God knows my emotions were all over the place as it was. I was so scared in case I would do something stupid in response, but at the same time hoping that he would never ever stop. It felt so good and just so right. Oh no, what on earth was wrong with me? I was in the middle of a crisis. I had a violent boyfriend that had finally completely broken me, both mentally and physically and here I was sitting in front of a drag queen that I totally respected, totally adored, totally wanted to be with... Oh no, I was drifting into my fantasy world again.

"Are you sure you're alright Marina?... Marina...?" asked Mark, obviously now very concerned about me.

"What...?" I said, suddenly snapping out of my ludicrous thoughts, but hardly able to string two words together, "Yes... yes... I'm... I just... I'm..."

"I know... you're exhausted. You're bound to be and I can fully understand that. It totally wears you down... but honestly, please don't you ever forget that I'm here for you Marina. O.K?" he said, patting my hand again.

Here for me... forget? I was never, ever going to forget. How lucky was I? Suddenly I felt totally overwhelmed and just wanted to cry, but this time with happiness. My heart felt weighted down with love instead of sorrow for once. He truly loved me. Wait a minute... I was reading far too much into it... again. What on earth was I thinking about? He was there for me... as a friend... nothing else. For God's sakes girl, pull yourself together. My thoughts were getting totally out of control and a bit hysterical to say the least. It was probably a reaction to everything that had been happening to me lately.

"Thank you, Mark... for being a friend... a good friend," I finally managed to blurt out, dragging myself back into reality, "You've got absolutely no idea what that means to me. It's so good to talk to someone that REALLY understands."

"Well, I mean it Marina and you know, to be honest, it's been really good to unload on someone that's been through the same thing," he said, squeezing my hand tightly, "So, please tell me that you're going to go straight to Ella and tell her that you're definitely leaving Ollie?"

"Well, actually, I was going to wait till later, when she comes out of college," I said, so glad that he had changed the subject and brought me back to my senses at last.

"Later? Why not now? You know what they say... there's no time like the present. Send her a text and let her know you're on your way?" Mark suggested.

"Oh, well I could, but I really don't think she'll have her phone on in class, so she probably wouldn't get it" I said.

"Oh, that's a bugger. Well, what about going to the college at lunchtime? Could you not catch her then," he asked.

"Well, I suppose so," I said, hesitantly, looking at my watch, "We usually get out about twelvish."

"Great! If we start heading now then we should get there in perfect time," said Mark, lifting his cup to his mouth, "Drink up. We've got places to go, people to see!"

I gladly did as I was told and quickly finished my cake and coffee, not only so we could get quickly on our way, but also because I just remembered that I was still absolutely starving! As we walked down the street, it felt so good, having someone at my side to support me. It made all the difference in the world, knowing that I didn't have to do this all on my own anymore. I had someone to help fight my battles, because he had been there himself already and knew exactly what I was going through.

The world suddenly seemed to be a much more beautiful place at long last, I thought to myself as we arrived at the station and luckily, we didn't have to wait too long until our train came. We sat, side by side with no need for words, feeling each-others pain, but also feeling a mutual support for one another, in a comfortable, silent kind of way. It didn't take us long to get to college, but I knew Ella would still be in class.   I sent her a text just saying that I was here, while Mark and I made ourselves comfortable in the reception area and just waited.

I still couldn't believe that Mark had been through the same kind of trauma as myself. The same hurtful agony. We had so much in common and it just made me feel somehow secure and at last, strong. I nearly jumped out of my skin though when my phone started ringing.

"Oh great! It's Ella," I said, looking at the screen then answering, "Hi there."

"Is everything o.k.?" she asked anxiously.

"Yes, everything's fine," I said, "I'm just sitting in reception. I'll see you soon."

"O.k., see you soon," she echoed, sounding a bit puzzled.

Literally within what seemed like seconds, Ella appeared with William and Hannah in tow. Oh no! Suddenly I felt totally self-conscious and weak again, knowing that she was going to see what Ollie had done to me. I had totally forgotten about my ugly fat lip. I could just about face Ella with it, but I didn't really want anyone else to see. It was too late though to run and hide when they all came rushing over, looking very surprised to see me with Mark. We stood up to greet them and of course Ella clocked my lip right away.

"Oh mother of God," she said, hugging me but then pulling back to examine my face, "What the hell's he done to you this time?"

116

I could hear William and Hannah gasp noisily as they noticed my battered and now very crusty horrible looking lip.

"Oh, Ella, I honestly don't know where to begin… but I know one thing… I just can't go back to him," I said, squeezing her tightly, "so, I was wondering… I mean it wouldn't be long term but...would it be o.k. if I come back and stay at yours... just for a bit?"

"Oh, for heavens sakes Marina… just for a bit? You can stay for ever and ever if you want, just as long as you promise me, you'll stay away from that evil bastard," said Ella, hugging me again with all her might, then she turned her gaze towards Mark, "Hello there, Mark."

"Hi there," he said, nodding his head and motioning his hand in a wave, obviously relieved at her response.

"Oh, sorry Mark... I haven't introduced you, this is William and Hannah," I said, realising that they had never met.

"Pleased to meet you," he said, stepping forward and shaking both their hands vigorously.

"Hi," Hannah said bashfully.

"How do you do," said William, eyeing him up and obviously very impressed by Mark's beautiful face and physique.

"Right," said Ella, "Let's get you home."

"Oh no, it's fine. You finish your classes and I'll just hang about till five. Honestly, it's not a problem," I assured her.

"Excuse me, but you'll not be hanging about anywhere from here on in," said Ella sternly, "Not with that evil monster lurking about. God knows what he could do to you, given half a chance. Come on, let's go."

"Me and Hannah better come too... Just in case," said William, eyeing Mark up again.

"No bother," said Ella, "The more, the merrier. What about you Mark? You're more than welcome to come back with us. I could rustle up a tasty lunch."

"Well, I can't refuse an offer like that. A tasty lunch sounds good to me!" said Mark, "Lead on MacDuff!"

We all chattered to each other as we went to get the train and in next to no time, we were at the right stop for Ella's flat. I felt a bit anxious and scared as we walked towards it, terrified in case Ollie was hiding, ready to just jump out of nowhere and bundle me into his car, driving me miles away from my friends.

I needn't have worried though. We managed to get indoors safe and sound. It felt like total sanctuary as I walked into the living-room and looked around at the familiar surroundings. I breathed a huge sigh of relief, but then suddenly everyone's kindness and attention was all too much for me and I started to feel all tearful again.

"Oh Ella," I said turning and hugging her tightly, trying hard to hold back my tears, "Thanks so much for this. You've no idea what it means to me. I definitely owe you one."

"Oh, don't you be daft now!" she said hugging me back, "You don't owe me anything. I'm just so relieved you've finally left that creep. It's going to be a new start for you and we're going to be able to have a laugh again. Right come on everyone and help me make this wonderful lunch I was talking about."

We all crowded into the tiny kitchen and mucked in, helping to create a fantastic, big pot of pasta.

"Marina... get the out the tomatoes and chop them, could you darling," ordered Ella.

"Yes Sir," I said, saluting and opening the fridge door.

"Hannah... could you chop up the bacon?" asked Ella, pouring pasta into a pot.

"Sir, yes sir," giggled Hannah and saluted too.

"William... stop ogling at Mark and open the tin of beans!"

"What.... I'm not ogling at Mark," he protested but obviously realising himself that he was, then scurried towards the cupboard.

"... and Mark...," started Ella, "... just you stand there and look gorgeous!"

"O.K.," agreed Mark, "I'll not argue with that. I mean I don't want to get in the way of you guys!"

"Although you could grate the cheese," added Ella.

"No bother. That's the one thing I'm grate at!" joked Mark.

We all laughed at his crummy joke, as we set about our designated jobs while Ella grabbed a multitude of other things to chuck into the mix. When the delicacy was ready, Ella piled it into bowls and then we all squeezed onto the couches with William and Hannah on one sofa, while I was squashed on the other one between Ella and Mark.

We all started to devour our amazing creation which had actually turned out to be absolutely delicious.

"Wait a minute... there's something missing," said Ella, putting her hands up in dismay.

"That's not humanly possible," laughed Hannah, "Cause we only put the entire contents of your fridge and cupboard into it!"

"It tastes alright to me," said Mark, tucking in, "In fact it tastes bloody amazing. To be honest... I don't think I've ever tasted anything like it."

"Or probably will again," I quipped.

"No, there's definitely something missing," Ella said again.

"A bit of salt maybe?" queried William.

"No," said Ella.

"Pepper?" I piped up.

Suddenly Ella jumped up and ran to the kitchen. We could hear her opening the fridge door and pulling out a bottle of wine, then we could hear clinking as she grabbed some glasses. Triumphantly she came back through with her cache.

"This is what's missing," she said, laying the glasses down and filling them all up, while we all cheered with delight.

She handed us all a glass then held hers high up in the air, saying, "Here's to happiness Marina and eternal freedom for my beautiful friend."

"Freedom," Mark, Hannah and William shouted in reply, holding their glasses up.

I giggled bashfully, saying, "Thanks guys. You've all been amazing. I really don't know how to thank you."

"Well, you can make a start by getting that wine down your throat and then just try to enjoy the rest of your life!" said Mark.

We all took big gulps from our glasses and then got stuck into our lovely pasta. I don't know if it was the alcohol already starting to take effect, but I felt so relaxed, so safe, so protected and so much happier than I'd felt in a long, long time. I just wanted the feeling to last for ever.

"Now you don't have to talk about it if you don't want to," said Ella, "But why the hell did that bastard do that to your beautiful face Marina?"

I felt a bit awkward at first, with them all looking at me, but then an inner strength took over and I began to tell them how I had come to get my fat lip. It was weirdly quite cathartic to be honest, sharing it with them and getting it out in the open, just like Mark had done with me.

"Well," I started, "I had got myself ready to go to Tail Feathers, the other night and obviously I had put on my make-up..."

"Obviously!" said Hannah, "Life wouldn't be worth living without make-up."

"My sentiments exactly," I agreed, "Anyway, Ollie said that I didn't need "all that muck on my face" and then he proceeded to wipe it all off."

"No way... the complete and utter gobshite," yelled Ella, obviously totally appalled, "What gives him the right to do a thing like that?"

"I think he thought it might put me off going out... but it didn't," I assured them all, "Nothing was going to stop me from going to Tail Feathers."

"And don't worry," said Mark, patting me on the back "Me and Ricky put it all straight back on for her!"

"They did and thank you Mark, I looked absolutely amazing... but...," I tried to continue, but could feel my voice embarrassingly start to shake.

I managed to control it though, when Ella squeezed my hand and then continued, saying, "...well, when I got back home, he was waiting for me... sitting in the kitchen... in the dark..."

"What a creep" yelled William.

"I know," I continued, "and then... he said... that I looked like a clown."

"More like he's the clown," shouted Ella angrily.

"Well, that was the problem... that's exactly what I said... and of course, then he punched me in the mouth for it."

"What a bastard," said William, "When I was at school, I used to get thumped by all the bullies and that's just what he is Marina... nothing but a flaming big bully."

"Oh, I know," I agreed, "but as if that wasn't bad enough, he made me go out for the whole day with him yesterday to say "sorry"... but made me go out... with no make-up on."

"Oh, what? Marina, you don't do no make-up," yelled Ella, totally outraged.

"Tell me about it and he knows that, but he knew fine well I'd be too scared to stand up to him," I said, "Oh God I just hate him so much."

"He sounds totally bonkers that one. You really should go to the police," said Hannah, "and get him done for assault."

"Oh, I know," I agreed, "But I honestly don't want any trouble and I'm away from him now, so hopefully that'll be the end of it."

"I doubt it Marina," warned Ella, "The guy's a true psycho. I don't think he'll ever leave you alone."

We all jumped with fright when Mark's phone started ringing and thankfully we didn't have to talk any more about my problems. He quickly pulled the phone from his pocket and checked it to see who was calling.

"Hey guys, it's Ricky! Sorry, I'll just take it... Ricky what can I do you for...?" he said, standing up and walking to the window, "... I'm actually at Ella's... you know Marina's friend... We're just having a lovely lunch... Come over? Yes, I think that should be o.k."

He looked over to Ella for approval and asked, "Is that o.k.?"

"Of course it is," she replied, nodding furiously, "The more, the merrier!"

We all nodded with her in agreement, totally delighted at the prospect of Ricky joining us.

"Yes, come on over," continued Mark, "There's no pasta left but you could bring a bottle of wine... The address ... Oh my God, I don't know! What's the address Ella?"

"It's number 168 and it's flat 2, North Main Street," she yelled towards his phone.

"Did you get that...," laughed Mark, "Excellent... Chow baby."

He switched his phone off, put it back in his pocket then took a mouthful of pasta as he sat back down, saying, "What a drama queen! He just hates being left out of anything!"

Everyone laughed and devoured the rest of their lunch, which thankfully diverted their thoughts, so they didn't speak any more about Ollie. The pasta went down an absolute treat. So did the wine, a bit too quickly, it has to be said and when Ricky made his grand entrance, we couldn't wait to open one of the two bottles he'd brought along as well as all the crisps and nibbles.

"My, this is a lovely little gathering," Ricky said, unable to take his eyes off of William as soon as he clocked him, "Well... isn't somebody going to introduce me?"

"Oh, sorry Ricky, well you've already met Ella," I said, standing up and motioning towards Ella.

"Hi Ella" he said, giving her a little wave, then went over and shook her hand, "Lovely to see you again darling."

"...and this is Hannah."

"Hello lovely Hannah," he said, giving her hand a quick shake.

"Hi there," said Hannah bashfully, too shy to look him straight in the face.

"...and this is William," I said, who had not stopped staring desirably at Ricky, since he stepped in to the flat.

"Well, hello William," said Ricky, giving him a long handshake and looking deeply into his eyes, very obviously captivated by him, "Charmed, I'm sure."

William played straight back, saying, "The pleasure's all mine sweet cheeks."

"Oh, get a room you two!" joked Mark.

We all laughed as Ricky squeezed on to the couch between William and Hannah, who must have felt like a gooseberry, poor thing, then we got stuck into his wine. It was very much appreciated and just what the doctor ordered.

"So? What's the special occasion for this lovely little gathering?" he asked.

"Well, Marina here has very sensibly left that fuckwit of a boyfriend of hers and has moved back in with lovely Ella here," said Mark, joyfully.

"Oh, that's fabulous news Marina," he said, but now leaning forward and scrutinising my face, "and oh my God now I can see why. What on earth has that maniac done to you sweetheart?"

"Used her as a punch bag...," said Ella, "...again! But even worse than that, he made her walk about all day yesterday with no make-up on!"

"No shit? What a rat. I'd rather jump off a skyscraper than have no make-up on," said Ricky, "If any man dared to do that to me, then I would most definitely need to hire a hitman honey."

"Well, he's not getting the chance to hurt her anymore," said Ella, hugging me "You're safe now my angel."

"We're going to look after you," said Hannah, raising her glass up in the air, now obviously under the influence of alcohol and yelled, "CAUSE WE LOVE YOU MARINA."

"We love you Marina," echoed William in a quieter voice, sneaking a cheeky glance at Ricky.

Everyone joined in, chanting "We love you Marina, we love you Marina."

"OMG! You lot are pissed," said Ricky, glugging back his wine and nudging William, with a wink, "I see I've got a lot of catching up to do."

I was totally staggered by all their support and good wishes. I felt like the luckiest person in the world as we spent the rest of the afternoon chatting, laughing drunkenly and drinking yet more wine. Ricky and William were getting VERY friendly while the rest of us just discretely watched their lovely little romance starting to unfold. It was wonderful to be hanging out with lovely, caring people and with no need for fear or malice.

I felt so relaxed and so happy. Relieved to be among normal people. People that actually loved me and didn't want to hurt me. The time just flew by as we chatted and laughed, watching Ricky and William getting more and more intimate. It was just really sweet and lovely.

"You know you've done a really brave thing today," Mark said, taking hold of my hand, "Well done my lovely."

I smiled and looked into his beautiful, twinkling eyes. I don't know if it was the wine taking effect, but I could actually feel my heart slowly melting, as I gazed at him. I just wanted to throw my arms around him and kiss his gorgeous face off, but unfortunately, I was jolted back into reality when my phone beeped really loudly with a message. My gut instinct told me it was bound to be from Ollie and the room immediately fell silent with anticipation as I read it.

"Well? Is it him? What does it say?" asked Ella anxiously.

I took a deep breath and read out the words, "I guess I'll be getting my own dinner then?"

"Is that it?" said Ricky, "All he's bothered about is his flaming stomach? Not even a "Where are you darling?" Or "Is everything o.k.?" What a total bastard."

"Oh, that's him all over. Believe me," said Ella, "She's well rid if you ask me."

I honestly didn't know what to think or say for that matter. I fully expected him to hound me with countless texts and calls, demanding to know where I was, who I was with or what I was doing but instead, that was all I got from him. I suppose it was a relief in a way, not to be harassed by him but it was a bit unnerving at the same time. It simply wasn't in his character to "just leave it". I somehow sensed Mark was thinking the same thing.

"Don't be intimidated by him Marina. You're on the home straight now," he said, patting me on the shoulder, "and just remember that and don't forget... we're all right behind you."

"I know," I said, nodding my head and feeling totally supported by my very dear friends but I still couldn't help worrying, wondering what the bold Ollie had planned up his sleeve next.

"Oh, for the love of God," shouted Ricky and I thought for a minute that he was somehow commenting on our conversation, but then he held up the empty bottle of wine saying, "Where the hell did that one go to?"

We all laughed and then Ricky turned passionately to William saying, "William darling, there's nothing else for it... we'll just have to go out and get some more."

"Oh, my God. I thought you were never going to ask," gasped William getting quickly up off the couch, obviously desperately wanting to get Ricky on his own.

"We'll not be long chickens," said Ricky winking and waving as they disappeared through the door.

"Something tells me they like each other," smiled Hannah, "Lucky bastards."

"Well, one thing's for sure... Ricky doesn't ever hang about," laughed Mark, "If he wants it, he just goes out and gets it... and I'm not talking about the wine!"

124

"Aw, I think it's really sweet," said Ella, "William's such a cutie. I really hope it works out for them."

"Oh, I'm sure it will… and don't worry! Ricky will treat him like a princess," joked Mark.

We all laughed but deep down inside I was secretly wishing Mark would treat ME like a princess. God knows I needed some loving and when Ricky and William got back, they were very obviously now well into each other.

"The emergency rations have officially arrived," yelled Ricky, waving bottles of wine up in the air.

"Woooo," we all very drunkenly cheered.

"Thanks guys," said Ella jumping up and grabbing the bottles, "So what are you lot having?!"

"Hey, leave the humour to us darling and just get the wine poured," ordered Ricky, "While me and my little friend William here get… shall we say… a bit better aquainted."

"Sounds good to me," said William, sitting down next to Hannah while Ricky squeezed on to the couch beside him.

"I think you need more seats Ella," joked Hannah, feeling a tiny bit intimidated by the duo.

"No, you don't darling. This is perfect," said Ricky, cuddling into William, "Just the way I like it… nice and cosy."

"Cosy," echoed William, looking intently into Ricky's eyes.

"Anyway," said Ricky, dragging his gaze very reluctantly away from William's, "What about this show you guys are involved in? Is there anything we can do to help?"

"All you have to do is turn up and do what you do best, which is to look good!" said Ella, "and we'll do the rest! Honest."

"Well… actually we couldn't help wondering… if you could maybe… provide the dresses?" I asked bashfully, "Seeing as you've got so many!"

"But,of course we can sweetie," said Mark, "That's no problem at all. So, what's the theme going to be again?"

"Mardi Gras," piped up Ella.

"Emmm, excuse me… grotesque Mardi Gras," added William, "Don't forget the grotesque! Basically, you'll be glamorous zombies."

"Oh, my goodness that sounds wonderful," said Ricky, "At last I'm glamorous... and Mark here's a zombie! Sounds absolutely perfect to me!"

We all laughed, but in my head, I was thinking that Mark was anything but a zombie. He was just totally glamourous and handsome in my eyes. My thoughts were diverted however, as we started chattering and discussing what we were planning to do for the show, so much so that we didn't even think about what the time was. After a while though, everyone began to realise that it must be quite late and it was… very late. We were all now a bit the worse for wear after the amount of wine we had drank between us, but Ella and I managed to see everyone to the door, as we all said our goodbyes.

"Oh my God, I can honestly say I haven't enjoyed myself this much in years," said Ricky, putting his arm round William's waist, "AND I've bagged me a man!"

We all laughed and hugged each other, feeling so ecstatically happy for them. That is, except for poor Hannah.

"Unfortunately I haven't bagged me a man! " said Hannah sadly, waving to us as she staggered through the doorway but then immediately brightening up, "But I've had a great time. See you tomorrow girls."

"Oh my God, yes," said Ella, suddenly realising it was only a Monday, "College! Here was me thinking it was the weekend! God we'll never get up in the morning! Better set the alarm Marina."

Mark hugged Ella then turned and hugged me really tightly kissing my cheek with his warm soft lips, which felt like velvet on my skin. My nostrils filled with the beautiful aroma of after shave coming from his body, then my heart melted yet again. I just wanted the moment to last for ever.

"Just let us know when you need me and Ricky for rehearsals and stuff," he said, as he went towards the door.

"Don't worry… we will," said Ella, while I just stood there, speechless and lost in my little fantasy world again.

"Bye now," said Mark, smiling his beautiful smile, as he stepped outside.

I managed to squeak "Bye" and then collapsed down on the couch as Ella locked the door.

"You fancy him, don't you?" said Ella, flopping down beside me and nudging me in the arm.

"What?" I said, pretending not to understand what she was talking about, "Don't be daft."

"You can't fool me," she said, pushing me gently, "I can read you like a book remember, but hey, I don't blame you. He's absolutely bloody gorgeous!"

"I honestly don't know what you're talking about Ella!" I lied, "I've just had a bit too much to drink, that's all."

"Yeah right!" said Ella, rolling her eyes, "Pull the other one! So, no more texts from that weirdo then?"

"No," I said, feeling thankful that she had changed the subject, "I really thought he would be annoying me left right and centre with texts and phone calls, just to get to me… but... nothing? Strange."

"I don't think it's strange at all... the creep's obviously up to something," said Ella.

"I know. That's the scary bit," I said, "and it'll probably be when I'm least expecting it."

"Don't you worry about him though. We'll get your stuff tomorrow. That'll let him know that you mean business," Ella said, patting my hand.

That was the trouble though. Me meaning business would definitely rub him up the wrong way. I think that's why I had a horrible gut feeling that something awful was going to happen and I wasn't far wrong.

The next day we dragged ourselves out of bed, feeling a bit hungover to say the very least and literally crawled to college. God did we feel rough! I was amazed how nobody made any remark about my lip, which was still a bit deformed and swollen. No one even stared. Not that I noticed it myself that much now or maybe I just didn't care anymore. It was a relief however and luckily the morning just seemed to fly in with a little bit of help from a lot of coffee.

On a Tuesday we had a big space between morning and afternoon classes which meant we got a long lunch hour. I decided it would give me enough time to pop to the flat to retrieve my stuff. Ella, William and Hannah came with me for moral support and when we got off the train, we were so busy talking that I hadn't even noticed that Mark and Ricky were standing waiting for us at the station exit.

"Hi guys," said Mark as they started to walk towards us.

"The cavalry's here," joked Ricky, joining hands with William.

"What are you two doing here?" I said in astonishment, but at the same time, so happy to see them.

"We're here to protect you, you doughnut!" laughed Ricky, "...and also, so I could see my lovely William of course!"

"Oh, my goodness," I said, hugging Ricky then Mark, "Thank you both so much for coming. I really appreciate it."

"You're more than welcome," said Mark, holding my hand and patting it, "God knows, you need all the support you can get Marina."

I was just about to start melting again as I gazed into his brilliant blue eyes but was quickly jolted out of my dreams with Ella shouting, "Come on you lot. We better hurry up or we'll be late back to class and we really can't afford to miss any time."

We did as we were told and hurried out of the station then hopped on a bus. To be on the safe side, we decided to get off a few stops before my street just in case Ollie was lurking about. We headed in the right direction and when we got within sight of the flat, I stopped and motioned to everyone else to stop too.

"It's probably better if you guys stay here," I said, cautiously, "I'll go on ahead and if the coast is clear then I'll give you a wave."

"I really don't think you should go in by yourself," said Mark anxiously, "What if he's in there... waiting to pounce?"

"There's no way you're going it alone" piped up Ella, taking my arm, "If he's in there then he'll need to take us BOTH on."

"Well, promise me you'll be careful girls," said Mark.

"We promise," I said.

"And if there's any problems then scream as loud as you can and we'll all come running to the rescue," added Ricky.

"Don't worry, we will! Are you ready to do this?" asked Ella, squeezing my arm.

I took a deep breath, trying hard to calm my nerves then said, "Yes, I've never felt more ready."

"Then let's do it," said Ella, marching me forward.

We walked confidently towards the flat, trying to work out if there was anybody in. The blinds were half open and half shut so it was a bit hard to tell. Hesitantly, we walked up the steps and I nervously got the key out of my pocket. We couldn't hear any movement from within, so I slowly turned the key in the lock and then gently pushed the door open. We stood for a minute, listening intently for any noises, but there didn't seem to be any signs of life. Looking at each other for encouragement, we bravely stepped inside.

"You sure you're o.k.?" Ella whispered, squeezing my hand.

I nodded, suddenly feeling more positive again and walked forwards into the living-room, with Ella following closely behind me. There was a horrible, stale smell of takeaway food, with a half-eaten pizza lying on the coffee table and a few mugs lying at the side of the couch. The place was absolutely covered in crumbs and empty beer cans were littered everywhere, obviously just chucked on the floor once Ollie had drained them of their contents.

"Oh, yuk. It's totally disgusting. What a bloody lazy slob," commented Ella, "He can't even tidy up his own flaming mess."

"Tell me about it. There's no changes there then," I said, turning around and heading for the kitchen.

The sink was chock-a-block with dirty dishes and the floor was splattered with coffee marks and gunk. As there wasn't really anything in the kitchen that I wanted, I started to make my way through to the bedroom but as I pushed the door open, I just stepped back, gasping with disbelief and horror at the sight that lay before me. All of my clothes were lying on the bed, ripped and cut to shreds. Totally destroyed beyond repair.

"Holy shit," shrieked Ella, as she came into the room behind me, "The rotten evil bastard."

She quickly got her phone out and called Hannah.

"You need to get in here... NOW," she shouted at her phone, as Hannah answered.

At first, I just stood there, unable to speak or even move for that matter. I was in total shock at the sight of the carnage in front of me. Eventually, I managed to take a step forward and lifted the strips of material that were once my favourite dress. I looked despairingly at pairs of jeans and tops, in fact every single item of clothing that I owned, which had all been totally annihilated by Ollie's evil rage. I

129

just couldn't believe that he could do such an awful thing. Through my shocked trance I could hear the footsteps of the gang coming into the flat, then I heard all their horrified gasps as they came through and saw the despicable scene.

They were all saying things like "Oh my God" and "What a pig" when it suddenly hit me. My make-up. Oh, please no. Surely, he couldn't be so nasty and depraved.

I barged anxiously past everyone, clambering to get to the bathroom, hoping and praying that everything was intact. As I pushed open the door, I actually felt physically sick as I surveyed the destruction. All my glass bottles of foundation were lying smashed on the floor with the contents splattered all over the walls. The mirror was scribbled all over with lipstick while the contents of the lipsticks lay broken and squashed in the sink. My powder pots were empty, having been visibly emptied down the toilet, while all my eyeshadows were lying, scattered and crushed all over the floor, obviously hammered and stamped on by his out of control rage.

I just stood staring at it all in total disbelief, unable to react, again numb with the shock, but then I could feel everyone else's shock and horror as they came in and stood supportively behind me.

My eyes suddenly shifted to the corner of the bathroom and my heart sank even further when I saw all my make-up brushes lying on the floor, every single one snapped in half and the bristles squashed and distorted. Not only were they an essential part of my kit but they had cost me a small fortune.

I could feel warm tears start to pour uncontrollably from my eyes as the enormity of it all began to sink in. He had managed to hit me where he knew it would hurt me the most, even more than a punch in the mouth ever had. He knew make-up was my passion, my work and my world. He knew I needed it to do my course and he had totally destroyed it all with his mad, psychotic behaviour. Why did he want to keep on hurting me like this? Why did he hate me so much and why could he not just leave me alone?

I felt Mark's arm come gently round my shoulder as he tried to comfort me.

"Come here you," he said, pulling me into a hug and soothingly rubbing my back.

I could feel my body shaking violently as I sobbed my heart out and there was just no way I could even try to speak. I felt actual physical pain as I looked over Mark's shoulder at the awful destruction that Ollie had caused. I just felt so completely deflated but weirdly, I also felt a strange kind of torture, as Mark held me. I wanted to hug him with all my might, to kiss him, to never let him go and to just keep smelling the aroma of his beautiful body. I felt totally exhausted with all my mixed-up emotions, but then thankfully Ricky stepped in and managed to pull me out of my muddled thoughts.

"What a total shit," he said, "If any arse-hole did that to my make-up then I would seriously have to wring his bloody neck. Either that or rip his balls off and make him eat them. You just can't let him get away with this Marina. It's absolute sacrilege."

Ricky then came over putting his arms around me and Mark, then everyone joined in, making a group hug, all cuddling and comforting me.

"Oh Marina!" said Ella, obviously battling to hold back her tears, "I'm devastated for you, but don't you worry... we'll help you to replace it all."

"... nice new clothes," said William.

"... and a nice new man," added Hannah, "Definitely a nice new man."

"Oh, thanks guys," I managed to say, sniffing back my tears but really wanting to add, "... It's o.k. ... I think I might have found him..."

There was just no way I could allow the gang to pay for new stuff though. Then I started to feel guilty and stupidly materialistic to be so emotional over some clothes and a bit of make-up, but then the enormity of it all hit home again and the tears started flowing. What on earth was I going to do?

"I'll not be able to finish my course without my kit... and then there's the show...?" I wailed, embarrassingly.

"Of course you'll be able to finish the course," comforted William.

"... and the show will take care of itself," added Hannah.

"It's going to be just fine," Ella assured me.

"Come on Marina," said Mark, gently guiding me out of the bathroom, "Let's get you out of here. I think you've seen enough."

131

I felt so defeated, that I couldn't even be bothered to gather together anything that was half decent and as we all headed for the front door, I turned, taking a last look back in the flat. I couldn't believe I was actually leaving my home totally empty handed. Ollie had truly left me with absolutely nothing. I mean I didn't have all that much anyway.

He had not only wrecked my body and spirit but also every single thing that was precious to me. There was one thing he couldn't destroy though and that was my friendship with my wonderful mates. What on earth would I have done without them all? I wiped back the tears as we left, knowing that I was undoubtedly doing the right thing by leaving him.

All that he had left me with was an intense hate for him. A feeling that I had never truly experienced before. It was a cruel turn of events but this was definitely going to be a new start for me and arm in arm with Ella and Hannah, we walked back to the station with Mark, Ricky and William following supportively right behind us.

"Now remember if there's anything we can do. If you need our help at all...," said Mark, taking hold of my hand, when we reached the station.

"...just you give us a shout," said Ricky holding my other hand, "and we'll come running to the rescue."

"Oh thank you so much guys," I giggled as they both kissed my cheeks, "I honestly don't know what I would have done without you all."

"All in a day's work," Ricky said turning to William and pecking him on the cheek, "and I'll see you tonight gorgeous."

"Ooooh! I can't wait," said William clasping his hands with a beaming smile.

We waved Mark and Ricky off as we boarded the train to go back to college, though God knows I really didn't feel up to going.

Ella linked arms with me while William and Hannah tried their best to comfort me too. I really appreciated their love and support, but at the same time my heart felt so heavy as I thought about all the awful things that Ollie had done to me. I was scared too, wondering what on earth the monster might do to me next.

CHAPTER 5

TWISTED

The next couple of days flew in, thank goodness. We were really busy at college trying to put everything together for our submission for the show, so it gave me something to really focus on and helped to keep my mind off things. Luckily, everyone was really kind and let me share their make-up kits, so that was a great help.

Mercifully, I hadn't had any more communication from Ollie and had settled well into my new surroundings, living back with Ella again. She very kindly let me borrow some jeans and tops and thank God I still had my job at the pub, so I knew that eventually I would be able to afford to buy a few make up essentials and clothes of my own.

Mark and Ricky were due in, so that we could practice their make-up and prosthetics which was going to be exciting for all of us. We were just setting up our stuff when they arrived, in their usual whirlwind fashion. William of course ran straight up to Ricky, giving him a big kiss, while we all stopped what we were doing and welcomed them both.

"Marina darling," said Ricky, reluctantly pulling himself away from William then putting his arm round my shoulder, "How are you sweetie?"

"Oh, I'm fine thanks, how's you?" I said, fully expecting him to turn back round to slobber all over William again.

He didn't though and said, "Oh, I'm good honey. Now... I don't want you to get annoyed ... but we've all clubbed together... and got a little something for you..."

I was a bit puzzled at first, not really taking in what he was saying but then Mark stepped forward and handed me the bag that he had been carrying. He kissed me on the cheek, then said, "There you go my love."

I looked round at everyone, totally gob-smacked, still not knowing what to say, then looked inside the bag which contained a beautifully wrapped present.

"Oh, my God guys! What have you been up to?" I eventually managed to say, feeling totally embarrassed and humbled.

I gently pulled the present out of the bag then carefully unwrapped the lovely paper, really expecting it to be chocolates or something, but instead uncovered a beautiful shiny silver case.

"Oh, my goodness. It's beautiful," I gasped, twirling it around and admiring it.

"Well go on then," said Ella, excitedly, "Bloody open it!"

I flipped the lock which made the lid jump open, revealing a multitude of make-up products. I could see eyeshadows, foundations, powders, you name it and it was there while attached to the inside of the lid was a fantastic selection of fluffy new brushes.

"Oh, flaming heck guys this is far too much," I said, feeling really emotional at their generosity, "It must have cost a bomb."

"You're well worth every penny," said Mark, patting my arm.

"Oh, thank you," I said, trying to look round at everyone without starting to cry, "Thank you so, so much. You don't know what this means to me."

"Oh, we DO know what it means to you and you downright deserve it," said Ella, hugging me tightly.

I was so happy I felt like I was going to burst. Their kindness was totally overwhelming and I was teetering on the brink of tears, but luckily Ricky put paid to that.

"Right come on, before we ALL start blubbing," he said, sitting himself down on a chair, "Now blast my face with some make-up for God's sakes!"

We all laughed at him then scurried about, trying to get things organised. I stopped and took a moment though to just simply marvel at my beautiful new case. I really was so, so lucky. What lovely, kind friends I had, spending their hard-earned cash and getting something that they knew was of the utmost importance to me.

I suddenly realised that I was just standing there in a little dream world, all of my own, while everyone else was busy doing all the hard work, so I lovingly sat my fabulous new kit down on one of the tables and hurried over to start helping to make up Ricky and Mark. I could see that Hannah and William were already getting stuck into Ricky, so I went over to help Ella with the lovely Mark.

"So, how's things been at the club?" I asked Mark as I rubbed some moisturiser on to his face.

"Yeah, good," said Mark, looking at me with his twinkling eyes, "It was really busy last night. In fact, my mum was actually in."

"Oh, that's nice. What about your dad, was he there too?" I joked.

"Wild horses Marina, wild horses!" said Mark laughing, "No, it's a pity you weren't there. You could have met her. You two would really hit it off."

"Oh, that would have been nice," I said, "God, I'll really need to make up my time, but unfortunately, I've just been otherwise engaged."

"Don't worry about it. You've got a good excuse and I promise we'll not tell that you've not been in!"

"She knows just about everything there is to know about beautification anyway," shouted Ricky.

"Don't be daft," I said bashfully, "I've got so much to learn from you two."

"Well why don't you try and come tonight because it's going to be amazing," said Mark, "There's some queens coming over from New York. They are an absolute blast. You would love them!"

"It sounds amazing. I want to come," wailed Ella.

"Me too," said Hannah, listening in to our conversation.

"Can I come Ricky?" whispered William, loudly into Ricky's ear.

"Why, of course you can darling," he said, cupping William's face, "We'll make a night of it."

"Wooooooh!" yelled Ella, "I can't wait!"

"Right, so you're ALL coming then?" laughed Mark, "That's brilliant! The more, the merrier I suppose!"

We continued working on Mark and Ricky, making some prosthetic moulds. The pair of them couldn't stop laughing and I must admit, they did look really funny at times. It was just such a joy working with them and the time just flew in. Once we had done all that we needed to do, Mark and Ricky scooted off to do some rehearsals while we quickly ran about, tidying up and as soon as we got finished, we all hurried home to get ready. We were so excited because we just knew it was going to be a good night.

Ella let me borrow one of her dresses, while she put on a glitzy jump-suit. We helped each other with our hair and make-up then eagerly headed for the station. Hannah and William were there waiting for us and in no time at all we were heading for the Tail Feathers.

Annoyingly though, it was absolutely pouring with rain and we all huddled under my umbrella as we approached the entrance. There was already quite a big queue, but I dragged everyone behind me as we clambered past angry customers, seething at us for being cheeky enough to try and get in front of them. When we reached the box office, I waved furiously at Molly to make sure she could see us.

"Hello, Marina my lovely!" she shouted, "On you go in."

"Thanks Molly," I shouted, giving her a big thumbs up, with the gang following closely behind me.

They tittered with glee as we not only jumped the queue but we didn't have to pay either and as we hurried quickly into the club, the waiting customers just tutted and complained even more.

"Wow... this looks amazing," said Hannah, gazing round the hall as we walked in.

William was utterly speechless, while Ella was looking frantically for a table for us.

"Over here," she shouted, spying an empty, while we hastily followed her, sitting down quickly in case someone else claimed it first.

"Shouldn't you be up in the dressing rooms helping Mark and Ricky?" asked Hannah.

"Should I?" I queried.

"Well, it is your work placement," William reminded me.

"...and you do have time to make up...," Hannah reminded me, smirking "Get it… make...up! Make-up!"

We all giggled at Hannah's really awful joke.

"God! You'd think they were trying to get rid of you or something!" said Ella.

"No, I think they've got a point actually!" I said, "You get the drinks in and I'll go and see if they need me."

I clambered out of my chair, squeezing past all the tables and chairs to get to the door then I went over to Molly who was busy serving someone. I stood back a bit and waited until she had finished.

"Is everything o.k. there, Marina?" she asked anxiously.

"Oh, yes, everything's fine thanks Molly. I was just going to pop up and give Mark and Ricky a hand to get ready if they need me," I said, "so would you be able to swipe me in please?"

"Of course I can love. In fact, I'll give you the number and you can just key yourself in," she said, scribbling on a piece of paper, then handing it to me, "There you go."

"Oh, thanks Molly," I said, looking at the numbers as I walked over to the door.

I carefully tapped in the code and the door clicked open. I quickly headed through, then climbed the big stairs up to the dressing rooms. I could hear voices laughing and talking from within.

Hesitantly, I pushed the door open and found Mark and Ricky... or should I say Giselle and Sabrina, sitting in the laps of two other drag queens. I quickly closed the door back over. I was shocked because they looked like they were getting very intimate. Not what I was expecting at all. I mean Mark had said that he wasn't gay but how could I have been so stupid to believe him? I was so disappointed that my hopes of getting closer to him were dashed and poor William. He was totally besotted with Ricky and would be absolutely devastated. I took to my heels and started running quickly back down the stairs but was suddenly stopped in my tracks.

"Hey, Marina," Mark called out to me, "Wait..."

"I'm sorry... I didn't mean to interrupt you," I said looking up at him, "I just wondered if you needed any help."

"Sure, we need your help sweetheart," said Mark, coming level with me on the stairs, "We were just rehearsing our act. You're going to love it Marina. It's so funny."

"Rehearsing...? I... oh," I stuttered, now feeling really stupid.

Of course, they were rehearsing. How stupid of me to assume that they were getting over familiar with the American queens. As usual, I had read far too much into it. What on earth was I like?

"Come on. You can touch us up if you think we need it!" he said, winking cheekily.

137

Touch him up? God only knows, I'd love to touch him up… in more ways than one!

"Great!" I said enthusiastically, following him back up the stairs.

Mark led the way and the queens all greeted me with wonderful warmth and affection as we entered the dressing-room.

"Guys, let me introduce you to Marina," said Giselle, putting her arm around my shoulder, "She's our wonderful make-up trainee..."

"...and very good friend," added Sabrina, standing up and putting her arm round my other shoulder.

"Marina, darling. It's such a pleasure to meet you," said one of the American queens, stepping forward and kissing my cheek, "I'm Frankie."

"... and I'm Regina," said the other queen, stepping gracefully forward then stroking my cheek and smoothing my hair, "Rhymes with vag..."

"Hush your mouth," said Frankie putting her hand to Regina's lips, "The show hasn't even started yet!"

I giggled at the pair of them. They were just naturally so comical.

"Oh, she's a pretty little one," said Regina.

"She is that," said Mark, smiling at me.

His words filled my heart with joy, more than he would ever know. As I looked at them all I honestly couldn't see what I could possibly do to improve any of them, but they had me adding bits of blusher here and bits of glitter there to their already perfect make-up and they were all delighted with their finished results.

"Oh my God," said Frankie, "Don't we look just awesome!"

"Even more so than usual sweetie!" said Regina, admiring herself in the mirror.

Just then the door pushed open and Matron came walking in, scrutinising everyone's make-up then looked over in my direction.

"What about me?" she asked, "Do you think you can work a bit of magic on me Marina?"

"Matron honey," said Frankie seriously, "The poor girl isn't a miracle worker you know."

Matron looked visibly offended by Frankie's comment, so I immediately took pity on her and welcomed her over.

"Grab a seat Matron," I said, getting the make-up brushes at the ready, "...and I'll see what I can do."

"Oh, thanks pet" she said, squashing her rather large bottom into the chair.

I started dusting round her stubbly chin which made me feel more inclined to want to shave her, rather than caking more make-up on! I tried to soften her bold eye and brow liner, then gave her a more smoky, sultry look, finishing off with a sparkly bit of glitter.

"Oh, my God," gasped Matron, when I stood back to let her see herself in the mirror, "I've not looked that good since... since..."

"Since 1969?" joked Regina.

"Why, you cheeky cuss," said Matron, visibly offended, "What I was going to say was... I've not looked that good since the arthritis got bad in my fingers."

"Well, that's what happens when you reach a hundred and fifty years old!" laughed Frankie.

"It's just as well I've got a thick skin," said Matron, winking at me.

"You know what they say Matron," piped up Regina, "Thick skin... thick make-up!"

"I honestly don't know how I put up with this lot Marina," Matron said, struggling out of the chair and then hugging me, "Thank you pet. You're a little treasure."

"You really are," said Sabrina, kissing my cheek, "Now you go back down to your lovely friends and just sit back and enjoy the show. You've worked absolute wonders on us all."

All the queens nodded in agreement and Giselle put her arm round my waist, saying, "We'll catch up with you at the end of the show. Thank you so much for your help darling."

"No worries!" I said, reluctantly pulling out of Giselle's hold, "See you all later."

I made my exit and walked back down into the club, feeling really pleased with myself, though to be totally honest, I still didn't know why, because I really hadn't done that much. They all looked fabulous already... well, maybe not so much The Matron, poor soul! I felt so sorry for her.

Ella stood up when she saw me waving frantically to remind me where they were sitting. I ran quickly over and sat down just in time for the show starting.

"You were quick," said Ella, shoving a glass of wine into my hand.

"I know," I said, "There wasn't that much left for me to do really. It's going to be amazing though. I can just tell."

"Does my Ricky look good?" asked William, inquisitively.

"Absolutely out of this world," I enthused.

"...and we don't need to ask about Mark... eh Marina?" Ella said, nudging my arm.

"What?" I said, trying to sound surprised, trying to ignore what she was implying.

William and Hannah glanced at each other, chuckling into their drinks.

"You're all reading far too much into things," I said, taking a big mouthful of wine.

"I don't think we are," joked Ella, looking away from me.

I just shook my head and tried to ignore them. It made me feel a bit awkward and embarrassed though. Obviously, I was attracted to Mark, but no way did I want to make a fool of myself. Not with my awful history with men. Not only that he was a good friend and I didn't want anything spoiling what we had. Luckily for me the show was quite loud so they couldn't make any more audible comments. Big Ron came strolling on, giving his usual funny introduction before the acts started coming on.

"Good evening ladies and jelly men. We have got a fun packed show with music, dancing, laughter... oh yes... and The Matron!"

The audience laughed then cheered at the mention of her name. She seemed to be the butt of everyone's jokes but was obviously also much loved.

"And now without further adieu, let's get this show on the road."

The music was brilliant and the first lot of performers looked fantastic. The humour was hilarious and below the belt as usual, but it was a real tonic and together with a bit of alcohol, it made for a very entertaining evening.

We were desperate to see Sabrina and Giselle and when they finally came on, the cheering and clapping from the audience was truly deafening. They were obviously really popular and loved by the crowd. We all felt so proud, because we actually knew them!

Giselle strutted her stuff and waved at the audience, while Sabrina looked out into the crowd.

"Hello boys," she cooed, blowing a sultry kiss to all the men, but then scowled and tutted, saying, "Girls... who needs them?"

Everyone laughed, while Giselle continued to strut about, then Sabrina said to her, "I'm Sagittarius."

"Aries," said Giselle, putting her hands demonstrably behind her neck.

"So I see," smiled Sabrina bitchily, looking at Giselle's armpits, then pulling a face, "You really should have shaved sweetie!"

"Cheeky," said, Giselle, "Oh, my God I had a total disaster yesterday."

"Why what happened?" asked Sabrina.

"I swallowed my veneer," said Giselle, giving a squinty smile.

"Is that all? I've swallowed a lot worse than that," mocked Sabrina, winking at the audience then clutching his crotch, "I can assure you."

"But seriously," started Giselle, "Has anyone ever been on one of those dating sites?"

The audience mumbled yes and no in response.

"Filling out your details is such a pain," she said, shaking her head, "Name?... What do you want it to be honey? Age?... Not telling you darling. Sex?... Obviously..."

"Dogs," shouted Sabrina, then pointed to a random woman in the audience, "Don't worry angel... I'm not referring to you! No, seriously... dogs... don't you just hate them? I mean... all those slobbers..."

"But you get all that unconditional love," pointed out Giselle.

"Oh, I get that from the audience honey!" japed Sabrina.

The crowd howled with laughter as their alcohol was obviously starting to kick in.

"If there's one thing I hate... it's politics," continued Sabrina, shaking her head.

"But sugar, you need to vote for a party," pointed out Giselle.

"The only party that gets my vote is one with plenty of champagne and plenty of dick. Sorry William," she said, blowing kisses over to him, "I'm only joking darling."

William blew lots of kisses back and we all felt so honoured to be acquainted with the pair. It was heart-warming to see them absolutely adored by everybody and when they finished their act, they left to thunderous applause.

Next up were the American queens, who came on after them and of course they were utterly hilarious too, with their disgustingly funny jokes. Their dresses looked so tight it was a wonder they could even breathe never mind talk! When they finished their performance, Sabrina and Giselle came back on and they all did a very seductive singing and dancing stint together, which is obviously what they had been rehearsing when I had walked in on them earlier.

They were so entertaining and ended their act with Sabrina kissing Frankie on the lips and Giselle kissing Regina. The crowd absolutely loved it and our ears were ringing with the wolf whistles and clapping at the end of the show. We sat back, exhausted with laughing so much and were happy to let the crowd disappear before we even attempted to leave our seats.

"I haven't laughed that much in years! They were brilliant," said Ella, sitting back in her chair and holding her sides.

"They're just so hilarious," praised Hannah.

"OMG, I'm so proud of my Ricky" beamed William, "He's gorgeous AND talented!"

We gathered ourselves together and once the hall had almost emptied out, we started to shuffle towards the exit. As we went out into the lobby, we started to head towards the main door but just as we were about to step outside, we heard a voice shouting to us.

"Hey guys," yelled Giselle from the security entrance and waving to us, "Come on up."

We all looked at each other, then we began to run towards her, laughing and jokingly pushing each other out of the way, in an attempt to be first through the doorway, then we excitedly followed Giselle up the stairs.

"Come in and meet the crew," she said, holding the dressing room door open for us.

Ella went gingerly in first, saying, "Hi everyone! You were all absolutely amazing."

"Oh, thanks sweetheart," one of the queens shouted.

"Well done everyone," said Hannah, shyly, going in next.

"Where's my Ricky?" asked William anxiously looking round the room, probably scared in case he had his arms round someone else.

"Here I am darling," said Ricky suddenly appearing out of the crowd of queens.

Mark and I laughed at them as they greeted each other enthusiastically, kissing and hugging, then Mark turned to me smiling warmly.

"So, what do you think?" he asked, "were we any good?"

"No, you weren't good…" I started.

The room immediately fell silent and I could see everyone turning and glaring at me.

"You were just brilliant!" I continued, with a cheeky little smile.

"Oh, thank God for that," Mark said squeezing me tightly, "I thought for a minute there, you hadn't liked us."

"There's no chance of that," I said, hugging him back.

I caught Ella and Hannah looking at us as we cuddled, then both of them smirked at each other. I just drew them a dirty look, but I was secretly enjoying every single moment of being able to feel his body close to mine. Mark pulled back, looking at me full on.

"So, did we make you laugh then?" he asked.

"Definitely," I said, "My sides are aching."

"That's the desired effect!" Mark said, pulling me back into a hug again.

"Though, I wish it was more than my sides that were aching," I thought to myself in a Sabrina, Giselle naughty kind of way.

Just then two women suddenly appeared. One of them came up behind Mark and put her arms round his waist then hugged him. I actually felt a pang of jealousy. Who did she think she was and how had she managed to get through security? Startled, Mark swung round, but then started to laugh.

"Mum! What are you doing here? You should have told me you were coming," he said, kissing her on the cheek.

"Oh, I just wanted to show you off to Isobel here," she said, motioning towards her friend.

"What a laugh we had," said Isobel.

"Thank goodness for that," said Mark.

"We'll not hang about though son or your dad will be wondering where we are," said his mum, "I just wanted to say hello."

"Oh, thanks mum. Wait, let me introduce you," he said, pushing me gently forward, "This is Marina. She's our very own little apprentice."

"Oh, pleased to meet you Marina," she said, shaking my hand, "You'll definitely learn a lot from my Mark. I'm Joan by the way."

"Pleased to meet you Joan," I said, feeling absolutely honoured to have been introduced to her.

She was lovely and when her and Mark had said their goodbyes, she went off with Isobel, while we continued to mingle with the crowd. Mark introduced everyone, while Ricky and William inevitably disappeared into a corner, chatting and petting each other. It was all just a wonderful experience. The American queens were so funny. I didn't want the night ever to end. We hugged and kissed everyone when it was finally time to go and when it came to Mark kissing and hugging me, I just wanted to stay in his arms for ever more.

"Take care Marina," he said, his eyes twinkling even more than usual.

"I will," I said, melting as predictably as ever and just wanting to kiss his enticingly beautiful glossy lips, hoping that he might feel the same way.

I felt like I was floating on air as we left The Tail Feathers. Everyone was on a high, as we headed for the station. We were all laughing and chattering away, but then suddenly I froze, when in the distance, I caught a glimpse of Ollie as he crossed the road. My happiness very quickly changed to terror, which stopped me abruptly in my tracks. My initial reaction was to try and hide behind everyone, to make sure he wouldn't be able to see me.

"What's the matter Marina?" asked Hannah, noticing my odd behaviour.

"It's Ollie," I said, cowering behind them and pointing up the street.

"Holy shit, so it is," said Ella, standing taller and stretching her arms out wide, in an attempt to hide me, "The cocky bastard."

"That's it, I'm calling the police," said William, quickly getting his phone out of his pocket.

"Oh, please don't" I hissed, "Just leave it. I really don't want any trouble."

"But he's a maniac," argued William, "He shouldn't be walking the streets after what he's done to you."

"Put your phone away William," said Ella, firmly, "If Marina doesn't want the police involved then that's her decision and anyway, it doesn't look like he's seen her."

Reluctantly William put his mobile back in his pocket, while the rest of us stood very still and watched intently as Ollie disappeared off into the darkness.

"Phew!" said Hannah, "Thank God for that. Well done for spotting him Marina."

"I just feel like I've got a permanent radar, watching for him," I said.

"Right come on," said Ella, rushing us all towards the station, "We need to get you home... pronto, in case he materializes again."

I actually felt quite terrified, as we sat on the train, heading back to Ella's flat. I found myself constantly looking over my shoulder, scared in case Ollie had somehow managed to sneak on the train and was in the next carriage, ready to pounce. I guess I was getting utterly paranoid but I just didn't want any kind of confrontation with him, especially in public. Luckily there was no more signs of him and we got home safe and sound. It had unnerved me though and took the shine off the great evening we'd had. I felt like I was never going to be totally rid of him, that he would always be there, lurking somewhere in the background, just to annoy me.

The next day went in really quickly and thankfully stopped me from worrying about things. We were busy at college with show preparations and then I was working at the pub that night, from six till ten. I had gone straight from college and Ella had arranged to meet me later at the station when I was finished, so that she could accompany me back to the flat, just to be on the safe side.

The pub was quite busy which was great because it kept my mind focused. All the usual old men were in, but a few younger ones had come in, brightening the place up and making things slightly more interesting.

I was busy chatting to a customer when my eyes were suddenly drawn to the doors as they were being pushed open and then to my absolute horror, in walked Ollie. I felt my heart sink as his evil eyes met mine. What the hell was he up to?

Unfortunately, I had nowhere to run and nowhere to hide. I had no lovely friends to protect me this time. I could only stand there, waiting anxiously to see what crazy scheme his unhinged mind had concocted this time. Luckily though, Bill my boss had clocked him right away and quickly came over to stand by my side for a bit of moral support.

"A pint of lager please, wench" Ollie said sarcastically, leaning on the counter and looking straight at me with his ugly, sneering face.

Bill never took his eyes off him, watching his every move, as I nervously began to pull the pint. Aware of this, Ollie stood up straight, obviously trying to make himself look taller and more threatening and stared brazenly back at him.

"Alright mate?" he said looking very cocky.

"Oh, I'M alright," replied Bill, "But the question is are YOU alright… "mate"?"

"Course I am," Ollie said, looking straight at me as I handed him his lager.

"Well, you'd better be," said Bill, "cause I don't want you causing any trouble in my pub. Capiche?"

"What makes you think there's going to be any trouble?" asked Ollie innocently, handing me the exact amount of money, "I'm just in here for a quiet drink. Eh Marina? Oh and keep the change."

I tried not to give him any eye contact as I took the coins from him and put them in the till, then stood at the other side of Bill well away from his stare. In pure Ollie style though, he just moved a bit further up the bar, so he was back standing in front of me again.

"So… how's things Marina?" he asked, putting on a fake soft voice.

I didn't answer him and then went to the other side of Bill again, trying to avoid his evil eyes.

"I miss you," he said, in a fake voice again, moving back down to face me.

"Right you," said Bill, getting annoyed at his behaviour, "That's enough. She obviously doesn't want to speak to you so not another word or you're out of here pal. Got it?"

"Hey just wait a minute there, "PAL", she's my girlfriend," retaliated Ollie, "I've got every right to bloody well speak to her if I want to and you can't do a single thing to stop me."

146

"Ex-girlfriend," I corrected him, but then instantly wished that I hadn't opened my big mouth.

"Not through my choice sweet-pea," he said, putting on a stupid, pathetic looking sad face.

"I'm warning you... one more word...," Bill reminded him angrily. But again the smart arse just ignored him.

"Marina, all I want is for you to come back. You know I love you," he said with a sickeningly false tone.

I cringed at his words and it felt like the whole pub was looking at us, waiting desperately to see what was going to happen next. I wanted the ground to open and swallow me up. Why on earth could he not just leave me alone?

"Right, that's it," said Bill, walking round to the front of the bar and pointing to the door, "Get out... NOW"

"I don't think so," said Ollie taking another sip from his drink, "I've paid for my pint, so I'm going to flaming finish it."

Bill pulled the glass off him and poured its contents on to the floor, saying "Either get down on your hands and knees and lick it up... or get out."

Everyone gasped and watched open mouthed to see what Ollie's reaction was going to be. Very visibly irate, he immediately snatched the empty glass back out of Bill's hand then smashed it hard against the wall. The shards of glass littered the floor but thankfully didn't hit any of the customers.

"It was shit anyway," roared Ollie, furiously at Bill.

Obviously used to vile hooligans though, Bill grabbed him by the collar, marched him to the door then pushed him roughly out into the street.

"You better start running pal before I call the police and don't even THINK about stepping foot in this pub again," yelled Bill, "You're barred."

"Wanker," shouted Ollie, straightening up and dusting himself off as he started to walk away, "I'll be back if I want to. You can't stop me, dickhead."

Bill stood at the door with his arms folded, watching until Ollie was completely out of sight just to be sure he was gone, then came back into the pub. He rushed over to me, putting his arm gently round my shoulder.

"Are you alright Marina?" he asked anxiously.

"Yes, I'm fine thanks Bill. Just a bit shaken," I said, "I truly don't know what's wrong with him. He's turned in to a total psycho. Thank you so much for standing up to him."

"Oh no bother pet. I've had a lot worse than him in my time, I can tell you but you're right there. He's definitely not right in the head," said Bill, "You want to be getting a restraining order put on him before he does something serious."

"I think you're right," I agreed, feeling a shiver go right through my whole body.

But it was just as I had expected. I knew he would rear his ugly head some time or another and by the looks of it, whatever was going on in that warped mind of his, he would never be able to leave me alone, not ever.

"Look Marina, just you get off home love. I think you've had enough stress for one night," said Bill kindly.

"Oh... that's really sweet Bill, but I'm fine," I assured him, "and to be honest, I could really be doing with the money."

"Don't you worry about that," he said, "I'll make sure you still get paid."

"Don't be daft," I said, "You can't give me wages for doing nothing. I'll just stay. Plus, it'll help keep my mind off things."

"O.k.," said Bill, reluctantly, "But only on one condition."

"What's that?" I asked.

"You get a taxi home. Just to be on the safe side."

"Oh God, I can't afford a taxi, but I've got Ella coming to meet me at the station. She's offered to chaperone me!" I assured him.

"Never mind the station. She needs to get you here at the pub," said Bill, "You're not safe to go anywhere on your own while that one's roaming the streets. You get on the phone to her."

I did as I was told and gave Ella a call. She wanted to come right away, but I assured her that I was safe and would finish my shift, which seemed to placate her.

I managed to keep it together as I pulled the pints and minutes before it was time for me to finish, in came Ella, not just on her own, but with Hannah and William for extra back up. It really was such a relief to see them all.

"Hi guys," I said, smiling at them, "You didn't all need to come."

"Oh, yes we did," said William, "and Ricky and Mark would have come too but they're busy with rehearsals tonight."

"Oh, no… you didn't phone them did you Ella?" I said, cringing at the thought, as I pulled on my jacket.

"Not me," said Ella, "It was young William here."

"Well, I just thought they should know because I knew that they would be worried about you," said William, "We all love you Marina."

"Oh, you're so sweet," I said, hugging William, then Ella and then Hannah.

"Did he hurt you?" asked Hannah, anxiously.

"No, thank goodness," I replied.

"No, but he would have, given half a chance," added Bill, "You get off home now and promise me that you'll always make sure someone's with you when you're coming and going Marina. Pardon my French, but I wouldn't trust that evil bastard as far as I could throw him."

"Me neither and don't you worry, I've got this lot to protect me" I assured him, "anyway, I think I'd be too scared to go anywhere alone now. Thank you so much Bill. I really appreciate all you did for me tonight. You're a hero."

"All in a day's work," he said with a wink.

I gave him a big hug and a peck on the cheek, saying, "Thanks again Bill. You're the best."

It was an anxious time as we headed back to the flat, scanning all around us just in case Ollie was lurking about anywhere, ready to spring out in front of us. Thankfully he wasn't and we all breathed a sigh of relief when we got home. William and Hannah saw us to the door, then went their separate ways.

"Oh, sanctuary," I yelled, falling on to the couch.

"It is indeed," said Ella, flopping down beside me, "and I would lock you in to keep you safe if I could, but I know that's just not possible."

"It's not, but I kind of wish you could too," I said squeezing her hand.

I was so lucky to have such a caring, lovely friend. It was hard to sleep that night though, because all I could visualise was Ollie's big evil face.

Thankfully, the next few shifts at the pub were hassle free, with no more unexpected visits from him. I was trying to fixate all my thoughts and attention on our college work and things were really coming together well, with our plans for the big show. Mark and Ricky came in whenever we needed them for prosthetic fittings and they had even managed to rope in Frankie, Regina and The Matron no less, which gave us a lot more work but also a lot more fun and laughs.

"Oh my God," said Ricky, "This is just going to be simply fabulous. If you lot don't win the competition, then there's something far wrong."

"What's the prize?" asked Regina, excitedly clasping her hands.

"Oh, well I think we all get certificates or something," said Hannah.

"Ooooh," she said, screwing up her face, "That's not much fun. Do you not win money or something... inspiring?"

"No, unfortunately," said, Ella, "But if we win then it really gets you noticed and it's good for our CV's."

"And hopefully gives us more chance of getting a good job," said William, "and earning good money."

"Oh, you don't need to worry about that," said Ricky, "I earn loads! I'll take good care of you Sweetie."

"Oh!" said William, running over and kissing him on the cheek, "I love you so much Ricky darling."

"Aww! Loves young dream," I said, laughing.

"They're so lucky," said Mark, looking at them wistfully, then turning his gaze to me.

"I know," I said, glancing at him but then feeling really awkward again.

"Marina?" Mark said, gently taking my arm.

"Yes?" I said, turning back to face him, trying hard not to show my embarrassment and to look as normal as possible, while at the same time hoping he was going to say that HE loved ME.

"Have you had any more run ins with Ollie?" he asked.

It wasn't quite what I was longing for him to say, but I replied, "No, thank goodness. Not since he appeared at the pub."

"That must have been really scary for you," sympathised Mark.

"Oh, God it was...," I started.

"Hey everyone," shouted Ricky, "Why don't we all go out for something to eat once we're finished here?"

This was met with a load of cheers in agreement from everyone and I was so glad that I didn't have to talk any more about Ollie to Mark, because it made me feel really anxious just thinking about him.

"Well, I guess it's a unanimous decision!" Mark said, looking at me and smiling, as he affectionately ruffled my hair.

"It certainly does!" I said, wanting him to keep running his hands through my hair for ever more, "We better get a move on and finish up here then!"

"Come and do me Marina, before we finish anything," Matron shouted, waving me over.

"No bother. I'm just coming," I said, glad for the distraction, before I made a complete and utter fool of myself with Mark.

I grabbed some stuff and rushed over to her. Once I had made her prosthetic mould, I just dabbled about with some make-up ideas, which Matron was absolutely delighted with.

"Gosh Almighty Marina, you're a true professional!" she enthused, as she peered in the mirror, "Do you know that? An absolute natural."

I just laughed, not really believing her words and then we teamed up with the others to do a mini rehearsal. It went really well and was an absolute hoot as usual, but after all our hard work making everyone up, we had to set about removing the make-up and all the prosthetics. Regina, Frankie and The Matron desperately wanted to keep theirs on though.

"Definitely not!" said Ella, sternly "We need to keep it all under wraps. We can't have anyone copying us or anything."

The queens groaned and complained but then let us strip them back to their bare skin. I was quite pleased, because for all I adored Mark in his full drag make-up, it meant I could see him as his true handsome self. I tried not to let him see me looking too admiringly at him though.

Once we were all cleared up, we headed on out and the queens kept us all laughing as we walked to the restaurant. We were lucky to get a huge round table, which made it very sociable as we shared pizza and garlic bread, while consuming copious amounts of wine. The queens wcrc hilarious and just seemed to bounce off one another. They lit up the whole room with their enormous personalities and good looks and we didn't have to worry about any embarrassing silences because there just wasn't any.

"So, Marky," said Frankie, looking at him admiringly, "Have you not managed to get hitched yet?"

"No not yet," said Mark, grabbing another slice of pizza, "But you know me... I'm always on the look-out."

"Well, don't forget..." said Frankie, with a cheeky little wink, "You know I'm ALWAYS available!"

"I'll bear that in mind," said Mark, giving a cheeky little wink back.

"Oh, Marky's saving himself for "the one"!" said Ricky, putting his arm round William and giving him a little squeeze.

"Oh, life's too short for all that soppy stuff," said Regina, "You want to just get out there and enjoy yourself. Plenty of time for "the one" when everything stops working!"

"... or you could end up like me," The Matron said, glumly, "Nothing working and STILL looking for "the one"!"

Mark just smiled warmly at them all.

"Well, I think I've found "the one"," said Ricky turning and kissing William gently on the lips.

We all looked on with delight then cheered and clapped with sheer happiness for them. It was just so sweet. They were both very obviously and completely in love with each other. I gazed round the table, looking at everyone, at my wonderful friends. These were the best friends in the whole wide world. Hannah and Ella, nattering away together, Ricky and William, cuddling and chatting, the queens making us all laugh... and Mark. Aaahh, my lovely, gorgeous Mark.

I don't know if it was the heat, the wine or all the excitement of the day but suddenly I started to feel a bit heady. I didn't want anything embarrassing to happen, so I quickly excused myself and rushed to the loo. The coolness of the toilets was soothing, but it wasn't quite enough to get rid of the dizziness that I was feeling. I desperately needed a breath of fresh air, so I headed out only to find Mark coming out of the gents.

"Fancy meeting you here!" he joked, coming towards me.

I chuckled but suddenly felt a bit giddy as the heat hit me again. Oh, no, please don't let me faint in front of him, I was thinking. How mortifying would that be?

"Are you o.k. Marina?" asked Mark, looking concerned.

"Oh, I just feel a bit funny," I said, "I think I'll just nip out and get some fresh air actually."

"I'll come with you...," said Mark, putting his arm round my shoulder as I headed for the door, "...don't want you keeling over or anything!"

"Oh... thanks Mark," I said, bashfully but really hoping that he wouldn't, just in case I made a fool of myself.

We stood outside the restaurant and as soon as the cool night air hit me, I immediately began to feel a whole lot better. I took in some deep breaths and enjoyed the gentle breeze against my face.

"Is that better?" asked Mark smiling, warmly.

"Oh, yes," I said, "A lot better thanks!"

As I took in some more deep breaths, I could feel Marks eyes still on me, so I shyly looked up at him, returning his smile and his gaze.

"You look beautiful Marina," he said, stepping closer to me.

What? Beautiful? Me? He must be needing his eyes tested. Evil Ollie had never actually said that he thought I was beautiful and meant it. I didn't know how to respond and blurted out a really stupid response.

"So do you... look beautiful!"

Oh no, how lame, but Mark just laughed then cupped my face lovingly with his hands.

"You're so funny!" he said, his eyes twinkling as he looked into mine.

He pushed his face slowly towards me then our lips touched. It felt wonderful. His warm velvet lips, gentle on my mouth. I had wanted this to happen for so long now. It was such a beautiful moment.

He drew back and looked into my eyes again then I pushed my face forward letting him know that I definitely wanted more. His gentle kiss turned into a deeper, more passionate one, leaving me breathless and giddy again, then I suddenly remembered where we were. Reluctantly, I pulled slowly away from him, looking nervously about just in case anyone had seen us.

"It's o.k. No one's spying on us, but I think it would be better if we just keep this to ourselves," said Mark, "Not that I don't want to tell everyone, but you know what the queens are like for gossiping!"

"Oh, my goodness, I was just about to say the same thing! You know what Ella's like!" I laughed, "She's even worse than the queens! Don't worry... my lips are sealed."

"They better not be," said Mark, pulling me towards him, then kissing me again.

It felt so good, like it was meant to be. I had yearned for this to happen for so long and it was such a relief to know that Mark actually felt the same as I did. I wanted the kiss to last for ever but realised we'd better re-join the company, before anyone started getting suspicious.

"I think we better go back in," I said, gently but totally reluctantly, drawing away from him, "We don't want any tongues wagging."

"Oh," he moaned, then tenderly rubbed my back, "I suppose you're right. Come on then gorgeous."

When we walked back into the restaurant together, I could tell from Ella's stare that she knew something was going on between us. She could just read me like a book.

"So where have you two been?" she quizzed.

"I found her outside," said Mark, "Getting a breath of fresh air."

"I was just feeling a bit woozy," I explained, sitting back down, "I was scared in case I was going to pass out or something."

"Oh, you poor thing," said Ella, fussing over me, "Are you sure you're o.k.?"

"Oh, I'm feeling a lot better now, thanks," I said, (in more ways than one but I couldn't tell her exactly how!), "Just too much wine I think!"

"Right come on then light-weight, we'd better get you home," said Ella, lifting her bag, "It's about time we were going anyway. Guys... we've had such an amazing time."

"...a really amazing time," echoed Hannah, swaying as she stood up, obviously having had too much wine as well.

I quickly grabbed her arm before she fell over, while Mark grabbed her other arm and managed to steady her. Hannah looked up and gazed adoringly into Mark's face.

"Oh my God, did you know you've got such beautiful eyes," she said, slurring her words a bit, then looking at me, "Hasn't he Marina? Have you actually seen them?"

"What... oh... yes, he's got really beautiful eyes," I said, smiling at Mark.

"Now come on girls, hands off," shouted Frankie, standing up in pretend rage, "You know I've got my eye on him. He's definitely not for sale!"

We all laughed and after settling the bill, tumbled out into the street to say our goodbyes. We worked our way round everyone, noisily hugging and kissing each other. It felt like electricity when Mark pulled me into an embrace. He brushed his lips across my cheek and whispered in my ear.

"See you soon my lovely."

I just melted again at the sound of his voice then literally floated all the way home. Unfortunately, though, as usual, Ella noticed. Nothing ever got passed that one!

"Are you sure you're feeling alright?" she asked, scrutinising my face, looking for clues, "You look a bit... well... strange?"

"What?" I said, coming down from my little cloud, "I... oh, yes... still feeling a little bit woozy."

"I thought so," said Ella taking my arm, "Oh well, straight to bed for you Mrs. lightweight. Honestly, you and Hannah need to man up when it comes to drinking!"

I just laughed at her, but straight to bed it was... not to sleep, but to visualize me and Mark kissing over and over again. Imagining feeling his beautiful body close to mine, his gentle lips all over my face and when I eventually did fall asleep, I slept like a baby.

When I woke up everything seemed like normal, but then when I thought about Mark I began to smile and the smile never left my face all day. That is until that evening. I was working at the pub and Ella insisted on coming to accompany me back home after my shift. Meanwhile Mark had text to say he would meet me once I had finished too. I didn't want to lie to Ella, so I told her the truth, well the sort of truth. I said that Mark was working and that he was going to make a detour to bring me home so that meant that she wouldn't need to come trailing out. Luckily, she bought it and didn't ask any more questions.

It was such a boring, slow night and I couldn't wait to get finished to see Mark. Just before I was due to clock off, he text to say that he was waiting outside for me. I felt my heart flutter at the thought of being with him and quickly went to the loo to tidy up my hair and freshen my make-up. After all, I had to look good for my man!

"That's me off Bill," I shouted, as I walked passed the counter and headed towards the door.

"No bother love. Have you got someone to see you home alright?" he asked anxiously.

"Yes... my friend's here," I said reassuringly, but not giving anything away.

"That's good! You take care now," he called, as I disappeared through the door.

I stepped outside and there was my beautiful Mark, standing waiting for me with a little posy of flowers in his hand.

"For you," he said, handing them to me.

I was flabbergasted.

"Oh, my goodness," I said taking them from him and smelling them, "Thank you so much. They're absolutely gorgeous."

"And so are you," he said, smiling his sexy smile.

We drew together into a warm embrace. It felt so good. I was so blessed to have him in my life.

"I've missed you," he said, linking arms with me as we walked up the street.

"I've missed you too," I said, "I can't stop thinking about you."

Mark stopped and pulled me into another embrace. I was floating on cloud nine again as we walked on up the street together, hand in hand. I suddenly came back down to earth with an almighty bang though. Up ahead I could see Ollie coming towards us, not on his own but arm in arm with a female. He had timed it perfectly, knowing that I would be finished work round about now, so he could just rub my nose in it. Or so he thought! I was just so relieved that Mark was with me. He clocked him right away and held my hand even tighter.

"Just stay calm Marina," he said, softly, "Don't be intimidated by him."

"I'll try," I said, holding my head down, hoping stupidly that he wouldn't see me.

Of course, there was no chance of that. I could see him staring and smirking at us as he got closer, then he stopped and revoltingly started snogging the woman right in front of us. It looked absolutely repulsive and I knew he had only done it to somehow make me feel "jealous". I motioned to Mark for us to cross the road to the other side and try and get away from them.

"Hey Marina," Ollie shouted over, roughly putting his arm round the female and pulling her towards him, "I've got me a REAL woman. Shame you can't get yourself a REAL man."

The woman, who was obviously very drunk, laughed hysterically at his foul comment, the bitch. I certainly wasn't jealous though, because she looked quite vile.

"Come on Marina," said Mark, rushing me up the road, "Don't let him get to you. He's not worth it. Just try and ignore him."

I wanted to, but as usual Ollie just wouldn't let it go and shouted after us.

"So… do you share each other's dresses then? Or is it just the lipstick and the bras?" he said, sticking out his chest and doing a stupid walk.

The woman cackled, drunkenly again at his jibes, but it just made me feel totally sick inside. I wanted to shout back at him. To kick him in the balls and punch him in the face, but then that would just be lowering myself to his depraved level.

"Don't think he'll fit your shoes though, with those big plates of meat," he yelled madly.

I could hear his demented laughter as we tried to get away from him. I had never in my life hated anyone as much as I hated Ollie. He had spoiled my special time with Mark, obliterating the lovely, warm feeling I was having. I felt really embarrassed and scared now in case it would frighten Mark away and make him not want to be with me. I mean who wants someone with loads of baggage and an arsehole like Ollie, always turning up out of the blue, making a complete fool of you. God knows he'd had enough of that in the past with his own father. He didn't deserve to get it from my ex as well.

I needn't have worried though. We managed to lose them, hurrying to get to the station. As soon as we got on the train, Mark held me tightly, stroking my hair and gazing lovingly into my face. I still couldn't believe how lucky I was to have someone that knew exactly what it was like to be tortured by a crazy person. He made me feel so safe and secure in his arms. We didn't need to talk. We didn't need words, because we had each other.

I wished the train would just keep going and take us as far away as possible, to somewhere nice. Just the two of us. That would be good. That would be so good. The train didn't keep going though and we were soon at my stop. Mark rubbed my back and kissed me gently, as my body visibly began to tense up.

"You o.k.?" he asked.

I nodded and kissed him again before we got off the train. We walked arm in arm and when we reached Ella's flat, Mark took me in his arms and held me tightly, as we stood at the bottom of the stairs.

"Thank you so much for being my bodyguard," I said, holding his hands and swinging them.

"No need to thank me," he said, pulling me to him again, "You're very precious to me you know, Marina."

"And you're precious to me Mark. I don't know what I would have done without you tonight."

"All in a day's work," he joked and kissed me again, "Anyway, you go and get some beauty sleep."

We kissed and said our goodbyes then I climbed the first couple of steps and turned, waving until Mark was totally out of sight. I dreaded to think what would have happened if he hadn't been there for me, to see me home after that awful encounter with Ollie. A shiver went down my spine just thinking about it, as I fumbled in my bag for my key. I was just about to put it in the lock when the door suddenly flew open.

"Alright Cinderella?" joked Ella, standing back out of the way, as I stumbled in.

"Yes," I said, "Fine thanks."

Oh no, had she seen me and Mark kissing?

Oh my God I should have been more discreet instead of throwing caution to the wind and being so blasé.

"Mark not coming in then?" asked Ella, looking down the street then closing the door.

"No, he... he was in a hurry... to get his bus" I stuttered.

She followed me into the lounge. Looking at me suspiciously as I sat down. I felt a little bit uncomfortable as she kept staring straight at me.

"Alright?" I asked.

She just kept staring at me then examined her freshly painted fingernails.

"So... is there anything... you want to tell me?" she asked, looking back up at me.

I hesitated for a minute. Had she seen us? Did she actually know about me and Mark? Or was she talking about something totally different and I was just getting the wrong end of the stick? Just stay calm and act dumb I told myself.

"What do you mean?" I asked.

Ella folded her arms and let out a sigh then raised her eyebrows questionably, saying, "Emmm... Mark?"

"Mark?" I said, still acting dumb, not knowing if she was trying to catch me out or not, "Oh yes... well... he walked me home... obviously."

"... and?" said Ella starting to get a bit annoyed, because I wasn't giving away any clues.

"And what?" I asked.

"Well, he obviously didn't JUST walk you home. Did he?" she said, wide-eyed, "Come on... I saw you both out there. So, what's going on Marina?"

There was no point even trying to cover it up with stupid excuses now. She had evidently seen us kissing out on the doorstep, so the cat was now officially out of the bag. I put my hands up in surrender.

"O.k., o.k." I said, "So we've got feelings for each other..."

"Oh, my God," said Ella, excitedly, "I knew it... I could tell there was something going on. The chemistry between you two lately has just been electrifying."

"What do you mean, the chemistry?" I asked thinking we'd hidden it so well.

"Oh, you know. Just the way you were looking at each other, stuff like that. Oh, Marina, I'm so happy for you. I mean he's absolutely drop dead gorgeous, but he's just such a lovely person too," Ella said, hugging me tightly, "Oh, my God, wait till everyone hears the good news!"

"Oh, well that's just it...," I said, gently pulling away, "We don't really want anyone knowing... not yet anyway. I mean it's really early days and... well, we've got the show coming up and we don't want it interfering with everything."

"Don't be stupid... it won't interfere with anything... but I know what you mean Marina," said Ella, motioning at her mouth, "Don't you worry, my lips are totally zipped."

"No, but are they?" I asked anxiously, knowing fine well what she was like, "We really DON'T want anyone knowing yet."

"Oh, my God I promise... I won't tell a soul," Ella said excitedly. I looked at her suspiciously, still not totally convinced that she would keep it to herself.

"What?" she said, looking falsely surprised, "I promise... I won't."

"You better not," I said, firmly.

I should really have told Ella about the encounter I'd had with Ollie, but I had kind of forgotten about it with one thing and another. Not only that I didn't want to talk about it and then spoil the good feelings that I had, so once we said our good-nights, I just floated off to bed and cuddled into my pillow, so wishing it was my Markie!

The queens were all coming back to college the next day for another rehearsal and fitting, so I was on tenterhooks that morning, worried in case Ella spilled the beans about me and Mark.

"So, did everything go o.k. at work last night?" Hannah asked as we huddled round the table at our coffee break.

"Yeah, fine thanks," I said, stirring my coffee.

"No weirdos hanging about then?"

"No... well, yes actually," I said, suddenly remembering my brush with Ollie, "I had just left the pub and as we were walking up the street, Ollie suddenly appeared out of nowhere, arm in arm with some random woman."

"How come you didn't tell me about this last night?" asked Ella, evidently annoyed.

"What? You weren't there? I thought you were going to be walking her home?" quizzed Hannah.

"No, Mark met her instead," said Ella.

I knew she was itching to tell but I emphatically raised my eyebrows, in warning for her not to say a thing.

160

"Mark?" said William, surprised, "So how come he was walking you home?"

"Well..." I said, nervously stirring my coffee again, "He... he was working and offered to come and meet me when he finished."

"He couldn't have been working," said William, puzzled, "Tail Feathers was shut last night, cause there was a burst pipe or something. So, my Ricky said anyway."

I looked pleadingly at Ella, hoping she would make up some excuse for me, but she didn't. Instead, she coughed politely and just looked up at the ceiling.

"Wait a minute," said Hannah, the cogs of her brain visibly starting to whizz round, "There's something fishy going on here isn't there?"

"Are you and Mark seeing each other?" yelled William, putting two and two together.

"No, of course we're not," I lied, stirring furiously at my coffee.

"You are," said Hannah, folding her arms and looking at me triumphantly, sitting back in her chair, "...aren't you? I could tell by the way you were looking at each other when we were at the restaurant the other night."

"Yeah," agreed William, "Big giveaway that was."

"Oh," I groaned, not knowing what to say and looking at Ella for support.

"Don't look at me," she said, putting her hands up to block out my stare, "I never said a word."

"O.k, o.k., so we like each other," I admitted, "But please don't let on to everyone else that you know. Pleeeease. We want to keep it under wraps... just for now any way. Just till we see how things go."

"Oh, don't worry Marina," assured Hannah, "It's our secret. We promise we 'll not tell a soul."

"We'll not tell a soul...," echoed William, "...but can I tell Ricky?"

"No!" I cried, "Definitely not. I shouldn't even be telling you lot. We just want to keep it quiet... till after the competition and stuff. Pleeeease?"

William groaned with disappointment and sat back in his chair in an obvious sulk.

"Anyway, that aside," said Ella, leaning forward, "What happened with Ollie. I can't believe you forgot to tell me! So, he was with a woman? What a shit."

"Yeah, they both looked stoned out of their minds," I explained, "He was kissing and slobbering all over her, just trying to make me jealous!"

"As if that would be possible with Mark on your arm," said Ella.

"Yuk," said Hannah, "He's just not right in the head that one."

"Tell me about it," I agreed, "I wish he would just disappear off the face of the earth and leave me alone once and for all."

"Well, with a bit of luck he will!" said Ella, "Anyway, we better get back and get some work done before we get into trouble."

We quickly gulped back our coffees and returned to class, picking up where we had left off before our break. We were putting the finishing touches to the prosthetic moulds we had made, so it was really satisfying. It made for a quick morning then in the afternoon, the queens started to stream in.

I could feel my heart start to flutter when Mark arrived with Ricky. William ran up to Ricky, hugging and kissing him and I was desperate to do the same with Mark, but just smiled at him bashfully.

"Hi," he said, with a cheeky little twinkle in his eye.

"Hi" I said back, aware of Williams eyes, firmly on us, watching our every move.

When I looked over at him, he was standing with his arms folded, looking at us in anticipation.

Sensing something was afoot, Ricky said, "What's happening here?"

William didn't utter a word, but motioned his head towards us and that's all it took. Ricky knew right away exactly what he was meaning.

"Is there something you want to tell us Marky?" quizzed Ricky.

Mark just shrugged his shoulders and looked at him in disbelief, not really knowing how they had worked it out. I could feel my body suddenly starting to shake, scared in case he would make a fool of me like Ollie always did, but I needn't have worried. He just chuckled, shaking his head and looked back at me.

"They know us too well Marina!"

"Go on... kiss her," shouted William, "You know you want to Mark!"

We looked shyly round at everyone as they all started cheering, then looked back at each other. Mark shrugged his shoulders again, then took me in his arms, kissing me gently on the lips. The cheers got even louder, making us both laugh as we pulled away from each other.

"Happy now?" Mark joked as he took my hand.

"No," shouted Frankie dramatically, as he came walking in, "I thought you were all mine sweetie... but hey ho! Suppose she seems like a nice girl."

It was just so surreal. One minute I'm being battered and thumped by an abusive, psycho boyfriend, then the next minute I've got all these wonderful, beautiful people cheering and happy that me and lovely Mark have a thing going on. It was just so amazing. In fact, it was all a bit unbelievable. It honestly seemed too good to be true. I felt like I really wasn't worthy of all the love and attention and was just waiting to waken up from what surely must be a dream.

Once everyone settled back down, we gathered ourselves together and started working on the queens. Predictably, it was an absolute scream. I just laughed and smiled the whole time. What a sublime job. It was everything I had ever wanted to do, transforming already lovely faces into complete works of art. Terrifying ones at that, with deformed chins and noses. Fake blood was oozing from scars on their faces and necks, while they still had their usual drag make-up layered on top. It really did look very professional, even though I say so myself!

The queens were all delighted with the finished results and we all felt so satisfied and pleased with ourselves for creating their vibrant but very scary looks. All our studying and training had finally paid off.

"God, Matron, I've never seen you look so good," joked Ricky.

Matron just drew him a dirty look which made her look even funnier because she had a prosthetic eye popping out of her head and for once you couldn't see any stubble because it was hidden under her huge prosthetic chin!

"They teach you well flower!" said The Matron, "I think I can genuinely say I've never looked like this in my life before!"

"Well… not since last week Matron," joked Mark.

We all laughed and then had a quick rehearsal, so the queens would know which order to walk in. Of course, they added in their own ideas with a bit of dancing here and some comical antics there.

I could just tell it was going to be fantastic on the big day, seeing them in their colourful dresses, topped off with their fabulous wigs. It was going to be brilliant and I just couldn't wait for the real thing. It didn't really matter to me if we won the competition or not because I knew it was just going to be so much fun taking part.

CHAPTER 6

THE COMPETITION

Now that our relationship was out in the open, things just felt so much easier and even better between Mark and I, if that was at all possible. I never once let my guard down though with regards to Ollie because I knew he just loved the element of surprise. I still always made sure that Mark, Ella or someone was with me at all times whenever I was out and about. I definitely felt a lot more relaxed and confident though. I suppose because I knew that I was loved by Mark, as well as liked.

It was such a busy time. Not only did we have the show coming up, but we also had assessments to complete and essays to do. I honestly don't think I would have got through it all if I had still been with Ollie. He would have made sure of that, without a doubt.

Luckily, we all passed everything with flying colours which was just as well, because at the end of the day, the qualification was the main reason for us being on the course. I think we had sort of forgotten about that very important point, with all the recent goings on as well as preparing for the competition. At least we knew that we were now fully qualified and worthy of getting a job at the end of it all, so it had been totally worth it.

I could hardly breathe with excitement when the day of the competition finally came. We had been given our slot which was last, but we were quite happy with that though, because it would give us more time to get ourselves organised.

We had a bit of a panic when Hannah couldn't get The Matron's prosthetic chin to stick. As usual the stubble was getting in the way, so after a quick shave and a restart, it stuck perfectly.

"I knew I should have got the razor out this morning. Oh yes, that's much better," said The Matron, looking at herself proudly in the mirror, as though having an ugly prosthetic chin looked better than a bit of stubble.

There seemed to be so much to do and it was a real worry in case we didn't get it all done in time, but I suppose that was part of the test, to see if we could cope in a stressful situation.

Thankfully though, everything seemed to be going to plan and the best bit was when the queens donned their dresses. They each wore a different bright colour, with their wigs complementing the colour of their outfits. The Matron had a basket of fruit to wear on her head, which looked absolutely brilliant though, how she managed to walk and balance it at the same time, I'll never know. I felt so proud of her, because after all, she wasn't as young as all the rest of the queens.

"You're definitely getting your five a day with that Matron!" joked Regina.

"Well, I'm telling you, it's been a long time since I've had five a day!" said Matron in her usual glum manner, "Just one a day would be quite nice!"

It was just so entertaining. We did some finishing touches, adding a bit more fake blood here and there to make everyone look that little bit more gruesome, then got nervously into position, back-stage, waiting patiently for our turn. We could hear the cheers and clapping from the audience as the first groups went on before us. My tummy was starting to do somersaults with nerves as our slot drew closer and closer. That's when I suddenly realised that I desperately needed to go to the loo. I glanced at my watch and knew that I would just about have enough time to go, because I really didn't want to risk wetting myself with all the excitement.

"Hey guys, I'm just going to quickly nip to the toilet, if that's o.k.," I shouted, looking towards Ella.

"Oh, God I better go too, come to think of it," she said.

We were all stopped abruptly in our tracks though when Frankie let out a piercing scream, yelling, "Oh no... one of my lashes just fell off."

Unfortunately, it had, landing right on her cheek and now her face was all contorted, trying desperately to stop it from dropping to the floor. Ella ran to the rescue and gently retrieved the rogue lash.

"Don't panic! I'll get it sorted," Ella assured her, "On you go Marina, I'll fix Frankie. Just you get to the loo before you flood the feckin' place."

"Aw thanks Ella," I said rushing towards the toilets.

I pushed open the door to the ladies, now totally desperate but so happy with excitement. I got the fright of my life though when the door slammed noisily shut behind me. I turned quickly round to see what had made it bang so loudly and was absolutely horrified to see Ollie standing there, with a mad, gleeful look on his face. I felt like I was frozen to the spot and unable to move or speak. It was like my worst ever nightmare.

"Thought you'd seen the last of me, did you?" he sneered as he stepped towards me.

"Get out," I managed to yell, "Get out and leave me alone or I'll... I'll..."

"Scream?" he said, shoving his face into mine, "Or why don't you get your fairy boyfriend to come and hit me? Oh no, wait a minute... he could just wave his magic wand, couldn't he?"

What happened next was all a blur, but I remember him slapping me really hard on the face and then wrestling me to the ground. I somehow managed to let out a scream but the next minute he had his hands gripped tightly round my throat and I honestly thought he was going to kill me. What had I ever done to him to deserve this? Why did he hate me so much?

It was a struggle now to breathe and although I tried with all my might to prize away his tight grip, I could feel consciousness starting to drift away from me. I was literally on the verge of passing out, when I was suddenly brought back round with the piercing sound of Ella screaming and shouting to everyone to come and help, while she tried with all her might to pull Ollie away from me. God only knows what would have happened if Ella hadn't come through to the toilet when she did.

Suddenly I could hear the queens as they came charging in. They took over from Ella and grabbed hold of Ollie, roughly dragging him off me as he kicked out and shouted in defence.

"Marina, holy mother of God, what has he done to you?" cried Ella, cradling me in her arms.

"I'm o.k.," I was able to croak, struggling to sit myself up.

167

Meanwhile Mark and the queens had pulled a raging Ollie to his feet. He honestly looked like a man possessed. Now it was his worst nightmare, surrounded by a load of drag queens and angry ones at that.

"I think it's about time you got a taste of your own medicine," said Mark, pulling Ollie's arm tightly up behind his back.

"Oh, I'm really scared… Bunch of fairies," Ollie yelled, looking totally humiliated.

"Well, we might look like fairies, but you're forgetting something… we've still got balls!" Ricky said, then punched Ollie hard on the chin.

"And nobody gets to hurt our Marina without paying for it," said The Matron, stepping forward and landing another punch square on his nose.

I had now managed to sit upright with Ella and Hannah's help, desperate to see the downfall of Ollie, which was comically being brought about by zombie drag queens. If it hadn't been so serious, I would have been falling about the place laughing.

It really was his worst nightmare, but what happened next was unexpected and totally shocking. He suddenly pulled out a knife from his pocket, just as Ricky stepped forward to plant another punch. We all gasped in horror as everything seemed to go into slow motion. Ollie pushed the knife into Ricky's neck. Blood spurted all over his face and dress and when he put his hand up to his neck, he looked totally aghast as he discovered that his fingers were now covered in blood. He looked back up at a now visibly petrified Ollie, before dramatically falling to the ground.

"Oh shit. I didn't mean to do that," shrieked Ollie, realising what he had done.

We were all so concerned about Ricky that somehow Ollie managed to wrestle out of everyone's grip, then started legging it out of the toilet. Poor William was distraught and dropped to his knees, nursing Ricky's head in his hands with tears streaming uncontrollably down his face.

"What have you done to my baby? Oh my God… don't leave me Ricky. Please... I love you so much," he wailed.

The rest of the queens had now taken to their heels, most of them stilettoes no less and were chasing Ollie, who was now running for his life, down the street, while Ella, Hannah and me tried to support William and Ricky.

I shivered at the thought of Ollie having a knife. Oh my God, was it actually meant for me? He really had gone too far this time. I could feel the tears starting to prick at my eyes as we looked on helplessly at William, lovingly holding his boyfriend in his arms, his hands now covered in blood. It was so heart-breaking to watch but then almost miraculously, we could see Ricky slowly opening his eyes, then unexpectedly he winked at William, shaking his head slightly.

"Please don't leave me," said William, who was so busy sobbing hysterically, that he hadn't even noticed, "I can't live without you."

"Well... you won't have to honey...," said Ricky, now struggling to sit up and trying to wipe the trickling blood from his neck.

We all gasped in surprise, honestly thinking he had just been breathing his last.

"Oh my God it's a miracle," yelled William, as Ricky now got to his feet.

"Well... no, not quite darling! Remember... I've got a prosthetic neck... and this...," he said, showing William his bloodied fingers, "...is the FAKE zombie blood, you doughnut!"

"Shiiiiit," laughed William hysterically, with relief, "I'm such a numpty! I totally forgot all about that! Oh my God... I really thought I'd lost you there. Oh Ricky... I love you so much."

We all started to laugh hysterically too, just so thankful that Ricky was alright. I hugged Ella and Hannah as we watched with delight at the pair of them kissing each other passionately. They were just so meant for each other.

"I love you too darling," said Ricky, reluctantly prizing himself away from William, "...but we need to catch up with the gang and try to get that bastard and give him what for. He can't get away with stabbing me!"

We all struggled, trying to get through the door at the same time, then ran as fast as we could to try and catch up with the others. Ollie had given good chase, but the queens had caught up with him and were now surrounding him like a hungry pack of wolves. It was so

169

satisfying to see him looking absolutely terrified as they all glared at him with their scary prosthetic faces. It must have been like a living nightmare for him and he honestly looked like he was going to have a coronary when he clapped eyes on Ricky arriving on the scene with William.

"What the hell... I thought you were...," he stuttered, looking at Ricky's blood splattered dress and neck.

"Dead?" yelled Ricky, "Well, maybe we're not as soft as you think."

Ollie looked nervously round at everyone, saying, "What kind of a weirdos are you?"

"We're very angry weirdos," said Mark, stepping forward, "and we don't like how you've been treating Marina. In fact, we don't like it at all."

"Oh God, you don't know her... she's not the nice girl you might think she is," lied Ollie, trying feebly to get around them, "She may seem gentle and lovely, but she's actually very manipulative... evil...she...she..."

Thankfully, his lies weren't working though.

"No sweetie... I think you're the evil one," said Ricky, pushing his face up against Ollie's, "Now tell me something, have you ever been beaten up by a mob of vengeful queens?"

"N-n-n-no," stammered Ollie, struggling to think what to say, "I mean I... I've got nothing against you lot... just as long as you keep it to yourselves."

"Well, we're not keeping this to ourselves," said Ricky, punching Ollie square in the face.

William then thumped him in the stomach, though it has to be said a bit feebly, saying, "... and that's for stabbing my boyfriend."

I watched on with total glee as all the queens took a hit. It was so satisfying watching Ollie getting what he deserved. I was just starting to really enjoy myself, when the squeal of sirens interrupted the proceedings and the next minute, they were all surrounded by police officers.

"Right, what's going on?" shouted one of the policemen.

"These bitches are beating me up," wailed Ollie pathetically, "I've done nothing wrong officer."

"He's a liar," shouted William, "He stabbed my boyfriend, so we were just rounding him up for you sir."

"Stabbed your boyfriend?" repeated the policeman.

"Yes," said Ricky, turning around to face him, with his fake bloodied neck in full view for all to see.

"Oh my God," said the officer, starting to speak into his mike, "We need an ambulance here... pronto."

"It's not actually as bad as it looks darling," said Ricky, hugging into William as they tried to hold back their giggles, "I think I'll live."

"Right you," said the policeman to Ollie, "I'm arresting you for attempted murder and for being in possession of a knife."

"But it was self-defence... you don't understand...," started Ollie, trying to retaliate and attempting to pull himself away.

"No, I don't think YOU understand," said another officer, getting his handcuffs at the ready, "You're coming with me."

We all cheered with delight when Ollie was led away, handcuffed and still pleading his innocence as he got bundled into the police car. I knew then that I could actually now breathe a sigh of relief once and for all, knowing that he had finally got his comeuppance.

"Are you alright my love?" asked Mark, turning to me, then clasping my hands tightly in his and gazing, adoringly into my eyes.

"I'm fine thanks," I said, so relieved to see him while trying not to be too gushy, but then suddenly remembering, "Oh my God.... the competition..."

"Oh no," yelled Hannah, "I think we'll be too late."

"No... we can't be... not after all our hard work," moaned William.

There was a hysterical roar then we all started running back towards the college.

"With a bit of luck, we might just be in time," panted Ella.

"To be honest, I really don't care anymore," said William, "I'm just glad I've got my man..."

"... But we're brilliant... We could have won it," wailed Hannah.

"Let's just see what they've got to say," I said, trying to calm the situation.

We must have looked a sight as we all ran breathlessly into the hall and the audience seemed to hush as we landed in front of the judges. I think they thought it was all part of the entertainment.

"We're so sorry we're late," said Mark, desperately, "But we were involved in a bit of a... of a..."

"Fracas," continued William, "We were involved in a fracas Sir and my poor boyfriend here was... was...."

"Stabbed your honour... I was stabbed," added Ricky, pushing forward his bloodied neck, "...but I'm o.k.... we're o.k....to do our thing... that is if we're allowed to???"

The judge stared in horror at Ricky's "stab wound" then whispered and confided with the other two judges. After what seemed like an eternity, he scrutinised us all, then said: "Actually you're not due on yet. There's one more submission before your slot."

With all the commotion, we had just assumed we were too late but on discovering we were well within time, we let out a joint sigh of relief, then whooped and laughed with joy as we started to make our way to the back of the catwalk. The audience were already on our side as they clapped and cheered us on, I think still assuming it was all part of the show.

It gave us some time to touch up everyone's make-up and rearrange The Matron's fruit basket, which was now sitting decidedly lop-sided on her head, what with all the running and everything.

"Nearly lost my grapes there!" she said, gently wobbling her head from side to side.

"What about your plums?" laughed Ricky.

"Oh, I think they're still intact," said Matron, grabbing at her crotch.

Thank goodness their jokes eased the tension a little bit, as we waited patiently in the wings again. I had never felt so nervous, even after all the stress of what we had just been through. I was just so scared in case the audience didn't like us, never mind the judges.

I needn't have worried though. The queen's totally stole the show with their wonderful personalities and even though I say so myself, outstanding make-up and prosthetics. We had a sensational show to offer and the audience DID love it. They clapped, whooped and cheered as the queens strutted their beautiful zombie stuff and incredibly with all their prosthetics intact, apart from Ricky's zombie blood that is! Each queen knew to dig their long nails elegantly into their prosthetic scars so that the fake blood would ooze scarily out, while still looking gorgeous and glamorous with their glorious make-up and lashes.

We honestly couldn't have wished for a better reaction. The tears started rolling down my cheeks, not only with pride and happiness, but also with relief, knowing that Ollie was where he should be, banged up in a police cell. At long last I was safe, together with all my adorable friends and we were putting on the best show ever.

The queens were on an absolute high as they came backstage from the catwalk.

"Well done guys," I said proudly, "You were absolutely outstanding."

"You all smashed it," yelled Ella, "It was even better than any of the rehearsals."

"Thanks girls," said Mark, grabbing me round the waist then twirling me in the air, "and do you know what? I don't care if we don't win cause I've got my prize!"

"Aw… me too," I said as his lips touched mine and I could feel his thick, waxy lipstick all over my mouth, but it didn't matter one little bit because I didn't care a jot what I looked like.

We all congratulated each other and then suddenly my bladder reminded me that I still hadn't been to the loo, even after all that. I caught Ella's eye and I could tell by her expression that she was thinking the exact thing.

"Toilet!" we both said at the same time, then started laughing.

We ran quickly to the loo, trying hard not to wet ourselves before we got there.

"Oh my God, we better not miss the results," said Ella as we quickly washed our hands.

"That would be just awful after all we've been through" I said, wiping my hands on my jeans because it would take too long to dry them.

We ran back-stage just in time to join the gang, as we all had to go back on stage in our groups. The queens pushed me, Ella, William and Hannah to the front, then we waited with baited-breath to see who had won.

Eventually one of the judges appeared with a piece of paper in his hand and cleared his throat as he walked up to the microphone.

"Thank you, ladies and gentlemen, for coming tonight," he said, "You've been a great audience and I think that you'll definitely agree with me, that all the presentations were absolutely first class... The students have obviously put their heart and soul in to providing us with an astounding show... which has made choosing a winner a very difficult task indeed... but anyway this is the decision of the panel... I'm very pleased to say that, in reverse order, "Tango in the night" came a well-deserved third."

The audience clapped and cheered as the students individually received their awards then the judge continued reading out the results.

"And in second place is... "Alien Invasion.""

Again, the students went up to receive their awards, with the audience cheering and clapping loudly. We were so happy for them all and stood rooted to the spot, holding each other's hands nervously, waiting to hear who had won. I didn't hold out much hope for us because to be honest, although we were good, I thought the third and second placed were actually even better than us.

"And without a doubt in first place...," the judge continued, "through a lot of adversities apparently... it has to be... Grotesque Mardi Gras. Well done everyone."

I just hadn't expected it and almost collapsed with disbelief when I heard that we had won. I was then being propelled along by Ella, William and Hannah, as we went to the front of stage, with the queens joyfully joining us, to accept our award. The audience was ecstatic and the whole room thundered with their applause and cheers. I still couldn't believe it. I was totally overwhelmed but tried my hardest to hold back my tears. The judge handed us the winning shield and Ella took it, thrusting it up into the air triumphantly.

We were all jumping about hugging and kissing one another, rejoicing in winning. We were so busy embracing each other that we hadn't even noticed that Mark had grabbed the microphone from the judge and it was only when he coughed into it, that we all stopped and looked towards him.

"Hi there!" he said nervously to the audience, "I hope you don't mind me taking this opportunity to thank William, Ella, Hannah and Marina for asking us to present their wonderful artistry and I think you'll agree with me... that they've done an absolutely first-class job."

He started clapping his hands and the audience joined in rapturously. I felt so humbled as he shared his appreciation with everyone. It was so sweet of him. He let them clap for a while, then put the microphone back up to his mouth.

"And I'm sure you won't mind me being so bold as to take this opportunity to...," he hesitated and looked over towards me, "...to ask someone extremely special a very important question."

Ella nudged me with her elbows, squealing and jumping with anticipation, as if she knew exactly what he was going to say. I on the other hand, was totally oblivious to his intentions.

"We've had a very hectic day today... in more ways than you could ever imagine... and it's made me realise that life is very precious... and that I love someone very much... Marina," Mark continued, stretching his hand out towards me, "Will you marry me?"

The audience sighed with delight at Mark's proposal, while I was catapulted forward by Ella and Hannah, landing right in front of him. He reached out and took my hand, then looked pleadingly into my eyes.

I felt breathless and a bit embarrassed, but somehow managed to squeak, "I love you too Mark... and yes... yes... of course I'll marry you."

Mark immediately threw the microphone down and pulled me to him, saying, "Oh thank you Marina. You've no idea how happy you've just me made me. I truly love you."

"And I truly love you," I said, then our lips met in a passionate kiss though I must admit, his prosthetic nose got in the way just a little bit!

The queens were jumping up and down, yelling with happiness, then everyone gathered around, hugging and kissing us and each other. I had never ever felt so happy. Not only did I have stellar friends, but we had won the competition AND the loveliest man in the world actually wanted to marry me. How lucky was I?

I just didn't want to come down off of cloud nine and was convinced that I must be dreaming as we packed up all of our stuff. The queens didn't want to take off their make-up and it was with great delight that we all piled into Ella's flat for a post competition party. Ricky and William had stopped off to buy some alcoholic beverages and we all couldn't wait to indulge, although I was already giddy with happiness. The shop assistants must have got the fright of their lives when they saw Ricky come in, with his neck and dress still splattered with the fake blood. Luckily, they served him though and as soon as they arrived back, Ricky pulled out one of the bottles of champagne and started to peel it open.

"Right, everyone... grab a glass," he shouted, "cause we've got an awful lot of celebrating to do!"

Excitedly, we all gathered round him and held out our glasses, eagerly waiting to get them filled. When everyone had a glass of bubbly, Ricky held his high up in the air.

"I propose a toast... firstly to Ella, Hannah, Marina and my lovely William for winning the competition," he yelled, "Well done."

We all clinked our glasses together, saying "cheers" then took a big glug.

"And I also propose a toast to my beautiful friends... Marina," continued Ricky, "...and the not quite so beautiful, Mark! May you have many, many years of happy, married bliss."

Everyone said "cheers" again, as Mark and I smiled at each other, then hugged and kissed.

"Can I pull that off now?" I said, tweaking his prosthetic nose.

"Definitely not," said Mark, pulling back and covering it protectively with his hands.

"Why's that Marky?" asked Frankie, with a cheeky little wink, "Were you planning on doing something with it later?"

"Frankie!" groaned Mark, thinking I might be offended by his slightly inappropriate joke.

"Right enough," I said, tweaking his nose again and winking back at Frankie, "I might just have a use for it."

"Oh no... our awful humour's starting to rub off on you," Mark said, but then immediately put his hand up to Frankie's mouth, "... don't even go there, sweetie."

I just giggled at the pair of them, but then Ricky let out a scream. We all turned and looked at him, worried in case he had taken a bad turn.

"Holy shit," he shrieked, "You know what this means?"

"What?" everyone cried, puzzled by his outburst.

"We've only got a wedding to arrange."

Oh, my God, so we did! I hadn't really thought about it to be honest. We all jumped madly about shouting and hugging each other. What a crowd and they hadn't even had a lot to drink yet! As you can imagine everyone was hyper, so it made for a really noisy but fun party. The neighbours must have been raging because the tunes were turned up high and we were dancing and singing at the top of our voices. It was simply awesome.

"Markie darling... just remember," shouted Frankie, "If it goes tits up... I'll always be here for you."

"I'll bear that in mind," said Mark, winking at him and pulling me close as we danced, then whispered in my ear, "I love you."

"I love you too," I whispered back.

We all watched as The Matron then took drunkenly to the floor. Somehow, she had managed to keep the fruit basket on her head, though it was looking decidedly dodgy as she started to twerk. Her poppy out eye suddenly popped right off and the fruit looked like it was about to do the same.

"Better watch you don't lose your grapes this time," laughed Regina, starting to twerk beside her.

"Hell, I lost my grapes years ago Regina," said Matron, shaking her ass so hard the whole basket finally fell from her head.

We all laughed then drunkenly scrambled about on the floor trying to grab a piece of fruit. Frankie managed to get the banana and seductively started to peel it in front of Mark.

"Want a bite?" he said, placing the tip of the banana suggestively in his mouth.

"No, you're alright," laughed Mark, handing me a couple of grapes.

"Hey Marina," shouted Ella, munching into a peach, she had managed to salvage, "Can I be your bridesmaid?"

"Oh, Ella, that goes without saying," I assured her.

"I've never been a bridesmaid," moaned Hannah.

177

"Aww... well you can be my bridesmaid too," I said, kissing her cheek.

"Wooo. Thanks Marina," she yelled with delight, "I can't wait."

Regina had come up behind me and said, "Aww, I've never been a bridesmaid before..."

"Me neither...," said Frankie, fluttering her eyelashes, looking pleadingly at me.

"Oh, sorry guys," I laughed, "I think two will be plenty if that's o.k."

We just laughed and carried on partying the whole night. At last, life was good and I could now actually look forward to the future with plenty of optimism.

CHAPTER 7

THE WEDDING

Mum and Dad were absolutely ecstatic when I phoned to tell them the good news and the next few weeks were totally taken up with trying to throw together the wedding. It wasn't something I had ever explored before, because I really didn't think that I would ever get married to be honest. The prices of some of the venues though, were positively extortionate and I began to wonder if we could actually afford a wedding at all.

I left the task of booking the church to my mum, as I knew that she was a church goer. After a little phone call to the vicar, we had a date to work around, but the next hurdle was trying to get somewhere for the reception. Unfortunately, everywhere seemed to be well and truly out of our price range.

Nevertheless, Mark and I arranged to go to this lovely, big hotel just to see if we might be able to work out a cheaper price with them. Of course, the gang wanted to come with us too, which wasn't a problem, because it would be good to get a second opinion on things, plus it would probably be a good laugh.

It was a lovely sunny day, which made the hotel and grounds look even more beautiful and enticing. I could just visualise myself, floating about in my wedding gown, as I mingled amongst the guests, with the blossoms on the trees and gentle music playing in the background. It would be perfect.

I was brought down to earth with a bang though when the wedding manager went through some prices with us, but we had to opt for the most basic reception that was possible. This was added on and that was added on to the price and then of course there was the VAT, so the final amount was simply way too much for our budget. We politely said that we would need to have a think about it, though there was absolutely no doubt that we couldn't afford it.

"Well, there's one thing, it would be lovely for the photos," said Ella, guzzling back her free glass of champagne, as we sat on elegant chairs on the beautiful lawns.

"But not very good for your bank balance, eh Markie?" joked Ricky, taking a sip from his glass.

"The cost really doesn't matter... I mean they might do a payment plan or something," said Mark, optimistically.

"Or you could sell a kidney," quipped Ricky.

"That's not very nice," Mark said, squeezing my hand, "And anyway, I don't mind the cost… just as long as your happy Marina."

"Well… It would make me happy for us to just save our money. I mean it is beautiful," I said, looking towards the hotel, "and it would be lovely to have the reception here, but it's just a ridiculous amount of money."

"You could nearly buy a new house for what they're asking for," joked Ricky.

"Slight exaggeration Rick!" laughed Mark, "It's your decision gorgeous. Let's face it though, I think they're all going to be pretty expensive."

"I know," I agreed, "I suppose we'll just need to accept that a posh do's going to cost a small fortune."

"Unless…," said Ricky, sitting forward, in a light bulb moment, "wouldn't it be amazing if you could have it at the Tail Feathers? I'm pretty sure we could sweet-talk Molly into letting us use it."

"Oh, my God," I laughed, "Why didn't we think of that before? I didn't know you could have wedding receptions there."

"You can't," said Mark, "But I'm sure the powers that be, would be up for it. I mean it could be the start of something big!"

"You've got a point there," agreed Ricky, "I know a lot of people that would love to get hitched at The Tail Feathers."

"It's not exactly photogenic though," said Mark, on reflection, "I mean, you won't get your photos on the lawn or anything."

"I don't really care," I said, taking Mark's hand, "It makes sense. All the queens will be coming so they'll love it and there's plenty of room to dance and stuff."

"I think it's a bloody no brainer," added William.

"Well, I suppose if everyone's agreed," Mark said, shrugging his shoulders, "Then, The Tail Feathers it is."

"Oh shit, it's so exciting," squealed Ella, "Now I really can't wait."

"Here's to The Tail Feathers" yelled Hannah, raising her empty up in the air.

We all clinked our glasses together, shouting, "Tail Feathers."

So that was how the reception venue was decided and we had got a free glass of champagne into the bargain. Mark phoned Molly the next day to see if it would be possible to have a wedding there and also most importantly, if it would be available on the day that the church was booked.

"I honestly don't see a problem," said Molly, "There's actually no shows booked for that date. In fact, I think it's a fantastic idea. Doing weddings would be a brilliant business venture. Why didn't I think of that?"

"See what we've started," laughed Mark, "That's great! Thanks Molly so, so much."

"No bother Mark," she said, "I'll work out a price for you, but I can assure you, it definitely won't break the bank."

"Oh, that's great! Love you Molly," Mark said, kissing down the phone.

"So, is that o.k.?" I asked excitedly when Mark came off the phone.

"Yip, that's it booked beautiful," he said, kissing me, then twirling me up in the air.

"Oh, Markie, it's going to be brilliant," I squealed, "I'm so excited."

I was so happy. In fact, that's an understatement. I was absolutely ecstatic. Things were falling nicely into place. Of course, I still had my dress to get. Ella and Hannah were desperate to help me choose and my mum had nipped over from Spain for a few days, so we decided to make a day of it, trailing round wedding shops, trying to find "the one".

It wasn't as easy as I had imagined though. I had an idea in my head of what I wanted, but when I tried dresses on, I just didn't look as good as I thought I would. That is, until we came to the last shop on our list. I felt exhausted and to be honest, a bit disheartened. The dress was on display in the window and though I didn't really think it was my cup of tea, I was goaded by everyone to try it on.

Reluctantly, I went into the changing room as the rest sat back with yet another free glass of fizz. I'd had a few myself but when the assistant zipped me up and I turned around to look in the mirror, I couldn't believe just how good I actually looked. Or maybe my judgement was getting clouded with all the free champagne I'd had. I started walking out of the changing room, trying hard to look elegant and willowy. My mum, Ella and Hannah all gasped then stood up as I walked towards them.

"Well? What do you think girls?" I asked, scared in case they didn't like it, "Another disaster?"

"My little baby," my mum gushed, dabbing the tears from her eyes, "You look absolutely beautiful."

"Breath-taking," squeaked Hannah, emotionally.

"Oh my God, that is definitely the one Marina," said Ella taking a photo on her phone, then rushing over and kissing my cheek, "You look absolutely stunning."

"Oh, well I don't know about that!" I said bashfully and turning to the assistant, "I think I'll take it."

"Praise the Lord," said Ella with relief, flopping back down on the couch and sipping at the rest of her champagne, "It's hard work this. Only thing is… now we need to go through it all again."

"Again?" wailed Hannah, "How's that then?"

"Because we need to get OUR dresses!" shrieked Ella.

We all groaned at the thought of it, but it was definitely a happy groan and it turned out to be an easier task than we thought. We had already seen lovely dresses in one of the big department stores and went the following week to get them. Luckily, the right sizes were in stock and when the girls tried them on, they both looked absolutely fabulous. We were going to be totally gorgeous.

"You know, Mark's never mentioned who his best man's going to be," I said, sipping at my Champagne, as Ella and Hannah twirled dreamily about in their dresses.

"For the love of God!" cried Ella, "Do you think he's forgotten?"

"Oh, well it's just got to be Ricky," said Hannah, "I mean they're joined at the hip that pair."

"That's true. I mean, it's not like he has a brother or anything. Hold on and I'll give him a call" I said, pulling my phone from my bag.

Ella and Hannah posed in front of the big mirror in their dresses, sipping on their champagne and waiting to hear my conversation. The phone just rang out though and I thought it was going to go to his voice mail, when Mark suddenly answered.

"Marina! What can I do you for, darling?" he said.

"Oh, hi sweetheart. Listen, I've just thought of something... You don't have a best man!" I said.

"Holy shit! How did we forget about that!" he said, then audibly relayed the conversation to Ricky and then I could hear them both laughing.

"So... who's it going to be then?" I asked, pretending not to know what the obvious answer was going to be.

"So... who's it going to be?" echoed Mark, "God I don't know... now who on earth could I ask?... Ricky, I don't suppose that you're by any chance available are you sweetie?"

I held the phone up for the girls to hear as Ricky yelled and screamed his deliriously excited reply.

"I think he's happy!" I laughed.

"Just a bit," joked Mark.

So that was another thing ticked off the list thank goodness. I knew mum would get her outfit back in Spain and that she'd take care of getting a good suit for dad. She was also organising the catering side of things for us and the wedding cake. That was her forte. She just loved anything to do with food, so she would be totally in her element. I was more than happy to let her get on with it, because truthfully that side of things didn't really interest me too much and not only that, I wouldn't have had a clue where to start.

It wasn't going to be too big a wedding, but we filled out some cheap, pretty invitations that we had just got in the supermarket. There didn't seem any point in spending oodles of money unnecessarily because there was plenty of other things to spend it on. We posted them off, desperate to get the replies back quickly so that we could work out our numbers. Meanwhile Ella's sister was quite good with flowers, so luckily for us she was going to do the bouquets at an absolutely bargain price.

It was all going good and I couldn't believe just how quickly and easily we had managed to throw it all together.

The time just flew in and before we knew it, it was the night before the big day. I still couldn't believe that it was really going to happen. We all went round to Tail Feathers to decorate it and to try and make it look more wedding like. It was great to have the place all to ourselves and we had free reign to do as we pleased. We had got little posies of flowers to put on each table, and gold and silver balloons to hang on the walls. It was just so exciting. O.M.G, we were actually going to get married.

"Oh, I just can't wait till tomorrow," I said, helping Mark hang up a big banner with our names on it.

"Me too," he said, bending over and kissing me on the lips, "It's going to be phenomenal. I can just tell."

"Hey, can we make it a double wedding with me and little William here?" Ricky said, squeezing William round the waist as he was reaching up to hang some more balloons on the wall.

"Aw, that would have been nice," I laughed, "but I think it's a bit too late to try and organise it."

"Only joking," said Ricky, "After all, it's your special day guys." William looked a bit disappointed, obviously thinking it was going to happen, but cheered up when Ricky put his arm round him again, giving him a big cuddle.

Meanwhile, Ella and Hannah were busy putting chains of flowers round the main doorway. Then we set each table with knives, forks and fancy silver napkins, finishing each table off with a sprinkle of glittery love hearts.

"Well, I think that's everything," I said, looking admiringly round the hall at our handy work.

"Doesn't it look good?" said Ella, "We're so clever!"

"Right, we better get off home and get our beauty sleep," said Hannah, shepherding us all to the door.

I took another admiring look back at the hall and felt so blessed to be marrying the man that I truly loved. Once outside, we all said our goodbyes with the usual hugging and kissing, then Mark drew me aside, taking both of my hands in his. He gazed lovingly into my eyes, making my heart flip with total happiness.

"Good night my darling," he said, kissing me, "Can't wait to see you in the morning!"

"Me too," I said, lifting his hands up to my mouth and kissing them.

We waved each other off, then as usual, I floated home with Ella and Hannah, who was coming back to the flat so that we would all be together to get ready for the big day in the morning. As soon as we got in, Ella made us all a well-earned cup of tea.

"Oh, my goodness, I was needing that," said Hannah, nursing her cup.

"Me too," I said, "You really can't beat a good cuppa."

"Oh, I know," agreed Ella, "Oh Jesus girls, I just can't wait for tomorrow. You must be absolutely shitting yourself with excitement Marina."

"Well, that's one way of putting it," I laughed, "God, I can't wait either. I just hope it all goes to plan."

"Oh, I'm sure it will," Ella assured me.

"It will if we've got anything to do with it," Hannah added.

"Oh, thanks girls," I said, looking at them both, "I honestly don't know what I would do without you both."

"Well, that's what friends are for! Right, I really need to get to bed. Night-night lovely," said Ella, pecking me on the cheek.

"Sleep tight Marina," said Hannah, hugging me, "You're so lucky, Mark's absolutely bloody gorgeous. I don't think I'll ever find my prince charming."

"But of course you will," I said hugging her back, "Remember, we all have to kiss a few frogs first!"

"I can't even get to kiss a few frogs!" joked Ella.

We finished saying our good nights and then went off to bed. I knew I would find it hard to sleep with all the excitement, but I tried desperately hard not to let my thoughts get in the way because I really did need as much beauty sleep as possible. I would look an absolute mess if I was washed out and tired with big bags under my eyes. I went over the order of things in my mind a few times and then very surprisingly began to drift off.

I started to dream about the wedding though, because it was obviously all that I had been thinking about lately. I dreamt that I was waiting for the wedding car to come and pick me up, but instead of waiting in the flat, I was standing out in the pouring rain. My make-up was getting washed off with the raindrops hitting my face and my beautiful white dress was getting wet and splattered with mud. What a complete nightmare.

Worse was about to come though. Eventually the wedding car came and took me to the church, but of course, it wasn't the right church. I was arguing with the driver, trying to tell him that he had brought me to the wrong place, but he wasn't having any of it and made me get out of the car. I reluctantly got out then made my way up the path, to the church door, which was shut, but then it started to slowly open and I warily went in.

As I began to walk down the aisle, I could see, to my horror that Ollie was standing at the altar. He turned around, sneering in his usual way, then started running towards me. I quickly took to my heels, trying my hardest to run away from him, but the weight of my dress which was soaking wet from the rain, was now holding me back. It was dragging me down and I was getting absolutely nowhere. I screamed when I suddenly felt him roughly grab my arm. I frantically started to wrestle with him, trying to loosen his grip on me but I just didn't seem to have the strength.

It really was a hellish dream, but luckily at that point I woke up. I sat up, sweating and gasping for breath with fear, fully expecting to see Ollie standing there in front of me. When I came to my senses though, I tried to relax back down into my pillows, but I was totally shaken by the frightening experience.

Thinking about Ollie was bad enough but to dream about him was even worse, because I had no control over it. I was scared at first to go back to sleep just in case I started dreaming about him again but luckily, after a little while, I drifted off and didn't budge until my alarm woke me in the morning.

At first, when I heard it, I just wanted to roll over and sleep a little longer, but then when I realised what day it was, I jumped up out of bed and ran through to the living-room. Ella and Hannah were already up and when we looked at each other, we were all hysterical with excitement.

"Oh my God, today's the day" yelled Ella, at the top of her voice.

"Woooo," I said clapping my hands excitedly, "I can't believe it's actually going to happen!"

"Right, we better get started," said Hannah, opening her suitcase, which was loaded full of make-up and beauty accessories, "Now where will we start?"

"At the beginning of course," said Ella, grabbing some stuff.

We painted our faces with blue beautifying face masks and put extra big rollers in our hair. We must have looked an absolute sight as we sat round the breakfast table munching on our cereal and toast.

"God, we look like a bunch of Smurfs!" joked Hannah.

"It'll be worth it though," said Ella, trying hard not to move her face too much, in case it cracked the mask, "We'll be drop dead gorgeous. I promise you… this is good stuff."

And it was. Our faces were positively glowing when we eventually washed it off. A perfect surface for slapping our make-up on to.

I felt a bit too nervous to eat much breakfast, with my tummy doing Olympics style somersaults, but I had managed to drink gallons of coffee. That was a pretty bad idea though because then I started to get the shakes. As if I wasn't trembling enough! I could hardly paint the nail varnish onto my nails as my hands shook so much, but I began to calm down when the girls started to fuss around, helping me to get ready. I felt really pampered as Ella carefully did my make-up and Hannah fashioned my hair. I felt even more relaxed as we sipped on a well-earned cool glass of bubbly.

"Aaahh, this is the life," I said, lounging back on my chair, "Getting beautified by my wonderful friends..."

"...and about to marry the most drop-dead gorgeous man in the whole bloody universe," interrupted Ella.

"What more could a girl want?" added Hannah, raising her glass.

Of course, we had Aretha blasting out in the background as we finished getting ready and yelled along to the songs, as we squeezed into our outfits. I stood back and sighed with delight as I gazed at Ella and Hannah in their beautiful gold brides-maid's dresses. They looked totally stunning. I was so, so lucky to have such incredible friends, who had supported me and helped me through a very dark time. The future was at last looking a lot brighter.

"Wow girls…," I said, "...and thank you."

"What for?" asked Hannah.

"For looking so God damned amazing," I squealed.

"Not as amazing as you," said Ella, kissing me on the cheek, "Just look at you. I've never seen you look so pretty!"

"You look like a princess," cooed Hannah.

I gave a little twirl, then I sneaked a quick glance in the mirror and for once, I actually believed them. I DID look pretty. At last, my confidence was coming back.

"Right girls... let's do this," I said, handing them their flowers, then lifting mine and giving them a little sniff.

As I looked admiringly at my bouquet, there was a knock at the door and for one split second, I held my breath in fear, scared in case it was Ollie, coming to break my spirit and ruin my day. I let out a sigh of relief though and my face broke into a huge smile, when Ella opened the door and there stood my lovely dad.

"Where's my beautiful girl then?" he said, with his arms open wide. I tried hard to swallow back my tears as he looked admiringly at my dress then back at my face.

"Oh, my goodness. You are one very breath-taking bride Marina," he said, positively beaming.

"Oh, thanks dad. You're too kind," I said hugging him with all my might, "I love you so much."

"Love you too sweetheart," he said, kissing me on the cheek.

I felt a bit nervous again when I could see the wedding car parked outside, but my nerves just melted away when I took dads arm and we stepped through the doorway, walking very carefully down the steps.

"O.M.G., I just can't believe this is happening," squealed Ella, walking behind us.

"Me neither," said Hannah, sniffing the flowers in her posy.

I still couldn't either, as we all climbed into the beautiful car. It really was like a dream come true.

"Oh wow, it's so posh," said Ella, making herself comfortable as she sat down.

"I feel like a film star," said Hannah.

I, on the other hand, felt like a queen in her golden carriage and it felt wonderful driving to the little church. I just couldn't wait to get there to see my lovely Mark. When we arrived at the church, we all scrambled out of the car, with Ella fussing over my dress, making sure that it was straight and Hannah fiddling with my hair. I could feel the nerves suddenly washing over me again, as I looked at the door of the church and then I started remembering my awful dream from the night before. Suddenly though, the mad, constant tooting of a car horn, totally diverted my attentions.

We all turned and looked to see what all the commotion was about, as a little red car pulled up behind us. Ricky, Frankie and Regina all struggled out, then turned and helped pull out The Matron.

They were all wearing the same gold dresses that Ella and Hannah had on, with the exact same posies! I just looked on in utter amazement, wondering how on earth they had all fitted in to such a tiny, little car never mind how they had managed to get the same bridesmaid's dresses to fit their rather larger sized bodies.

"Hey honey," said Ricky, rushing over to me and planting a big kiss on the side of my cheek, then quickly but gently rubbing off his transferred lipstick, "I hope we're not stealing your thunder, but Ella here had the brilliant idea of us ALL being your bridesmaids. I really hope you don't mind gorgeous."

Ella looked at me nervously, obviously waiting to see what my reaction would be.

"Oh, my goodness, of course I don't mind," I laughed, "I'm absolutely delighted and just so glad you're all here. You all look stunning."

"Oh, so do you honey. You look like a little fairy princess," said Frankie, "That Markie is one lucky guy."

"Oh, thanks Frankie," I said, blowing him a kiss.

"You look almost as good as me," joked Regina, striking a pose.

"Don't listen to her," said The Matron, muscling in, then gently kissing me on the lips, "No one could ever look better than you Marina. You're absolutely beautiful."

"Oh, thank you Matron. You're so kind... But wait...," I said turning to Ricky, "I thought you were going to be the best man?"

"Still am sweetie," he said giving me a twirl to display his dress, "Just not in a suit and tie."

"Oh Ricky," I laughed, "what are you like!"

We all quickly got into position and for one split second I wondered if Mark would be in a bride's dress too. I mean, it wouldn't have mattered a jot because he looked brilliant in or out of drag and I really didn't care what he was wearing. Just as long as he was here. I needn't have worried though. As we entered the little church, I looked down the aisle at Mark, who turned slightly to look at us. He was in a beautiful crisp silver suit, with a dazzlingly white shirt and metallic gold tie. He looked fantastic and started chuckling to himself when he saw the queens, strutting their stuff behind me, alongside Ella and Hannah.

I had chosen a nice romantic, classical piece of music to walk down the aisle to but was totally taken aback when a triumphant drag queen type of song started blasting out. The queens were dancing and singing along, waving their bouquets up in the air. It made me laugh out loud and I knew that the queens must have had some influence on the choice. I honestly couldn't have wished for a better tune though. It really was so apt.

I just glided down the aisle, with everyone commenting on how lovely I looked. I really did feel like a fairy princess. I saw William standing up and gesturing both his hands to Ricky, who waved his bouquet back at him. As we passed my mum, I gave her a big smile, but I could see that she was starting to well up, so I turned my gaze to Joan who blew me a big kiss. Mark's dad Rodger on the other hand, just stared stony faced straight ahead, but I didn't care, because when I reached the altar Mark turned to face me, smiling broadly.

"You look beautiful," he said, gently taking my hand and kissing it.

"So do you," I said bashfully.

"Hope you don't mind the music choice," he whispered, "I've got a feeling Ricky might have had something to do with it!"

"I don't mind at all," I chuckled, "It's brilliant!"

Ricky clambered from behind us to get to Mark's side, rearranging his fake boobs in the process. He smoothed down his dress and hair, then clutched his bouquet tightly in front of him, giving us a huge smile, while dramatically fluttering his false eyelashes. He was so funny!

"Well... what a wonderful... vibrant... gathering we have here today..." started the minister, first looking at me, then at Mark and then at all my "bridesmaids" behind us, "...and of course we are here to celebrate the wonderful union of Marina and Mark, so let us begin by all coming together and singing... Jesus loves me."

It wasn't your normal wedding hymn, but it was the only one that we all half knew so at least there wasn't going to be an embarrassing silence! We all sang loud and proud and when the hymn was finished, the minister continued.

"Love is the gift and love truly is the giver. Love is like gold and makes the day shine, love forgets self to care for one another and love changes life from water to wine. Mark and Marina..." continued the minister, "Are here today, because they love each other. They have had a bit of a bumpy ride lately but this in turn has made their love even stronger... as it is God's wish to unite two hearts with love. Love indeed conquers all and there is no better excuse than love to bring two people together in holy matrimony. If anyone has reasons for Marina and Mark not to be joined together today, then please say so now or for ever hold your peace."

A cold shiver suddenly went through me and for one awful moment I was fully expecting Ollie to crash through the church doors, behind us then come running down the aisle, declaring his eternal love for me and totally spoiling everything.

Instead though, Frankie started to raise her hand up in the air, obviously wanting to declare her undying love for Mark. Regina promptly dug her hard in the ribs though, bringing her back to her senses. She immediately brought her hand straight back down, shoving it into her mouth and biting down hard on it, to control her emotions.

The minister continued with the sermon and then we proceeded to the vows.

"I, Mark Roger Turner," started Mark, holding my hand, "take you Marina Burton, to have and to hold from this day forward; for better, for worse, for richer, for poorer, in sickness and in health, to love and to cherish, till death us do part."

Then it was my turn. I tried hard not to shake but was so scared in case my voice would start to wobble. I took a deep breath and just hoped for the best.

"I, Marina Burton, take you Mark Roger Turner, to have and to hold from this day forward; for better for worse, for richer, for poorer, in sickness and in health, in suits AND in dresses!" I added with a cheeky smile.

This was met with laughter from the congregation and a very contented smile from Mark.

"To love and to cherish," I continued, "Till death us do part."

191

Phew! I did it without mucking up my lines and my voice didn't wobble. Not once!

"Lovely, now may we have the rings please," the minister said, looking to Ricky, who was just looking back at him with a totally vacant expression.

"Oh God, yes," said Ricky, remembering that this was his job, but then biting his lip in embarrassment for taking the lord's name in vain in a church.

Discovering that his bouquet was getting in the way, he thrust the flowers into Marks hands for him to hold, while he started wrestling with the big locket that he had on a chain round his neck. He seemed to be having great difficulty getting it open though.

"Shit," he said as he struggled with it, then bit his lip with embarrassment again, realising he had now just sworn in front of the minister, "I'm so sorry your worship."

Just then, the locket popped open and Ricky managed to catch the rings before they fell on to the floor. He smiled with relief as he handed one of them to Mark.

"Oops," smiled Mark handing it back, "Wrong one Rick."

"Oh, Jesus," said Ricky, then looked like he was going to have a breakdown when he realised that he had just taken the lords name in vain – AGAIN!

When at last we each had the right ring, Mark handed Ricky his bouquet back then we placed the rings on each other's fingers.

"They have declared their marriage by the joining of hands and by the giving and the receiving of rings. I therefore declare that Mark and Marina are now husband and wife," the minister said triumphantly.

"Another one that got away," whispered Frankie loudly, then sadly shook her head, while Regina just glared at her to keep quiet.

I couldn't believe it, we were actually married! Mark was now my wonderful husband and I was now his very lucky wife! It was just so surreal. I felt like I was in a bubble, still a bit scared in case it would suddenly burst.

"You may now kiss the bride," said the minister.

"Just try stopping me!" said Mark, kissing me gently on the lips to the delight of the congregation, who started clapping and cheering.

192

After we joyfully signed the register, I felt so proud walking back down the aisle, arm in arm with my husband and with all my lovely bridesmaids following behind us. My dad smiled and gave us a little wave, but I could see my mum sniffing back her tears and dabbing her eyes, while trying hard to smile at the same time. Joan was beaming with absolute joy but Roger, of course, was barely able to look in our direction, which was sadly to be expected I suppose.

It really was a bewildering, mixed up, weird old world but I honestly didn't care, because I was so ecstatically happy.

Lots of photos were taken outside the church, with the queens trying to muscle in on all of them! I didn't mind a bit though, because I loved each and every one of them dearly and they were more than welcome to be in every single one of my wedding photos! They really were my "sisters", along with Ella and Hannah of course.

We got showered with confetti as Mark and I climbed into the wedding car. We waved madly to everyone as it started to pull slowly away and as we drove along, we just looked at each other, laughing in disbelief that we were actually now married. It really was all a bit bizarre.

"I love you wife," said Mark, pushing his face towards mine.

"I love you husband," I said, kissing his luscious, gorgeous lips.

I would happily have driven off into the sunset, just the two of us, but I was also really excited about the reception and thankfully, it went like an absolute dream. When we arrived at Tail Feathers, Molly was standing at the door waiting to greet us. I had never seen her look so good. She was dressed to the nines and had obviously had her hair specially done.

"Congratulations you two! Oh, my goodness, you both look fabulous," she said, hugging us tightly, "I hope you're very happy together. Now come on in and let's get this party started!"

She ushered us through to the main hall, which somehow looked even better than it did yesterday, with all the decorations. Molly got us in to position and we stood at the door waiting for our guests to arrive. One by one they streamed in, shaking our hands and hugging us, as they headed towards their seats. My poor mum was still bubbling as she cuddled me.

"I'm so happy for you both," she sobbed.

"Oh, thanks mum," I said, squeezing her tight.

"You wouldn't think it with the state of you," said Dad, trying to drag her away, "Come on pet, or you'll have us all crying!"

Joan and Rodger were next to give us their good wishes. Well, Joan that is. Rodger just looked sternly ahead, saying absolutely nothing.

"Congratulations you two," said Joan, kissing us both, "We're so pleased for you... aren't we Rodger?"

He still didn't say anything, just making a grunting noise.

"Thanks mum...Dad...," said Mark, looking at Rodger, trying to get some kind of response from him but he just went marching on into the hall.

"Sorry darling. Just ignore him... you know he doesn't like these kind of things and the poor man's starving," said Joan, trying to apologise for his rudeness, then scurried after him.

"This will be absolutely killing him," whispered Mark with a big smirk on his face.

"Poor Rodger," I chuckled, "You can't help feeling sorry for him."

Meanwhile, the guests continued to flow happily in and once they were all seated, Mark and I began to walk across the hall to absolutely rapturous applause and cheers. We made our way to our table, waving to everyone as we went. We didn't have a top table as such and had also decided not to bother with the usual embarrassing speeches, mainly because we knew Mark's dad wouldn't have a nice word to say about him. In fact, he wouldn't have any words to say at all probably, going by the reaction we'd had from him so far. Instead, my dad just said a few words before the meal.

"It is with great pride that I am standing here today... celebrating the wedding of my one and only beautiful daughter Marina... to the outstandingly wonderful Mark. It is obvious how very much in love with each other, they both are...," he said, lifting up his glass, "and I wish them many, many years of health, wealth and happiness."

"Health, wealth and happiness," everyone echoed, raising their glasses.

Everyone that is, with the exception of Mark's dad, who sat with his arms tightly folded and scowling bitterly, evidently not wanting to be present. Even a coat-hanger in his mouth couldn't have forced a smile on his face. I almost felt a bit of sympathy for him, because

194

after all it probably wasn't his fault that he was so narrow minded. Perhaps it was something to do with his upbringing how he had treated Mark. A different generation I suppose. Stiff upper lip and all that. Anyway, I wasn't going to let him ruin our day and just tried to ignore his negativity. I couldn't for the life of me though, work out how Joan had managed to persuade him to come to The Tail Feathers, let alone the wedding. I mean, it was a drag club after all, but then maybe she had forgotten to mention that bit!

We all got stuck into the buffet, filling our plates with lots of lovely food. My mum had made a great job organising it all and it was the best way to feed everyone because they could just help themselves. It was absolutely delicious and all washed down with a lot of alcohol.

Then of course, it was time for the dancing. Mark and I started it all off with our first dance which was of course another drag queen anthem. This would obviously just rub Rodger's nose in it even more!

I felt like I was floating on air as I gazed, now a bit wine fuelled, into my new husband's beautiful blue eyes as we glided around in each-other's arms. Mum and dad then followed us on to the dance floor, along with almost everyone else. Amazingly, Joan actually managed to drag Roger up to dance, albeit grudgingly, especially as it was a song about a transvestite. His face was like absolute thunder. Meanwhile the queens whooped and spun each other around with delight.

"Aren't you just the most perfect couple," said Ricky, as he and William danced beside us.

I just smiled, looking dreamily back into Mark's eyes, knowing it was completely true, but then the next minute, Ricky had twirled over next to Rodger and loudly sang the words of the song straight into his face. He immediately stomped off the dance floor, obviously irate and disgusted at being forced to socialise with a load of queens then sat back down at his table. Thankfully, Joan didn't seem at all perturbed and just kept dancing, joining up with a welcoming Ella and Hannah. She definitely wasn't for sitting down and just about took over the whole of the dance floor!

"Oh no," groaned Mark, looking anxiously at Frankie, who had stopped in her tracks in front of us.

"Holy Moly... he's your absolute double," Frankie said, first looking at Mark then eyeing up Rodger.

"Don't even think about it," warned Mark, reaching out to grab Frankie.

But before anyone could stop her, she had bounded over to Roger.

"Oh my God Mark's dad, would you do me the honour of dancing with me?" Frankie asked, with a beaming smile and holding out her hand.

"Bugger off," said Roger, grumpily, folding his arms and turning away from her, obviously totally repulsed.

"That's no way to speak to a lady," said a very disappointed Frankie.

"And you're no lady," said a very irritated Rodger.

Unfortunately (or maybe on reflection, fortunately) the queens had been watching and when they saw Mark's dad's negative reaction, they started clapping and chanting in response. They didn't know anything about Mark's history with his dad, but they could evidently sense the friction between them and couldn't help but notice Rodger's disgust for them all.

"Dance, dance, dance, dance...," the queens shouted at Rodger.

Then everyone started to join in the chant... even Mark's mum! Of course, Roger now looked totally humiliated and was visibly squirming. Due to the reaction from the crowd though, he was very reluctantly pressurised into getting up on the dance floor with a now extremely delighted Frankie, who twirled him energetically round and round the hall. I could feel Marks body start to shake uncontrollably with laughter at the awkward sight of his father and I couldn't help but join in when I saw Roger's angry, red face. It was so funny. He was definitely getting his comeuppance today!

"I can't believe this is happening," laughed Mark, delighted at his father's embarrassment, "I would have gladly paid good money just to see this! This really is the very best day of my life!"

Frankie sang along to the music as he forced Rodger grudgingly to strut about the dance floor, alongside of him. It was definitely judgement day for poor old Rodger and when the dance was finished, Frankie planted a great big kiss on his cheek, leaving a huge lipstick stain.

"Thank you darling... and remember.... if you ever decide to bat for the other side... then I'll always be available for you," she said, with a cheeky wink.

"I can assure you, that I won't EVER be batting for the other side," Roger said, storming off, clearly totally traumatised by the whole experience.

He sat grumpily back down, folding his arms again. Just then, The Matron went over, gyrating her hips as she stood in front of him and holding out her hand. She obviously liked what she saw and desperately wanted a dance too.

"Come on Rodger," said The Matron enticingly, "I'm more your age pet."

"Oh, for crying out loud. Just leave me alone you lot," he yelled, standing up, then heading for the door.

"Oh, please Mr. Rodger," begged The Matron, chasing after him, "Just one dance."

"Bugger off," shouted Rodger as he disappeared through the big doors.

The Matron looked really upset at his reaction, but then turned to face the crowd again. Shrugging her shoulders, she smiled and boogied back on to the dancefloor.

"Oh, well... his loss," she said, starting to do her famous twerk.

"Holy shit, I love this life," laughed Ricky, "and I love you my William."

"Oh, honey, I love you too," said William, planting a big kiss on his lips.

We couldn't have foreseen what was about to happen next, as we all watched Ricky go down on one knee, holding William's hand and looking pleadingly up at him.

"William... will you marry me?" he asked.

"Ricky," said William looking over at me, "It's a bit bad timing. I mean this is Mark and Marina's special day."

"It can be your special day too you plonker," I shouted, "and for God's sakes just say yes!"

"Are you sure Marina?" William asked.

I nodded my head frantically in approval then William looked back at Ricky, saying, "O.M.G. sweetie... yes, of course I'll marry you. Oh, Ricky, I love you."

We were deafened with ear-splitting with cheers as they kissed and cuddled each other. It had been on the cards for a while, so it might as well happen today of all days. It just made everything seem so complete.

"For heavens sakes," yelled Ella, "You know what this means guys?"

"What?" we all replied.

"We've only got another wedding to arrange!"

We all laughed and whooped with delight, just knowing that it was going to be another wonderful experience.

"Where's Molly?" shouted Ricky, "We need to thrash out a deal!"

Mark just looked at me and we both laughed then kissed and hugged and danced the rest of the night away. It was such a fantastic start to the rest of our lives together, sharing it with the loveliest people in the whole wide world.

It really had been the best day of my life. I was so lucky to have Mark, but I just wished I had met him first and not Ollie. It would certainly have saved a lot of heartache. It's a true saying though, "what doesn't kill you makes you stronger."

The abuse that Mark and I had both individually suffered had in a strange way made us stronger and together we would be even stronger still. To think that if it hadn't been for a bunch of queens, then I would still be stuck in a Godawful relationship. My life really had been totally turned around by drag, but I can honestly say that my life was now anything BUT a drag! I couldn't imagine being any happier. It was definitely onwards and upwards now for me and my lovely Mark.

ABOUT THE AUTHOR

Thank you so much for reading my book. I really hope you enjoyed it. I live in central Scotland with my family and on leaving school, attended art college, then qualified as a nurse. I worked in hospitals, but specialized in aesthetics.

Due to my "people" skills in the workplace, I have come across a variety of characters, throughout my career, which has been invaluable in my writing.

Life's a Drag was written through my own love of make-up and also from my personal experience of mental and physical abuse, in a previous relationship. I would like to think that the book gives hope to anyone in the same situation and to prove that through adversity comes countless possibilities.

I would also urge anyone experiencing any form of abuse not to suffer in silence. There are so many organizations available to help, so please do get in touch.

Printed in Great Britain
by Amazon

27508865R00119